An Irrational Lesson on Witch-Boy Wooing

Magical Husbandry: Book 2

Cynthia Diamond

To all my LGBTQIA+ readers. I hope I did right by you.

And to L.A. Witt who taught me to pour on the "suffer sauce." As usual, this is all your fault...You instigator.

contents

Chapter 1

The winter's chill bit through Rowan's way too thin coat, prickling his skin and making the twisted muscles in his thigh tense. He rubbed his hands over his jeans—which were also way too thin—trying to soothe the cramping. Winter would be so much easier for him without the snow.

Carefully he toddled up the slippery drive, duffle bag slung over his shoulder, his sneakers crunching in the packed ice. He'd only been out of his car a second and already his toes were drenched. He patted his bag, feeling for the boots he'd packed instead of wearing on his long drive. Footwear was the last thing on his mind as he left his apartment. "Deep breaths, Ro. Deep breaths." He sucked in frigid air through his nostrils. "Nothing is coming after you."

His sister's grand house towered over him, smoke wafting from its many brick chimneys and warmth smiling from its tall glowing windows as if to say, "welcome back, Rowan." It took all his will power to not sprint up to the porch and bang on the door.

A snap cracked in his ears. Rowan spun, feet slipping on the frozen drive, a defensive spell glowing in his outstretched palm. A bending pine branch shook off its snow before springing back into place. His heart slowed, arm lowering back to his side. 'It didn't follow you. It's not in this realm."

It had been his mantra as he sped down Highway Five, white knuckled grip on the steering wheel. That thing only came at night. Only seen in his dreams.

He dragged his stiffening leg up the porch steps, mind racing. He had driven all night to get to Big Bear despite a second week of no sleep. Nightmares. The memories of... He shook that loose as fast as he could. What was he going to tell Ivy and Aster first? *Fuck it, don't tell them anything. Don't worry them.*

Rowan stared at the front door, its wreath a woven delight of juniper and pine branches laced with golden lights. But there were no cords or batteries powering that twinkle. Definitely cottage magic. A sign that Ivy was well again. Well and happy. Guilt surged. His problems would only be a burden to his already overburdened sisters; Ivy with her anxiety, and Aster with...well... Gods only knew what she had been through. And then there was Callum. *Sweet Hecate, Callum. How am I going to face him?*

This was a mistake. He couldn't arrive two weeks early to Yule without an announcement begging for sanctuary. Besides, his family came to *him* for help not the other way around. That's how it had always been. One of them would call and he'd come running, not this opposite day bullshit. *Forget it. Go home. It's just in your dreams, nothing else. You can handle that, right?*

He turned to leave when a loud, groaning creak shook the porch boards. The windchimes hanging from the eaves jingled happily. Rowan stiffened, giving the door a pat. "Uh, good to see you too. But I'm just leaving. Don't let them know I dropped in, okay?"

The windows flanking the heavy oak door shook, as if the house was laughing.

"I'm serious! Don't tell Ivy I was-" The door swung open, banging against the inside wall and he rolled his eyes. "Ooooor you can ignore me and let everyone know I'm here. Okay. Cool."

There was a mad chitter. A blur of brown fur dashed out the door and a raccoon skittered between Rowan's ankles beaming with shiny black eyes. He chirped, grabbing handfuls of his jeans.

"Good to see you too, Maximus," Rowan chuckled.

Maximus began to tug him through the door. Of course, he had as much success with that as a chihuahua pulling an SUV down the street by its teeth.

"No, no, no!" Rowan tried to gently shake him free. "Go on now. Move along and go do... racoon things." The raccoon screeched, continuing the tug-o-war with his pants. Rowan waved his hands, hissing sharp shhs which went unheeded.

Clack-clack-clack. Rowan froze as the sound grew closer. That was the sound of hooves. Hooves belonging to a large, curious creature that was racing towards the door. *Callum! Shit!* Rowan lifted his leg in hopes of shaking Maximus free, but the furry menace just squealed in what could only be described as racoon-ish delight, swinging like a tiny trapeze artist. "Why are you so tenacious?!"

A blur of air moved towards him, tall and broad. It hovered in the threshold and Rowan's heart shot into his throat. He braced himself as he lowered his leg with a nervous, and very fake, smile. "Heeeeey...I uh...I bet you're wondering why I'm back?" *Because I'm wondering the same damn thing myself.*

There was a pop and the blur formed into a tall, handsome male with golden skin and black horns curling over his thick caramel mane. He was bare except for the leather loincloth tied around his narrow hips. His fur coated legs were thick and muscular, ankles connecting to huge cloven hooves. And he wasn't Callum. A strange disappointment needled Rowan but he smiled all the same. "Finn! Hey!"

Finn lifted Rowan up in a tight bear hug, crushing the air from his lungs. "Rowan! Brother!" His fangs glinted in glee as he gave another squeeze. "My Witchling will be so pleased to see you!"

"Can't breathe, buddy!" Rowan slapped Finn's arms, feet, and raccoon dangling from the satyr's towering height.

"Oh! My apologies." Finn put him down, dusting him off with the brush of his long bull's tail. "I forgot you're fragile."

Rowan chuckled awkwardly as he tried to pry Maximus's tiny claws from his jeans. "Dude, I'm not fragile."

"Compared to my kind you are. It's adorable. Witches are adorable! Who knew?!" Finn patted Rowan's head, grinning as if he bestowed the greatest compliment ever. "Does Ivy know you're coming?"

"Uh, not really, I..." Any story Rowan had half-assed for his arrival popped out of existence. "I'm uh...Here because..."

"Ah," Finn wagged a finger. "You're here for my brother Callum, aren't you?"

"What? No!" Rowan finally yanked Maximus free, trying to hide his blush. "No, no, no. I'm not here for Callum. I'm-"

"Finn, is someone at the door?" Ivy called.

Rowan waved his hands at Finn in the universal gesture for "shut the hell up" but the satyr snaked an arm around his shoulders. "Look who's come to Yule early!" *Dammit. Busted.* Finn led him inside, the buzz of protection wards raising the hair on his arms.

"Oh, my Gods! Rowan!" Ivy laughed. She looked radiant, her blue eyes bright, and her form plump and healthy.

Rowan wiggled his fingers and sang a pathetic, "Surprise?"

"No shit!" Tendrils of her fiery red hair spilled from her messy bun as she darted to him. flinging her arms around his shoulders.

Rowan melted, embrace timid before squeezing her tight. Gods, he needed a hug so badly. And now he was here with his twin where everything should feel right. But it wasn't right. It hadn't been for ages.

He clenched his jaw, gently untangling himself. *Dammit, what am I going to tell her? She can't worry about me! She has Aster to take care of and-* "Ow!" Maximus had climbed to his hip, murder mittens digging into his flesh. The little bugger was like Velcro. "Max, take it down a notch, buddy. Ives, a little help?"

"Sorry. He's a hugger." Ivy clicked her tongue and Maximus released his hold. He ran up her side and draped himself across her shoulders like a stole. "Go sit down. Warm up that leg of yours. I'm sure it's killing you."

"Nah, it's fine," he lied.

She twirled her fingers, the door shutting on its own. "Why are you here so early? You said you weren't coming until Yule because work had things tied up tight."

Work is not a problem. Can't miss work during the holidays if you're unemployed. Rowan took a deep breath, pressing a hand against his chest for the talisman buried under his button-down shirt. The pewter brushed his palm, its energy calming him. "If it's going to be a problem I can head back to San Francisco."

"Like hell you will! You know I still hate the idea that you decided to move up there." Ivy took his bag, handing it to Finn. "Now you're here and you're going to stay."

"But I-"

"Don't defy the hospitality of a cottage witch, Ro. Especially if they're your sister. Besides, Auntie Lia and Auntie Rosie will be thrilled you're back in time for Krampusnacht."

"They're still doing that?"

"Seven years and counting," Ivy replied. "Not even your horrible Krampus impersonation scared the public off."

Rowan rolled his eyes. "It was one time! Besides, they needed someone to dress up as Krampus that year. Was I supposed to say no?" When Ivy smirked, a little laugh escaped him. "You're needling me, aren't you?"

She gave him a wink. "Of course, I am." Another twist of her wrist and the brass chandelier overhead brightened, casting the huge living room in a cheerful glow.

The house had gone from dilapidated to grand in only few months, now dressed in its lovely Yule attire. A giant tree stood beside the hearth, tinsel shimmering on the boughs like silver dew. Various glass baubles, pinecones, and candles with ghostly flames nestled in the snow coated branches. The wide staircase was a riot of red and green holly wrapped around the ornate banister, its runner a bright crimson.

"Aunty Dahlia is still decorating I see," Rowan said.

"There's no stopping her when she's on a fabulous mission," Ivy replied. "Though Finn and Callum took over tree trimming duty."

"The pinecones were my idea." Finn puffed his chest. "It's a strange custom, but a fun one nonetheless."

Rowan jabbed finger guns at the two. "Well make sure to clean up afterwards or you may catch Tinsil-litis!"

Finn's brows knitted in confusion while Ivy groaned, pinching the bridge of her nose. "You've been sitting on that joke since you walked in, haven't you?"

Rowan grinned. "You needle me, I needle you." Before he could release another horrible pun, the flames in the huge fireplace roared in a heartfelt hello. He gave the stone mantle a pat. "Thanks for ratting me out," he muttered. A light tinkle of laughter whispered through the ceiling beams.

"Why so early?" Ivy asked.

The truth sat on the tip of his tongue. *Just tell her. Explain why lost your job and you're lonely as hell.* But the words stalled as soon as he saw the twinkle in her bright eyes. After so many battles with life, death, and her own mental health, Ivy was finally carefree. Gods, he couldn't take that away from her. "I just thought it would be fun to show up early. It's not a problem, is it?"

"When have you ever been a problem, Ro?" Ivy gave his cheek a peck. "Aster is going to be thrilled to see you."

"As well as Callum!" Finn added, bounding to the stairs. "I'll let him know you're here!"

"No!" Rowan dashed past Ivy, almost tackling Finn to the ground.

"Why not? He's been pining for you since you left. Your aunts even commemorated it."

He swept an arm towards the new painting hanging over the mantle; a nude satyr leading an equally nude, ginger haired male elf down a forest path. The satyr was huge and beautiful, from burly, scarred torso to the long dark hair trailing between his shoulder blades. The golden Celtic knots that traced his spine were twisted from the lines that crisscrossed his body. Gods, Rowan loved those scars, remembered how they rippled, how they felt against his lips...

Nope. Stop. Don't go there. Too late. He was there. Hell, he had already bought a condo and was about to move in. He rubbed his eyes, stared, then rubbed them again. That elf looked suspiciously like Rowan. "They... commissioned that?"

"Indeed!" Finn replied. "They had your little sister-Oof!" He sighed as Ivy elbowed him. "Witchling, must you?"

Ivy gave Rowan a sheepish shrug. "Sorry. I tried to stop them, but you know how Auntie Dahlia and Auntie Rosemary are. And Aster just ran with it."

Rowan rubbed his burning face, forcing his laugh to not sound uncomfortable, and failing dismally. "It's fine."

Ivy shook her head. "It's not fine."

"No Ives! It's really-"

"We're witch twins, Ro." Ivy tapped her temple. "I know when you're uncomfortable."

The softest ping of her anxiety touched the back of his mind, reminding him of their shared link. Rowan cleared his throat. "Maybe a little uncomfortable, but I'll get over it."

"Good!" Finn wrapped his arms around both Rowan and Ivy, Maximus letting out a yelp as he was added to the group hug. "Now we feast and revel!"

"Rowan!" a sweet voice called from the stairway. Aster flew down to the living room, flinging herself into the group hug. "This is an awesome surprise!"

Her strawberry blonde hair was in a tangled bun, her outfit old sweats she clearly was living in. But at least there was a sparkle in her eyes, one Rowan hadn't seen in far too long. Gods she had been through so much. *Why are you here? You should be dealing with this alone, not dragging them into your dream crap!*

Rowan wiggled himself free of the sibling sandwich. "Well, I missed you two. And I'm..." *Fired. Can't get work. Totally screwed my career. Haven't slept in two weeks.* "On leave." Aster's mouth dropped open as Ivy sucked in a long gasp that rivaled a bathtub draining. "It's nothing! I'm just taking some time off."

"Ro, you never take time off," Ivy said. "And when you do, it's because someone here needs a hand, not for fun."

"Yeah well, I'm working on healthier habits." He shoved his emotions deep before Ivy could detect them.

Calm and cool. Yup. That was him. The rock in the storm. The family lighthouse. Always had been, always will be, nightmares be damned.

Aster smiled. "Well, I'm glad you're on leave. It's been boring as hell around here without you!"

"Hey!" Ivy laughed. "A little credit, huh?"

Aster batted her eyes, giving her most saccharine smile. "I'm used to your bullshit, Ives. It's time for Ro's bullshit."

"I'll hunt a feast!" Finn announced. He pressed a kiss to Ivy's forehead, murmuring loud enough for all to hear. "Witchling, I expect you to pleasure me well tonight for providing for you."

"Sweet Brigid, in front of my siblings, Finn?" Ivy cried.

Finn cocked his head. "That's how we're playing to-night?"

"No!" the twins said in horrified unison.

Finn gave them a grin, releasing them from his hold. "I figured. But it's fun to tease." He clacked his way to the door, grabbing the bow and quiver beside it before marching out, his tail high and his chin even higher.

"See, this is the bullshit I'm used to." Aster tugged on Rowan's arm, leading him to the couch. "Come on. Tell me all about what you've been up to. What cases have the authorities given you? Have you been crossing the veil? Any new dead people you've led towards the light?" The painting over the mantle almost vibrated off the wall. Once again, Rowan's cheeks were aflame. Aster wrung her hands. "Oh, you saw the painting."

"It's hard to miss your own ass over the fireplace," Rowan replied.

"Please don't be mad at me." Aster gave him her the patented, *I'm too cute to scold* pout.

As usual, Rowan fell hook, line and sinker for the routine. "I'm not. It's...nice."

"Does it look like you and Callum?" She rubbed her chin, studying her work. "Be honest. I'm totally open to criticism."

"You did a great job, Azzie. It's amazing. But...did we have to be naked?" The chandelier tinkled, and Rowan looked at Ivy. "The house is laughing at me, isn't it."

"My house is a perv and likes naked people in it," Ivy said matter of factly.

Aster smiled. "It's not a pervert. It just loves love. And I think it's sweet."

Ivy ruffled her little sister's already mussed hair. "Yeah, well wait until it keeps you up all night with erotic dreams. Then we'll see how sweet you think it is." She headed to the kitchen. "Sit, Ro. Relax. I'll get you a glass of wine."

"I'm not in a wine mood right now," Rowan said.

Aster leaned in, whispering, "Callum's been camping out in the new wing."

"Oh yeah?" His voice cracked as he looked back to the stairway, waiting for any sign of blurred air or loud hooves on hard wood. "The new wing huh?" The one the house had created just for him and Callum only a few days before Rowan ghosted.

"It's probably just him wanting to move out of the basement. It's cold down there you know. And easier to escape Aunt Rosie's constant questions about satyr mating rituals." The corners of Aster's mouth quivered, as if a giggle were about to bust out at any second. "Speaking of which, do they know you're here?"

Rowan shook his head. "No, this was kind of a last-minute thing. I'll probably go see them tomorrow."

Ivy looked to Aster. "Azzie, mind getting that wine for us?" Her inflections said more than just wine was needed. Privacy was also requested.

Rowan sighed. "Aster, I don't need-"

"Too late! I'm getting it!" Aster called as she hurried to the kitchen, leaving the two alone.

Rowan flopped onto the couch, a pang shooting up his leg. "You worry too much."

"I have anxiety. It comes with the territory." Ivy took his hands. "You know you can tell me anything, right Ro?"

"What's there to tell?"

"Well for one, your leg is hurting. Don't lie. I see it in your face."

"Okay fine. The cold is getting to the injury but that's it." Rowan spread his arms wide. "Now, I'm on vacation in my favorite perverted house with my two amazing but annoying sisters." Ivy puckered her lips, unconvinced. Not surprising since his nervous vibes were probably pinging off her like sonar on a submarine. It was time for a big ol' change of subject. "How's Aster doing?"

"Good. She's painting again and overall, she's happy." Ivy sighed. "But she never wants to leave the house. We've tried and tried but she won't set foot past the porch. She won't use her magic. And she has panic attacks about...you know who."

Rowan shook his head. "Her King of Shadows, huh?"

"The one and only. She's convinced she killed him while she was still that monster. And since we haven't seen him in a while, I'm starting to agree."

"She needs a therapist."

"And she's been seeing one. They have sessions online so it's a start." Ivy sunk onto the couch, the lines in her face deepening. "Honestly, her panic attacks in the night have been stressful."

And you just brought your nightmares into the middle of it. Rowan's belly knotted as he shoved those thoughts deep down. No, his issues weren't going to be his sisters' issues too. He gave Ivy's shoulder a squeeze. "I got your back. If Aster has a problem, I'll handle it for you. You need your rest too."

Ivy smiled. "Coming to our rescue as usual, Ro. I'm glad you're here." She gestured to the stairs. "Get settled and relax. Take a soak in the tub. I mixed some good healing salts that will help with the muscle cramps. And Aster will bring your wine up."

"I don't need the wine."

"You need the wine, trust me. I can feel it." Ivy rose from the couch with Rowan. "I'll let you know when dinner is ready. Finn's been on a rabbit kick lately." When

Rowan made a sour face, she added, "And I'll make sure our resident vegetarian has something to eat too. No bad meat vibes for you."

Rowan stood, smiling through the shock of pain that sizzled down his thigh. "Best twin ever."

Dread crept up the back of Rowan's neck, its fingers as cold as the outside. He looked out the window to the frost dappled trees, half expecting glowing green eyes staring right at him. A flutter of wings and a crow landed picking through the piles of ice.

"You good?" Ivy asked.

Rowan deflated with a relieved sigh. Nothing but a crow. *Of course, it was nothing. That thing is just in your head.* "All good." He climbed the stairs trying to forget his fear.

The gaslight sconces ignited one by one as he walked down the hall, the door to his former room swinging open with a happy creak. "You missed me, I see.". The floorboards rippled in the affirmative. "Well, I missed you all too."

The sight of his room warmed his heart. Everything was set just as he'd left it; a neatly made bed piled with blankets, fur rugs covering what would be freezing floors, and curtains drawn tight, keeping out the chill. Familiar. Warm. Safe. This grand old house had felt more like home than any puny apartment he'd resided in.

A sharp stare stabbed him in the back. Rowan swallowed, waiting for the distinct icy breeze to trickle past his neck but no, this was different. He peered over his shoulder towards the towering door at the end of the hall. It was solid oak, carved with intricate designs of leaves and branches, its knob a shiny brass. And it was cracked open. A hulking dark shadow crouched on the other side, his eyes reflecting like a cat's, one bright sunny gold, the other as blue as the dusk sky.

Rowan swallowed the lump in his throat. "Hey Big Guy." He waved as if that would add panache to his stupid greeting. Dammit, why did this have to happen now? Sure, it was only a matter of time before their paths would cross again but he was hoping it would have been later. Much, much later.

There was no response, only staring. Rowan pointed to his door. "I, uh, decided to show up early." Silence. Rowan turned from the beautiful shining eyes that wouldn't look away, focusing on his very soggy shoes. "Yeah well, I guess I'll see you around then? I'm glad you're okay, Cal." A snort came from the shadow and the door shut with an abrupt click. Rowan rubbed his forehead. "Guess you're still pissed at me."

The fireplace burst to life as Rowan stepped inside his room. He gave the wall a pat in thanks, wishing the welcome would have delighted him more. Unfortunately, it was overshadowed by the satyr lurking beyond that door. He tossed his duffle onto the dresser, sitting at the end of his bed. And here he thought he'd sneak in under Callum's radar. Great, now things would be even more awkward.

The bedroom door swung open with a creak. Rowan stiffened, expecting to see Callum. Was that a good thing? A bad thing? Gods, he didn't even know. After the disaster that was their last encounter, it could go either way. The hall was empty. The hearth sparked and the door swung open and closed, beckoning him out.

Rowan grumbled. "I know what you're trying to say, and the answer is no. He doesn't want to see me, and I shouldn't see him."

But sweet Hecate I want to see him. Despite all the things his good sense told him, he missed Callum. Missed their talks and their strolls. Missed his crooked scarred smile. He especially missed how he groaned at his god-awful dad jokes. *And you miss that ass. Don't deny it.*

Rowan got up and closed the door. "No. This crap may have worked with Finn and Ivy, but Callum and I are a completely different story. So, no." He gritted his teeth as he unpacked his bag. "No matchmaking. No accidental meetings. And *absolutely* no erotic dreams. Got it?" The walls creaked with disappointment. Well, at least he got his point across.

The evening continued with a welcome home dinner, sibling chatter, and ridiculous innuendo from Finn. Even the spirit of the rabbit everyone had for their meal had serenely crossed the veil, leaving Rowan to eat his vegetable casserole in peace. But there was no sign of Callum, which made stomaching dinner harder than anticipated.

Finn grinned over his wine glass. "Not going to ask where my brother is?"

"Don't be a dick," Ivy scolded.

"I'm not a dick. I'm excited for their reunion. Every-one is. Especially since Callum has been sulking for an entire month." Finn pressed a wrist to his forehead dra-matically. "Pouting in the new wing of the house, wailing why? Whyyyy?! Dear Gods, where has my witch-boy gone-Ow!" He frowned as Ivy smacked him with her spoon. "What?"

"You're exaggerating," Aster laughed. "He hasn't been that bad. Just grumpy."

Gods I hope so. Rowan shrugged. "It's his business if he doesn't want to come to dinner. He's probably having a..." *Panic attack?* The idea of Callum all alone, fighting his demons in a dark, empty room made Rowan's gut turn. It was sheer will alone that he didn't launch himself out of his chair and run to comfort him. "...a quiet night in." he finished, shoving a bite of carrot into his mouth.

No, he won't run to the rescue. He wouldn't play white knight this time. After what happened, Callum didn't want to see him. End of story. And he'd do every-thing in his power to keep out of the satyr's path until Yule had passed. Easy peasey.

Later that night Rowan climbed into bed, burying himself under mountains of blankets. The warm air and the crackling fire were serene, the house embracing him like an old friend. Yet he couldn't close his eyes. That shade waited on the other side of sleep just like it had for days. Waiting. Wanting. Ready to devour him with its empty gaze.

He rolled into his side, punching his pillow. "Its just a shade. You can scare it off like always." Yet that was getting harder and harder to do each night. "Its just a shade. It will be gone by morning. It will be gone as soon as you wake up. Go to sleep.

The hours ticked by and soon his body grew heavy. His lids fluttered close, sleep finally taking its hold. It was just a shade. A bad dream that vanished when he woke. His last chilling thought echoed in his head before he drifted way. *But will you actually wake up this time?*

Chapter 2

*O*h, woah. Where did you come from?"

A butterfly sat in Rowan's outstretched hand. Its huge orange and black wings fluttered as it crawled across the witch's fingers. "It's so late in the year. And it's night." Callum's heart pounded, riveted as Rowan held it up to the moonlight. Gods he was beautiful with his hair full of fire, cheeks dusted with freckles, and eyes as blue as the summer sky. "How are you even out here, buddy? Monarchs usually can't last in this cold."

Because it was a sign. Orlaith. That butterfly was exactly like the one that had painted her back and now it sat in Rowan's palm. She was here in the forest beside him. She had returned on this autumn night to give her blessing.

The guilt that had once curdled Callum's belly disappeared. No shame now. No dishonoring the memory of his former mate. This is what she granted. And who he wanted.

The butterfly took to the skies, sparkling in the silver light before vanishing amongst the stars. A smile curled Callum's mouth. "Thank you," he whispered to the air.

He dared to brush Rowan's cheek with his knuckles. Rowan stilled, heat in his bright cerulean eyes and his scent fresh with the musk of his arousal. Callum never thought there'd be another like Orlaith and yet here he was; Her complete opposite. A stunning witch-boy with a gentleness and sweet nature that needed to be tasted. I'm ready to love again. Goddess, I want to love again.

And this time, he would keep his true one safe. Callum inched close enough to feel the witch-boy's breath, to see the pulse in his throat flutter.

Rowan smiled at him. "You're grinning."

Callum nodded. "Indeed I am witch-boy," he murmured, before slanting his mouth over his in a heated kiss.

Callum shook the memory free, his long deer-like ears flattening against his skull. He paced in a circle for the tenth time then looked back to the door. His witch-boy had returned? For him? Of course not. Why would he? Yet a small part of him, one he was starting to loathe, hoped he'd factored into Rowan's sudden arrival.

Callum hadn't seen the witch-boy since before the snow had fallen and he was positive he didn't need to see him again. But when that cheerful voice tickled his ears, it became a drug and he crouched by the hallway door, hoping to catch a look at Rowan. Just a look. Nothing more. Perhaps it would rekindle Callum's resentment and he could go back to brooding in peace.

Alas, one glimpse of Rowan had done him in. Gods, he was still lovely; a boyish face made wise from his forty-two years, his slender frame still solid and lean, and that smile. Oh, by Dionysus, that stunning smile. It took every ounce of strength to not dash out and take the witch-boy into his arms, all offenses forgotten.

Callum did another circle, grumbling under his breath. *Leave the wing and see him. No. Stay put. Don't chase after him. But perhaps a quick greeting would be in order since he's already seen you.* He rested his hand on the brass doorknob, eager to turn it. *Look at you. Crushed yet again by a witch. You're pathetic.*

"Indeed, I am." He clenched his jaw and forcefully yanked his grip away. Resentment returned, sending him to the new wing's living room.

Months ago, the house had taken upon itself to create a twin version of itself for Callum and Rowan to reside in, thinking that their eventual union would end in joy, not a grim reminder of what Callum had lost.

It was the exact layout of the original house, but the décor was that of the warlock who once lived there, all leather, dark wood, and trophies of stag heads. Not a single branch of pine, or soft nest of moss for its new resident. Clearly the house was still attached to its old master. Callum hated it. It reminded him too much of the past. And for some daft reason Callum decided to live there.

Finn said it was melancholy and dramatic of him to stay. Afterall, Rowan had vanished the day after they fucked, giving a lame excuse before disappearing. But it was the closest Callum could be to the witch-boy without a direct reminder. He groaned. All right, in retrospect, it *was* melancholy and dramatic.

He stared at the waxy scars that covered the back of his hands. *No need for a reminder of why he ran. You're covered in the reason.* They twisted up his arms in gruesome maps of puckered flesh that continued across his chest and back. One even wound up his face, slicing his lips and across his brow. The coven had intentions of removing his eye. Thank the Goddess it never came to that, but the damage had been done.

Hot sick rose in his throat. "Fuck that coven! "He kicked the settee, his hoof cutting through the supple leather. The antlered chandelier overhead shook, a rumble of irritation rattling from the walls. "Oh, shut up!" Callum snapped at the ceiling. "You'll just mend it as usual!"

No sooner did the words leave his lips, the leather patched itself together, smooth, and soft as if nothing had happened at all. Callum jerked a thumb at the repair. "See? Maybe now you'll change the décor here to match its new tenant."

There was a creak in response. The door to the hallway had opened no doubt. Callum rolled his eyes. "If you are insisting, I go out there to talk to him, I won't. *He* must come to *me*." Loud thuds made him bristle. "I don't know what you mean by that racket, but I'm staying right here." He flopped onto the settee to demonstrate, folding his arms tight across his chest.

Hours ticked by and the sun had long since set. The silence of sleep filled the air. That was when Callum's stomach decided to growl. Dammit all, he hadn't eaten since that morning, opting to skip dinner knowing that Rowan would be sitting at the table. He shoved a hand against his belly, but the gurgles only grew. The door to the hall slammed over and over, each crash louder than the first.

"Stop! You'll wake the dead!" Callum snarled. He jiggled as the floorboards rippled. "You want me out, then?! You'll have to push me out, you damned-"

A wild gale swirled through the room, lifting Callum in the air. It threw him up the stairs and into the main house, dropping him onto his belly with a thud. The door slammed behind him, a smug click of its lock following.

"Well, fuck off too, you creaky shack!" Callum spit his braids from his mouth, struggling to his knees. After a barrage of crude hand gestures at the hallway, he took a deep breath, collecting his composure. "Fine, I wanted to leave anyway. Get myself a bite to eat."

His belly rumbled as he set off down the stairs. The glow from the Yule tree warmed the otherwise dim room, creating a cheerier than usual mood that eased his sourness. He'd eat his fill then return to his wing and continue his solitude. Callum was a champion at disappearing. If he could hide in this house for eighty years, avoiding Rowan would be just as easy.

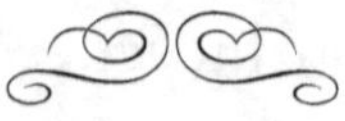

Rowan shot up from his bed, the warmth of the room slapping his icy flesh. His heart slammed against his ribs, nightmares racing through his mind. The car flipping over and over. The sound of crunching metal. Mom and Dad coated in blood, dangling upside down by their seat belts. Then darkness blanketed him. The shade wrapped itself tight, sucking his life and replacing it with a cold despair that made him weep. *Your fault! This is your fault!*

He slid out of bed, catching himself as his leg cramped. After a breath, he limped to the fireplace, eager for its glorious heat to coax the stiffness from his limbs. His flesh thawed but the guilt remained. Gods dammit, not even Ivy's house could fight that feeling. Just when he thought he had outrun it, it had caught him in its boney fingers.

Puffs of white escaped his lips. Rowan frowned. How the hell was his breath fogging the air? He kept his room like a furnace. He groped the talisman around his neck, thumb circling the sigils carved into its worn surface. "I'm not alone. I'm not alone, I'm not alone," he chanted, wishing the words would sink into his stubborn brain. They never did, only hovered before him like a good idea he couldn't quite formulate.

He shoved himself away from the fireplace, blowing into his palms in hopes of bring them back to life. "Walk it off, Rowan. A quick walk and it will all disappear from your mind."

Usually, a brisk trip around the block cleared his head. But this was Big Bear in the winter, not San Francisco. He couldn't jump into his sweats for a little stroll unless he had a snow shovel. A lap around the house would have to do.

Rowan snatched his robe and slippers from the closet and limped downstairs. "It's just nightmares," he muttered. "You always get a little upset around this time. And you're stressed. Of course, you're bound to have nightmares." *That shade followed you here. It found some way to get to you, again.* "No. The wards are too strong." *Then all those years of therapy must have worn off. Which one is it?* "Rowan Bennett. Calm the fuck down. You're fine, you're fine you're fine. It's just a damn shade!"

Shades had hitched rides with him tons of times before. It was a risk that came with being a veil walker. A few cleansing spells and poof, off they went. Except this one.

Rowan rounded the yule tree, flopping onto the couch, face buried in his hands. This was more than just some spirit not wanting to cross over. This felt personal. And creepy as fuck.

Heavy clacks exited the kitchen. Rowan stiffened, lifting his head to see Callum marching out, tearing his fangs through a huge hunk of leftover rabbit meat he'd probably scavenged from the fridge.

Gods, he was still gorgeous, a hulking Clydesdale of a male with the grace of a panther. Puckered scars crisscrossed over every inch of him. Rowan had always loved how they rippled when he breathed. Fire's warm light chiseled the satyr's form from the tip of his huge, curved horns all the way down to his fur coated legs and cloven hooves. Slung around his thick hips was his loincloth, adorned with a strap of leather. His long dark hair was woven tight to the sides of his head, the rest tumbling down his back in a riot of beads and waves.

Off came the dagger on Callum's belt and he cut a few slices meat free, wrapping them in a cloth and slipping them into his pouch. His comforters. There was never a time Rowan saw Callum without his pouch and dagger. A lusty sigh escaped, and Rowan slapped a hand over his mouth. Callum paused, lifting his head to sniff the air. His dark brows lowered along with the rabbit at his chops.

Crap! Rowan sunk down in hopes he could hide between the cushions, curling up tight. But Callum looked right at him, his deer-like ears perked. Rowan should say something. Anything.

"Hey." He winced. *Brilliant, Ro. Brilliant.* Callum vanished with a pop, his meat dropping to the floor. The clatter of his steps hurried to the stairs. "Wait! You don't have to go! I'll head back to my room so you can finish eating!" He looked at the mess on the floor. "Though you may want to get another helping."

A long pregnant silence made Rowan squirm, finally broken by Callum's sharp voice. "You were supposed to be gone for good."

Ouch. Rowan shook his head. "I never said that."

"You implied it when you ran." Callum cleared his throat, pitching his voice to Rowan's. "I have to go, Cal. I have a...thing."

Rowan shrank back into the couch, wishing it would swallow him. "Yeah, I did say that didn't I?"

"Then I'll leave you to your...thing." There was a growl, then more steps storming away.

Rowan climbed over the couch after him. It was too late to hide. Now it was time to talk to him and clear the air. "Wait a second Cal!" A shock of pain buckled his knees and he tumbled. "Aah Fuck!"

Strong hand snared his waist and Rowan was hauled up against Callum's invisible form, the touch of his palms burning through his robe and onto his waiting flesh. The last of the nightmare's chill fled, as he absorbed the satyr's warmth. Gods, he was like a glorious, sexy radiator.

"You're hurt?" Callum's voice was so deep. All vocabulary left Rowan's brain, registering only that sexy snarl. "Who hurt you?"

Rowan shook his head, managing a raspy, "No one."

"Then why did you fall?"

"It's an old injury that acts up in the cold."

The musky scent of pine and earth wrapped around him, heavy. Lustful. *No, Rowan. Step away from this. Say good night and go to bed.* That's what his brain said. His hands were busy testing hard, hewn muscle and raised scars. A shuddering breath whispered from Callum, his arms growing tighter. *Do* not *get a boner, Ro!*

The brush of Callum's tail thwacked his ankles, a thump-thump-thump hitting the floor behind them. Another whisk shook Rowan free of his onslaught of horniness. "What was that?"

"Nothing," Callum said all too quickly.

"Is your...tail wagging?"

"No!" Another thump-thump-thump betrayed the satyr. He released Rowan and the air shimmered. Callum reappeared; his squirming tail locked under his elbow. "See?"

Rowan covered his snorty laugh, but it kept on coming, making it hard to stop. Callum grinned. Oh Gods, he was grinning *that* grin. The one that made his eyes twinkle and gave his scarred face a roguish light. The very one that had brought Rowan to his knees the first time.

A sharp stab cut his mirth and he hissed, clutching his thigh. Callum scooped him up, carrying him to the couch and settling him. Rowan's head spun. *What just happened? Did he just princess carry me? Did I like it?* His cock twitched. *Oh yeah, I liked it.*

"So, you've returned then, Witch-boy."

"Just for Yule," Rowan replied.

Callum looked disappointed. "Then you'll disappear again. Head to what you call home."

"Yeah, I guess I..." The nightmare came roaring back. Crash of metal on metal, the smell of burning oil, the iron taste of blood. Green eyes. Sharp dagger like teeth. His palms turned clammy, edges of his vision feathering into black.

Callum pursed his lips, tracing worried lines across his face. "What's wrong? Why are you up at this hour?"

Rowan swallowed as he fiddled with the ties of his robe. "Nightmare. That's all."

"That's all," he echoed, the words heavy with queries. "Do you get nightmares often?"

All the time now. And they grew more vivid every time. Rowan slapped on a smile and shrugged. "They come and go. Nothing I can't handle."

Rowan half expected Callum to leave but he just nodded. "I understand nightmares all too well."

"I'm sure you do." Rowan shoved his hands into his robe pockets. "But they're just nightmares. I mean, how bad can that be, right?" When Callum arched a brow, Rowan's blush heated. "Okay, yeah. Nightmares can be bad. But I won't let them take over my life."

Another grim nod before Callum looked at his hooves. "I'm glad one of us is brave enough to declare that."

"I'm not brave. I've had my moments. But since they just happen in my sleep, I can endure them." *Or can you?* Sleep deprivation was becoming a serious issue these days.

Callum fished in his pouch, retrieving a small bottle filled with a shimmering blue liquid. "Drink this. It will help you sleep without dreams."

"I can't take your calming potions, Cal. You need them."

"Finn has endless supplies to make me tinctures for eternity. I can spare one." He wiggled the bottle at him.

"You're of no use to anyone without sleep. Do your sisters a favor and drink the potion."

Dammit, the satyr knew exactly what button to push to get him to comply. With a sigh, Rowan plucked the potion free. "Fine."

Callum placed a hand over his before the bottle met his lips. "Drink when you get back to your room."

"That potent, huh?"

"You wouldn't even make it off this couch after a sip. You'd be asleep in moments."

Rowan nodded, tucking it away in his pocket. "You know, sleep is a *blanket* statement." Callum narrowed his eyes, and Rowan giggled. "Sorry. Couldn't resist."

Callum's grumble rolled into a gruff chuckle. "Your jokes are still awful."

"Yeah, but you laugh. Everyone always says the jokes are bad and yet they always laugh."

"Hopeful thinking, Witch-Boy."

Oh, Gods the last time Rowan heard that nickname they were naked and pressed together. The sounds of Callum's groans, the heat of his mouth. Claws digging into Rowan's hips. The slap of a tail on his ass as Callum's enormous cock slid inside him.

Rowan grabbed a pillow, throwing it in his lap. What was it about Callum that turned him into a hormonal teenager? *Uh, look at him Ro! No, no don't look at him! It will only make the boner worse!*

Callum crossed his tree trunk arms, a slight pout on his lips. "A thank you would be nice."

"Oh! I...sorry I..." *Was too busy thinking about your dick.* "Thanks, Cal."

"You're welcome." Callum scooted away. "I know I am the last male you want to be near, so I appreciate the sentiment."

Rowan blinked. "What do you mean?"

"Running away after the first fuck leaves a bad impression," Callum smirked.

Rowan rubbed the back of his burning neck. "Oh...yeah." *Gods, you really stepped in it Ro,* he thought. *You really were an asshole.*

"It was my scars, wasn't it?" Callum murmured. "I was comely once. I had many bedfellows. And I have other attributes that you would enjoy..." The corner of his mouth twitched in a brief tease. "That you *did* enjoy. But I wasn't always this twisted mess."

"Are you joking? Callum, scars are hot. *You* are hot. Sweet Hecate you're the hottest guy I ever laid eyes on." Finally, the dark clouds drifted from Callum expression. His smile returned, twisting the split in his lips. Rowan softened. He reached over, hooking his pinkie around Callum's. "I'm...I'm sorry. I shouldn't have bolted. That was really shitty of me, but I was super overwhelmed at the time and I..." He bit the inside of cheek before he confessed more than he dared. "I don't expect you to forgive me, but you deserve an apology."

More silence. It urged Rowan to hightail it up the stairs, down that potion and sleep until all this bullshit finally passed. *Sleep. Ugh. No more sleep. Just sit.* At least here it was peaceful. Here he was safe with Callum.

Callum's calloused palm slid over his knuckles. "Thank you."

The air went thick as paste, trapping them in the goop of their awkwardness. "How about a truce?" Rowan asked. "Since I'm going to be here through Yule, it's best if we just get along."

"There'd have to be war to have a truce, Witch-boy." Callum's tail flip flopped against the back of the couch, and he snatched it, clearing his throat. "I'll accept this truce and your apology."

A glimmer sparked inside Rowan, one that cut through the lingering nightmare plaguing him. "Cool," he said, then groaned. *Can you try to say something decent for once, Ro?* "I mean awesome. Uh, cool and awesome." *That was worse.* Rowan pushed himself to his feet. "Well, I better get to bed before I sound stupider."

"Stay," Callum charged. "I'm sure neither of us are ready for sleep."

Rowan couldn't fight the delicious command, loving how it vibrated up his spine. "Yeah, I can sit for a while, sure." Another smile curled Callum's lips and just like that, Rowan eased himself back onto the couch, the relaxed vibe overwhelming and wonderful.

Well, they had their words, they made their amends. Now what? *You know what you want to do.* No question about it. He'd give his right hand, and his left, for a replay of that night in October.

Callum's pointed tongue wetted his bottom lip. Oh yeah, whatever Rowan was thinking, Callum was thinking it too. But no, he couldn't. There was too much going on. Rowan had his sisters to worry about. He had his job, or lack thereof. But the claws dancing over Rowan's bicep was filling him with other ideas. The sharp tips made their way up, brushing his collarbone then lifting the talisman from his neck. "You never told me what this was," Callum said.

"It's from my parents." Rowan swallowed, as Callum gave the talisman a little tug, pulling him closer. "It helps with…"

Callum's mouth was right there for the taking. Rowan balled his fists, fighting the oncoming arousal spike that was sailing right to his crotch. *Too fast! Too fast! Hakuna your tatas Ro!* He had to sort out his own shit before diving on Callum's dick. But by the Gods, he wanted it so badly. Callum moved in closer, the danger reaching a fevered pitch.

"Did you hear about the woman who loved making archery supplies?" Rowan blurted. Callum pulled away, blinking in confusion as Rowan snapped his finger. "Every day she went to work, she quivered with joy."

"By the Goddesses tits, Rowan!" Callum groaned. "Don't make me regret this truce!" And just like that, Rowan could breathe again.

Chapter 3

*B*lood *gushed down Callum's back in sheets, hot and thick, pooling under him as his wailed, "No! Stop! I beg you!" Down came her dagger, slicing, scraping, tearing his meat away. He could hear Finn begging between his screams, and the angry curses of the warlock. His baby brother would be next on the altar. And Callum would be gone, unable to save him. He was supposed to save him! He was put on this earth to protect his brother!* Sweet Goddess, if one of us survives, please let it be Finn!

The silver haired witch smiled. She was beautiful, with her ruby lips and her lavender eyes. She had been beautiful when she had arrived that summer morning, setting foot into their territory without fear. She was beautiful when she introduced herself, wise enough to only use her first name. And she remained beautiful as she'd peeled the flesh from Callum's back.

"Such delicious anguish from such a strong male," She purred. Her blade glinted, its blood stains turning black in

the moon's light. "You alone can power my coven for years, my strong one." A chorus of cackles joined hers, the surrounding witches cheering in delight at his torture. "Say her name again, my sweet."

"Stop..." Callum whimpered. "Don't do this."

"Say it!"

"...Orlaith.

But Orlaith was dead now. Callum had tried to leap in the spell's path but was too slow. It hit true, cleaving Orlaith's neck. Dead. She was dead.

After that was a berserker's rage. He'd cut down every witch he saw; piercing them with his arrows, cutting them to pieces with his dagger. And when the blade broke, he slashed them apart with his bare hands, the bright scarlet glow of his eyes matching the blood that coated him. The coven had howled in horror, frightened long enough for him to grab Finn and run. They had escaped to the warlock who hid deep in the forest in his fortress of a home. Callum vowing that Finn would not die. The coven may have taken his mate, and their herd, but they wouldn't take his baby brother. Or so he thought.

Soon the coven had Finn in their clutches, rope around his neck, knife as his throat. His tear-filled eyes pleading as he whimpered, "Cal. Help me! Please!" Callum had lowered his claws and fell to his knees. That was the day he was finally broken.

"I let her die. I let them all die!" Callum cried.

"Cal, wake up."

The dagger came down again.

"I let her die!"

"Callum!"

Callum gasped, his eyes snapping open. Rowan was there, not the silver haired demon that carved him to pieces. Rowan. Sweet, kind Rowan. "It's okay. It's just me," he said.

Relief was a cold bucket of ice water on Callum's clammy skin. "Witch-boy?"

"You're having a panic attack," Rowan said. "But you're going to be fine. Just listen to my voice." Callum nodded dumbly as Rowan held out his hands." I'm going to touch you, is that all right?" Once again, Callum nodded and was rewarded with firm yet gentle palms on his shoulders. "It's going to pass, Big Guy. I promise. It always passes."

"It...it always passes," Callum lunged, wrapping his arms around Rowan's shoulders, despair pulling him deep into the dark. "Gods, am I doomed to spend the rest of my days too frightened to face anyone? To do anything?!"

"Of course, you won't," Rowan said. "But healing takes time."

"I've been healing for decades! I want it to end!" His claws curled against Rowan's back. "I want to walk free again. I want to face the world, not be a coward."

"Hey. You're not a coward." Rowan's thumbs brushed his cheekbones, their gazes locking. "You're a tough bastard, Cal. And when you're ready, you'll face the world out there. Hell, you might even walk right into the middle of town. And if you need it, I'll walk right beside you."

Callum's terror melted away as soon as Rowan's gentle smile appeared. "Truly?"

"Tell me when you're ready. We'll march arm and arm." His warm hands stroked Callum's back, coaxing him to stillness. "Say it one more time. Make me feel it. The feelings always pass."

"The feelings always pass." Callum swallowed the last of his fear, collapsing against the witch's chest. He was safe. His gentle, caring witch-boy wouldn't hurt him. None of his family were like the silver haired one. This is where he needed to be, wanted to be. The steady beat of Rowan's heart soothed him to stillness. "I fell asleep?"

"A few hours ago. I didn't want to wake you. Then you started getting restless." Rowan smoothed Callum's unruly locks. "Want me to walk you to your wing so you can get some rest?"

The mere idea of being alone made bile rise. Callum shook his head hard, fingers curling into Rowan's forearms, desperate to keep him close. *Don't leave me.* It sat on the tip of his tongue, held back by whatever pride inside him remained.

Rowan fished the potion bottle out of his pocket. "Okay. Then we'll sleep here."

Callum shook his head. "That's for you."

"How about we split it?" Rowan popped the cork free. "Because I don't think either of us are going to fall asleep easily tonight." He took a quick sip then handed it to

Callum. With trembling hands Callum took the bottle, downing the rest.

The two laid back, Rowan resting his head on Callum's shoulder. "You need to talk about it?" he asked.

"Perhaps in time," Callum replied. "Perhaps I'll be brave enough again."

"Meh, you're brave just for surviving this." Rowan squeezed Callum's knee. 'I got your back."

The tiniest of smiles softened Callum's lips as he inhaled the witch's clean, crisp scent. He wasn't alone. He could revel in that, tonight. "You are a wonder, Witch-boy."

The heat of Rowan's blush tickled his flesh. "No. I'm not."

"Yes, you are. A complete wonder."

Glorious numbness, took over, his thoughts going slack. The last thought before sleep wasn't of blood, or pain, or the silver haired witch. It was of Rowan. *He needs to know how special he truly is. He needs to know it as strongly as I. And I will be the one to show him.* A smile rested on his lips as he drifted off to sleep.

Chapter 4

When Callum woke, Rowan was gone. He sat up, still groggy from the potion aftermath, wondering if last night was just a glorious dream. It must have been. Things didn't wrap up in such a nice, neat bow like that, especially for him. Something under his hand crunched. A folded note was wedged under his palm, laying where Rowan once was. Carefully, he opened it, reading the neat, precise handwriting.

Cal,

Had to run to my Aunts' place this morning and didn't want to wake you. I'm glad we're at a truce. Thanks for the talk last night. And the potion. Hope we can talk again soon.

Rowan.

An elated laugh squeaked from his throat, giddy pitter-patters dancing a little jig inside his chest. It wasn't a dream. There was a truce. That meant there was a chance. Callum tucked the note away in his pouch as proof, not that anyone beyond him needed that reassurance but he'd take all he could get. He marched up the stairs into the main house. The mission was clear. And there was only one witch in particular that could help him.

After getting chased out of Ivy's bedroom for—ahem—various reasons, he went to the *other* only witch in particular who could help him. One who wouldn't be occupied in such a carnal manner.

Callum bounded down the hall, nostrils flaring as he took in the air. The delicate scent of jasmine caught him, and he snapped his fingers. *Good, she's in her room.* Two steps and he was in front of Aster's door, throwing it open. "I need your help!"

Aster screeched in surprise, her sketchbook tumbling from her lap. She scrambled for it, giving him a glare. "Seriously, Cal? After our talk?"

"Oh. Our talk. Yes." Callum bowed his head, tailed tucked between his legs. Slowly he backed out of her bedroom, closing the door behind him. He held his breath, counted to ten, then knocked.

"Come in," Aster called.

Once again, he flung the door open repeating, "I need your help!" just in case she missed it the first time. When she nodded in approval, he strode inside.

"See? He can learn," she murmured to her sketchbook before setting it aside, pages open to a drawing of a shadowy horned figure, his huge wings spread off the page. Callum tightened his mouth, saying nothing. He'd caught her more than once whispering to her drawings, looking hopeful for a reply.

Aster was still clad in her sleep clothes, dark circles under her light blue eyes and her strawberry blonde locks pulled up in a messy top knot. But he couldn't deny the loveliness beneath her exhaustion. All the Bennett witches were breathtaking in their own way, Rowan being the most fetching of all. "You, okay? You're practically vibrating." She gasped, grabbing his arm. "You're not having a panic attack, are you?"

Callum thumped his chest. "No. I'm vibrating for good."

Aster wrinkled her nose. "Probably not the connotation you wanted there, Cal."

"I assure you; it is. Tell me Rowan's desires and wants. All of them."

"Me?" Aster cocked her head. "Shouldn't you be asking Ivy that? *She's* his twin."

"I tried. She threw me out of her bedroom." He flicked a finger against his ear. "I listened for sex and heard none! How would I know her mouth was full at the time?"

"Oh, my Gods!" She buried her face in her hands, clucking out a chortle.

"It's not funny," he grunted.

"Yes, it is." Aster bit her lips closed, turning red as her shoulders shook with mirth.

The harder Callum glared, the louder her giggles grew. He huffed. "Fine. It was funny when Ivy bit Finn's shaft but the book she threw at me was not funny at all!" Aster fell back onto her bed, clutching her belly as the hysterics took over. He threw up his arms, beginning to regret his decision on which sister to talk to. "Will you help me or not? This is important!"

She sat up, struggling with her composure. "For the sake of Ivy's sex life, I'll help." She patted the mattress beside her, and Callum obeyed with a sit, tail flipping in nervous jerks. "Okay, can you tell me why you suddenly want this info? Yesterday you didn't even want to talk to him."

"We came to a truce last night."

"So, you had sex?"

"No. Cocks were not out. But an understanding was reached, and we're fine to be in each other's presence."

"Well, it's a start I guess." Aster tapped her lower lip. "Okay, so Rowan's wants and desires...Well, in the looks department you have it made. Rowan loves the big burly types. And the scars are-"

"Hot." Warmth filled his belly as Rowan's declaration echoed in his mind. He squared his shoulders, head held higher than before. "Rowan told me last night. I'm hot."

Another giggle trilled from Aster. "Cal, you're so cute."

Well, that deflated him fast. He folded his arms giving Aster an irritated snort. "I'm not cute! I'm carnal, virile, and strapping! In other words, hot!"

"You're wagging your tail like an eager puppy!" She nodded to it slapping the headboard in a frantic thump-thump-thump.

Callum snatched the renegade appendage, shoving it into his lap. "Then I'm a carnal, virile, strapping puppy!" He frowned, ignoring yet another barrage of laughter. "But this isn't about what he thinks of me. I'm on a quest to make him understand his worth."

Aster balled her fists against her cheeks letting loose a high-pitched squeal that made his ears flip back. "You want to make him feel good! Oh sweet Artemis, that is so precious!"

"Indeed. I made him feel good with my shaft once. Words will be next." Another squeak and Callum clapped his hands, hoping that would sober her from her giddy nonsense. "Now, his desires and wants, please?"

She cleared her throat, sitting up as if at a lesson, counting off each of her brother's wants on her fingers. "Let's see, his favorite color is yellow,"

"I know that."

"He loves good vegetarian food."

"That I also know." By accident. Callum had brought him four kills from his hunts before Rowan confessed, he couldn't stomach the idea of meat.

"He's also an animal lover. Used to pet sit for everyone when we were kids and was nuts over Aunt Dahlia's cat, Betty Davis. You know he was kind of jealous that Ivy got a familiar even though he wouldn't say it."

"That information could come in handy later. Anything else?

Aster gasped. "Oh! He's a *complete* word slut!"

"Word... slut?" Callum's ears perked. Did those words even go together? If they did, it sounded complicated. "Explain."

"Shakespeare, poetry, super romantic songs. He totally melts for that. He had a musician boyfriend back when he was in high school who used to write songs for him. And he loved it." She wrinkled her nose. "Then the guy cheated on him, and the novelty wore off."

Callum gnashed his fangs, a growl rolling from his throat. The mere thought of some bastard human hurting his witch-boy was intolerable. Perhaps his head would be a good present for him. "Where is this male now?"

"Easy tiger," Aster replied. "He's been out of the picture for decades. I doubt Rowan even remembers his name."

Erased from Rowan's mind? That was acceptable. Instead of violence, he'd fill Rowan's thoughts with his sweet deeds as his form of justice. "Then I'll write him poems. Dozens of them! Hundreds! True ones! Yes, I can work with this." He clasped Aster's shoulder. "Thank you, Aster. I owe you a favor."

Aster smirked. "My favor is knocking from now on."

"Consider it granted." He wrapped his knuckles on the headboard as an example. "Fetch me a pen and paper! I must capture these words while they are fresh!"

"...Please?" Aster added.

Callum sighed. "*Please* fetch me a pen and paper." Aster gave his knee a pat and went to her desk, leaving her open sketchbook beside him. He picked it up, thumbing through countless drawings of the gargoyle; his eyes bright, body sculpted from darkness, the images so detailed they looked ready to leap to life. Satyrs called his kind the King of Shadows. His heart cracked, feeling her loneliness on those pages.

"Oh, you're not supposed to see that." Aster hurried over, grabbing for her book like an eager child. "I should have put it away."

"I don't judge such things, little sister." Callum handed it to her.

She tightened her mouth, running her fingers down the dark charcoal. "I know this looks crazy. But it helps to sketch him. Like if I keep his details fresh on the paper I'm manifesting him, keeping him alive." She closed her sketches with a sigh. "When I was out there on the mountain with my curse, he would talk to me. Just crack stupid jokes or piss me off or make me laugh... He made me feel human again. Reminded me I wasn't completely the monster my coven..." She winced. "*That* coven turned me into." The twinkle left her eyes as they welled with tears. "Gods, I wish I could see him again, not just a drawing. I wish I knew if he were alive or not."

Callum's jaw clenched. He knew how strong hope could be. And how devastating. *No, she's too young, too fresh to be crushed like that. Let her dream a little longer.*

"Your King of Shadows isn't dead. He's probably hiding somewhere, bemoaning how you bested him." When she opened her mouth to protest, Callum pressed his wrist against his forehead and moaned, "How?! How could she be stronger than me?! A King of Shadows, bested by a witch?! Hooooow!?"

A ghost of a chuckle haunted her mouth. "I was a twenty-foot-tall monster at the time, not a witch."

"And I'm sure you would have bested him even more in your true form."

The laugh finally broke through and she cupped Callum's cheeks. "Thanks for the pep talk. I need to keep believing he's okay. If I believe it, and keep sketching, it will be true right?"

There was a knock at her door and Ivy—who didn't look happy but then not completely unhappy either—entered. A riot of colorful flowers wrapped in bright blue paper rested in her hands. "Is Callum in here?" she asked.

"Yeah." Aster poked at the flowers. "Are those for me or for him?"

"Me!" Callum rushed over, plucking the bouquet from Ivy's grip. "Where did you find these in this season? A magical meadow?"

"At the grocery store." Ivy folded her arms across her ample bosom, face stern. "There. You got your flowers. *Now* will you learn to knock after this?"

"Only if you learn to make louder noises when sucking my brother's cock," he replied.

Ivy sighed.

Aster cackled.

"Aster, I need a mirror." Callum winced and quickly added. "*Please*, I need a mirror." He unwrapped the flowers from their paper prison, cutting the blooms from their long stems with his claws and piling them by color on the bed. "Where is Finn? I must work with him with my words."

"He's busy...icing his dong." Ivy turned pink before slapping her hands on her hips. "What's this all about?"

"I'm making Rowan feel good." When Ivy's eyes widened in horror he snorted. "Don't worry. No mating, this time."

"Of course, I'm going to worry!" Ivy replied. "So what? You're going to seduce him? It's not like I'm against Rowan getting laid but the last time-"

"I'm going to show him how special he is with deeds and words." Callum shook his dark mane, weaving blossoms into his braids while Aster, held her mirror. "I vow I will woo him without courtship. It will be good for him."

"Oh Gods..." Ivy groaned. "Cal, the primary objective is great. But what if Rowan reacts like last time? Are you going to sulk forever? And what about *his* feelings? Something is up with him, Cal. Something he's not talking about, and I don't want it to get worse."

Callum swallowed. Rowan had been so haunted last night, his nightmares bringing out his ghosts. But wooing could only make it better, right? How would pouring on praise and gifts make things worse? Besides, Rowan said there was a truce, said they should get along. He said that scars are hot... *You're so blind. He said that to placate you.*

Callum looked at his reflection. At the long gash that split his eyelid. The puckered flesh that twisted his lip. The countless lines that trailed down his chin, blanketing his chest. Scars are hot... Hot...

Hot...

Fire...

The silver-haired witch's dagger, glowing hot from the flames...*Such delicious anguish from such a strong male. Your power is delicious...*

She wanted to take his eye, then his tongue. Wanted to feed them to Finn who was beaten and bound, waiting for his turn. *You couldn't protect your brother. You couldn't even save your mate.* Callum's throat thickened, his heart clenching. If he couldn't save them, he could never protect Rowan. *You* will *make things worse.*

"Cal?" Ivy asked. "You, okay?"

Weakling. Weak, twisted, and broken. You will never be the warrior you once were. Burden! You make things worse!

"Callum?" Aster called.

A failure to your herd, to your brother, to Orlaith. And someday to Rowan too. Callum bared his fangs, emotion rising like a volcano.

"C-Callum, you're uh..." Ivy gestured to his eyes as she backed across the room, her voice trembling. "Getting *really* emotional."

Callum turned towards the mirror, flashing red eyes staring back. He slapped his hands over his eyes, inhaling a deep breath, then another. The fury ebbed and slowly, he peeled his fingers away. When Ivy slumped in relief, he knew his gaze had returned to normal. "My apologies. I know that bothers you."

"No. I got you worked up and said something shitty. *I'm* sorry." Ivy sat down beside him with a shame filled smile. "Let me make it up to you and finish your braids." Callum gave a compliant grunt and she thread her fingers through his hair. "Aunt Rosemary taught me this when we were kids. It's a given to wear flowers in your hair when your aunt is a green witch."

"Ivy used to braid mine every Ostara," Aster added.

"Rowan's too." Ivy plucked a daisy from the pile.

Callum scoffed. "How in the seven hells did you manage to braid Rowan's hair?"

"There was a really short period when he decided to grow it out." She grinned. "Oh yeah. He had a hippy phase. It didn't last long. He couldn't stand it when it touched his cheeks. Would flail like he walked into a spider web."

Imagine the clean shaven and impeccably cut Rowan, with a head of thick fiery locks down his back. The idea seemed so strange and yet so enticing. What would it have been like to wave his fingers through that mane? "Be sure to place the yellow ones in the front," Callum, said, lost in that daydream. "Yellow is his favorite color."

"Already on it," Ivy tied off the last braid, giving his head a little pat. "So, you want to make Rowan feel special, huh?" Callum nodded as she draped her handy work over his shoulders. "Good. He needs to know."

"Tell me about it," Aster added. "Rowan the Light-house takes care of everyone but himself. A little pampering would do him good."

"I appreciate the encouragement." Callum said.

"I'm happy to give it," Ivy replied. "You're a good guy, Callum. And I trust you. But a word of advice from his twin. He's stubborn and skittish as a cat. Relationships scare the hell out of him for some reason. He's never had one that lasted over a month or two. So just..." She pursed her lips, as if trying to find her words. "Just be gentle and slow."

"Gentle and slow..." Callum pressed a fist to his heart. "You will never see anyone move with more care around your brother. I will woo him like I make love to him."

Ivy pressed her hands over her ears. "Ooookay too much info there, Cal."

The sound of tires crunching on snow came from out-side followed by the sound of a car door shutting. "He has returned!" Callum rose, realizing his pen and paper had gone ignored. "There's no time to write a poem. Dammit!"

"Just go with your gut!" Aster patted his shoulder. "Make it sound fancy! Remember! He's a word slut!"

Ivy blinked at her. "Seriously? You told him that?"

Callum wet his dry lips. Go with his gut. Make it sound fancy. He could do that. Hells, he had written Orlaith a sonnet right on the spot when he'd wooed her. Surely, he could do that same for Rowan... maybe. *No! There is no maybe! You can do this!* He patted his braids. "The flowers are in place, yes?"

"You look as pretty as a Rose Bowl parade float," Ivy said.

"I don't know what that is, but good!" He stepped to the door. "Don't come downstairs!"

"You know the new rules!" Ivy called after him. "Loincloths *on* in the living room! And slow and gentle! Slow and gentle!" She groaned. "Gods, why do I have the feeling this is going to be anything but slow and gentle?"

He headed down the stairs, ready for battle. But instead of his bow and dagger, he was armed with words and knowledge. *Go with your gut. Make it fancy.*

The front door opened and Rowan stepped through the threshold, wiping his wet boots on the mat. Callum leapt across the room, hooves skidding across the hardwood floor before he fell to his knees. The tremendous thud made Rowan jump and he jerked his head up, hand still resting on the doorknob. "Uh, hi Cal," he said. "You...okay?"

Callum's pulse quickened, sweat coating his palms. Gods above his eyes. His beautiful blue eyes. Dammit, what was he doing? He was supposed to say something, wasn't he?

"The flowers are nice." Rowan cocked his head. "Did you lose something, or do you need help getting up?"

What was wrong with him? This hadn't been so hard with Orlaith all those decades ago. Why was it now? He took a deep breath. *Go with your gut. Make it fancy.* He cupped his hands to his heart, willing it to slow. *Let the words come. Let them flow through you like music. Tell the witch-boy what you think of him!* With a sudden gasp, he took Rowan's hands, pressing his lips to his palms.

Rowan instantly turned bright red, looking over his shoulder then back to Callum. "Okay, this might be a bad time to-"

"An ode to my Witch-boy!" Callum bellowed. "Oh, my beautiful male! My Rowan! Eyes like sapphires and hair as bright as the fire that burns in my loins!"

"Your what?" Rowan squeaked.

"How they burn for you!" Callum pressed Rowan's hands to his heart "Feel me burn! Burning with lust! The need for your flesh is strong! To smell you! To taste you! To suckle you and drink your sweet nectar!"

Rowan's mouth hung open. "...My what?"

It was coming much easier now, each word flowing like water. "Honey and cream! Sweet and rich! Oh, to feel you spend upon me! Such a dream within a dream to feel your heat dribbling down my hard flesh!"

"Oh Gods. This is *really* graphic." Rowan looked around then back to him, still wearing that beautiful shade of red. "What are you doing?"

"Wooing you with words," Callum replied. "I was told you're a word slut."

"Word...?" Rowan light brows lowered, and he released an exasperated grunt before screaming, "Aster! Gods dammit!"

"I have pictured the day I will possess your body! Naked and writhing, our cocks like two entwined snakes on a tree!" Rowan shut his eyes, clearly overwhelmed by Callum's talent for words. Sure, it might not have been gentle and slow, but it seemed to get results. "Moaning snakes bewitched with lust!" He leapt up, taking Rowan by the waist and pulling him close. "Touch my lust snake, my Witch-boy. Let us tangle together."

Rowan cleared his throat. "Cal..." Callum held his breath as he leaned in, whispering, "My aunts are right behind me."

"Your...aunts?" Callum leaned to the side, spotting two women on the porch.

Dahlia was tall and dark as a tower, dressed in a heavy black fur coat with a hat to match. The other was Rosemary, small and plump in a rumpled puffy jacket of bright green. Both wore enormous smiles which contrasted with Rowan's deep frown.

"Oh Lia!" Rosemary cooed. "We're witnessing a true satyr mating ritual!"

"Indeed!" Dahlia clutched Rosemary's shoulders, giving her a tiny shake of glee. The two women rushed inside; hands clasped with eagerness.

"What are they doing here?" Callum asked.

"They came for dinner tonight," Rowan groaned. "Closed the shop early for family time."

At one time Callum would have been terrified of the two women but after months of them forcing themselves into his personal space, he had grown accustomed to their slightly unnerving presence. Yet he still couldn't help but take a step back. "Perhaps I will continue later, Witch-boy."

"Nonsense!" Dahlia stepped in front of Rowan before he spoke. She twirled a regal hand at Callum. "Don't stop because of us, Callum. Please continue."

"Beautiful poetry!" Rosemary sighed. "I especially like the snake part. Don't you, Rowan, dear?"

When she patted Rowan's arm, his mouth turned up into a smile. A somewhat pained smile but a smile all the same. "It's... vivid."

Callum's pride swelled. Fuck slow and gentle. Bombastic and riotous was getting results. Dahlia took Rosemary's arm and ushered her towards the couch. "We'll sit and observe. You won't even know we're here."

Callum pressed Rowan's palm to his lips. By the Goddess, he was trembling at his words! Aster was right. Rowan was indeed a word slut. "Prepare yourself, Witch-boy. There is much more to come.

Chapter 5

The bell over the shop door hadn't even stopped ringing before Rowan announced, "Can we just not talk about it?" as he hurried inside.

He shook his head, dashing past the tables of crystals, shelves of books, and his aunts, side by side behind the counter, beaming at him as if he'd won the lottery.

"Nope. I'm going to set up my table in the back and get to work," he said. "Not talk about yesterday's poetry slam."

Never mind that it had gone on for hours. Well, more like fifteen minutes but it felt like hours. There was an entire paragraph dedicated to Rowan's ass; its shape, its color, the number of freckles it had (apparently fifty-two), and of course what acts Callum planned to perform on it. He hadn't spared one damn detail, making Rowan want dissolve into the cracks in the floor. Instead, he had opted to hide in his room and avoid everyone for the rest of the night.

"Maybe just a little bit of talk?" Rosemary batted her eyes. "For research! I'm writing a book on Satyrs and their mating habits, you know."

"Darling, you're not writing a book." Dahlia's red lips curled into a sly grin. She pulled a key from the pocket of her Morticia Adams style dress. "Rowan dear, the tarot room is locked. You can't sequester yourself just yet so you might as well talk to us. We're all ears."

Rowan blew out a puff of air, scattering the hair from his forehead. Fighting his aunts was like boxing a hurricane. "Okay fine. Just lay it on me." He spread his arms out wide, head tilted back as he waited for the firing squad.

"It was so very charming, Rowan!" Rosemary shook her fists, hearts practically forming in her eyes.

Dahlia pressed her hand against her chest with a dreamy sigh. "The part about your backside gave me goosebumps! Such imagery!"

"Did you really have to listen to the whole thing?" Rowan asked.

Rosemary gave a sage nod. "It's good research for my book."

"You are not writing a book," Dahlia scolded. "You simply can't help yourself when satyrs are involved."

"But they are fascinating creatures. Filled with mystery and lust. So much lust." Rosemary gasped. "Lia! I just had a brilliant idea. Callum should come to Krampusnacht! With his horns and hooves and his huge size he would be an amazing Krampus for the children!"

"Oh yes!" Dahlia cheered. "Good idea, love!"

"Oh no," Rowan replied. "Bad idea. Very bad idea." He could already see the terror in Callum's eyes. Gods, the idea of being amongst all those humans and witches would scare him shitless.

"What harm would it be to ask him? I'm sure he'd have a lovely experience!" Dahlia shrugged. "Besides, he couldn't do a worse job than you did."

"Really?" Rowan said flatly.

Rosemary shook her head. "The police were called, Rowan. It was bad."

"And on that humiliating note, I better set up the tarot room." He held his hand out for the key but was promptly ignored.

"Rosie, my love, fetch Rowan some tea." Dahlia said.

"I'll make you my special blend," Rosemary cooed. "Lavender and rose hips for your nerves and your relationship." She bounded off, her gray curls bouncing along with her long green skirts.

Rowan shoved his hands into his pockets, Dahlia's smug smile a heat seeking missile. "You have more to say. I can feel it."

"Of course I do, dear. You saw the painting, yes?" Dahlia asked. "The one we commissioned from Aster?"

"Hard to miss," *Especially if it was your own ass on display. Freckles and all.* "I know you and Aunt Rosie really want me to get together with Callum, but it's not going to happen."

"Why not? You are perfection together. Two strapping males who have been through so much sadness in their lives that- Ah, ah, ah! Don't you shake your head at me, Rowan Connell Bennett! You have been on your own for far too long and loathe it."

Rowan sighed. "I don't loathe being alone, Auntie Lia." The lie was bitter on his lips.

"You can't fool a witch who practically raised you. You hate being alone and have since you were a child. It's why your father made you that talisman." On reflex, his hand went to his sweater, tracing the outline of his pendant, Dahlia giving him a knowing look. "It's a wonder why you moved away from here in the first place."

Because I was able to leave the bad memories behind. He rubbed his leg, the dull ache a token of what had happened. What he had done.

Rosemary returned from the back, pressing a steaming mug into his hands. With a grateful smile he took a sip, hoping the aroma of rose hips would overpower the phantoms dancing in his mind. "I'm not in the market for a boyfriend. It's just not the right time."

Rosemary clasped her hands before her, eyes gentle. "Rowan dear, it's never been a right time for you."

"It's true. You never had a boyfriend," Dahlia added.

"Yes, I have," Rowan said. "I've had a lot of them." His lips parted then sealed as he tried to recall at least one relationship that wasn't a fling, a booty call, or just a fun one-night stand. Nothing. Nada. The big goose egg. "I have my career to worry about." *You mean you* had *your career.* "Ooookay!" He stood, forcing a laugh into his sharp tone. "I really should get into that card room." He held out his hand again. "Please?"

Dahlia placed the key into his waiting palm. "At least ask Callum about being our Krampus? A night out would be good for you both."

Sweet Hecate, once Dahlia and Rosemary had a life plan for someone, that plan would come to fruition come hell or high water. And since he didn't have the patience to fight or the heart to tell them to back off, Rowan nodded in reply, not daring to give them a verbal agreement. He handed his tea back to Rosemary, gave both a kiss on their cheeks then hightailed it into the card room, shutting the door before they could follow.

The room had already been prepared, not that he expected less of his aunts. Pillar candles were lit, and a stick of incense burned in the corner making the air taste of sandalwood and spice. The small table was dressed in a violet cloth with two plush velvet chairs at the ready. They even set out the beautiful tarot deck he'd left behind. The one that he hadn't used since he'd left town.

His dad had taught him how to read Tarot with that deck. Every week he'd sit with Rowan, teaching him the skills of grounding and centering, how to listen to the spirits that whispered the meaning of the cards he drew. And every lesson ended with him telling Rowan how proud he was of him.

Heartache spread to his limbs, stiffening every joint and pinging every nerve. *No, stop thinking about that.*

Stop it right now. He clutched his talisman, chanting "I'm not alone. I'm not alone. I'm not alone."

He closed his eyes, shoving his grief aside to imagine what color Callum would turn if he asked him to be Krampus for a bunch of kids. Probably some shade of purple. There would be no way Rowan would subject Callum to that form of torture. He'd sooner play the Krampus himself again. Not like anyone would want him to. Which was for the best.

But what if Callum said yes? Afterall he'd just confessed how he wanted to leave the confines of the house. Callum worked hard getting his panic attacks under control, using his rescue potions less frequently. Maybe he'd be willing to try. *Maybe* you *should at least try.*

A sour taste filled Rowan's mouth. Try? Try at what? Dating a satyr? He was in his forties. It was way too late in the game to change the life he'd settled for. Yet there was something about Callum that made him feel safe and wanted, made him want to lower his guard and just be himself, not the fortress he'd always been. Not to mention the oddly endearing poetry. Sure, it was awful but so sincere that it tugged at Rowan's heart. How many guys in the past wrote him poems? None. That's how many.

Rowan shook away the temptation. No. What mattered was his sisters and those spirits on the other side of the veil. It is why he chose to be a veil walker over a healer. The law enforcement for his kind needed him. *Yeah, but you're not needed now since you've refused to cross the veil.*

He rested his head in his hands. "You need to get back to work and back to your life. It's just a shade. Push it back across the veil where it belongs."

Cold consumed him, bony fingers brushing his cheek. Rowan stilled. No, it wasn't in this plane. It only existed in the veil, in his nightmares. Yet he felt its stare upon him. Rowan clutched the table. "You're losing, Rowan. It's not here. Manifest good things." He took a deep breath. "Blessed Hecate, please show me something good."

The candles flickered, flames splitting into two sweeping horns, long ears, and a strong jaw. Callum. Rowan breathed out his anxiety, concentrating on the satyr dancing in the fire.

Callum with his comforting embrace and his twitching ears always ready to listen. His eagerness to please. His sweetness under all that stony hurt. Someone in this world who wanted Rowan just as he was.

The flame snuffed out, smoke trails swirling from the wick like a ghostly hand. But the thought still tickled his brain like a hard-to-reach itch. *Maybe you don't have to be alone. Maybe, Callum is what you need.* He swallowed. *At least ask him about Krampusnacht. The worst he could say is no.*

The knock at the door snapped him out of his trance. He shuffled his deck calling "Come in," Callum's silhouette still burning in his gaze. *Don't think about it now. Think about it later.* But it was always later. Now never occurred when it came to this type of thing.

Rowan straightened, plastering on his best smile as his first customer entered. He shoved Callum to the back of his mind, yet the satyr remained, still smiling. Still tempting him.

Chapter 6

The wraith waited out in the snow dusted street, attention locked on the shop's door. Strangers bustled in and out of the establishment, their emotions licking its flesh as they passed. A teaspoon of sadness here, a dab of fear there, a peppering of anger on top, all of it making its empty belly growl. But none of these beings were worthy of its hunger. None of them were Rowan.

It longed to be inside with him, but the wards had forced it out right after a fleeting touch of Rowan's cheek. It was flung outside, drained, and worn. And there it waited.

The time ticked by. No sign of him. The longer the wraith waited, the weaker it became, having deprived itself of other nourishment beyond the witch for far too long. Damnit, it would have to eat something soon or fade back into the realm of the dead for good.

It reached out, snatching a silver thread of despair from a young girl's heart. She stumbled, oblivious to the wraith's presence and tears rained from her eyes. Her friends consoled her as she fell to her knees and sobbed. It slurped the sorrow down, the girl's thoughts flooding its tongue; flashes of an argument with a boy, cruel words exchanged, and then the sadness as he stormed away. It was fine. Perhaps even tasty. Yet the food soured its belly.

How could it betray Rowan like this? How could it take another so easily? No, Rowan was all it wanted, all it needed. It whispered a soft apology, spitting the remains into the air before it could be sated. The weakness returned, making it dizzy. *I must latch onto him now or lose him completely.* Rowan. Its prize. Its love. Its obsession.

The wraith had known Rowan wasn't some average veil walker the moment it had seen him. He had arrived in the realm of the dead, curiously peering at the wraith, as if was just a mere shade. Of course, it played into that sham. If Rowan knew what it truly was, he would have fled like every other walker.

It still remembered his gentle smile. How he talked so softly, so warmly, as if to comfort it. Silly witch, thinking it needed such cajoling. But it was charmed none the less, and curious enough to take a taste of him while he passed. It didn't expect pure ecstasy.

His guilt had tasted so fresh, so new, despite the decades that had passed. The accident. His parents. His sisters in peril. One taste became another. Then another. And with every sip, his despair grew. Yet Rowan soldiered on despite his huge loving heart being torn to pieces. A huge loving heart that now belonged to the wraith alone. *My beautiful, loving prize.*

A month had passed and it had latched onto him in the living realm, unable to fight the addiction to Rowan's sorrow. They were inseparable. They were bound. That is until he came here and went to that fucking house. So many damn wards that drained its power. So many obstacles between it and Rowan.

There was a tinkle of a bell and the shop door opened. Rowan. The wraith shot up, only to waver, still dizzy from hunger. Its prize kissed his aunts goodbye, then hurried to his car. *Why are you waiting!? Go after him!* It stumbled again, fingertips brushing his ankle as he slid into the driver's seat. The car started and off he went. *No! Dammit, no!*

The wraith tore a chunk of rage from a passing man, shoving it between its lips, restoring what little strength it had. The man ranted and raved at a pedestrian as it took to the air, following Rowan's car as it twisted up the mountain roads. Down it swooped, latching onto the car's bumper and crawling over its trunk. It pressed its face against the back window. Oh Gods, it missed him so much. How could it miss him so much after only a day? Even after seeing his dreams last night before that damn house threw it out? *Because he is yours. Your prize for all time. Bound forever.*

The air around them rippled and a shock of agony sliced through the wraith. It screeched as the wards took hold, tossing it from the car into the prickly treetops of the tall pines. What strength is had gained from the stranger was gone, and it flickered, almost slipping past the veil. The wraith clung to the tree before it was sucked away, roaring, "Damn you!" to the sky. No, it wouldn't end like this. It needed to see Rowan. It had to slip into his dreams again somehow.

Movement below caught its attention. Two figures wandered through the snow, female by the looks of them, wearing thick winter coats and overstuffed backpacks. One was strong, her body thick with muscle, her skin golden, and her long-braided tresses as dark as night. The other was so pale it was like she was encased in ice, her white, blonde hair stick-straight and tied in a severe bun.

The wraith scurried down the tree. Yes, it would consume their emotions, devour all it could. Anything to go on another day and see its Rowan again. Auras of magic radiated around the two. The wraith paused, tilting its head. Witches? Yes, this area was ripe with their kind but these two smelled different. They lacked the forest that tinted the mountain folk.

"The cabin is in the other direction," the pale one said, thin hands shoved deep into the pockets of her puffy white coat.

The strong one ignored the statement, striding onward with determination in her mahogany eyes. "Did you notice that house? We should investigate. See if there's anyone living there."

The pale one shook her head, her expression as serene as the other's stormy. "Mother said we needed to settle first, Threnody. The cabin is just ahead. We'll settle and wait for further instruction."

The cranky witch, Threnody it seemed, rolled her eyes. "The longer we wait, the more time those assholes have to run. Or worse, grow stronger."

The pale one sighed. "It's not Mother's will."

Threnody clenched her jaw, stopping in her tracks. "*I'm* Mother's will. She put me in charge of this mission." She thrust a finger into the small witch's face. "We investigate. And if the killers are there then…"

"Then what? What will we do, sister? Attack? Force ourselves through the wards you can feel from here? You're being so reckless." She snorted a soft chuckle. "And here I thought you wanted your revenge."

Threnody clenched her jaw. "This isn't about revenge. It's about justice."

"It's about your emotions. Your lack of control." The pale witch said. "You've lacked control since Aster died, sister."

"I don't have time for your bullshit Judith." Threnody spun on her heels.

But Judith didn't back down. She folded her arms across her bony frame, the corner of her mouth lifting "It's as if she'd taken a piece of you with her. Aster dies and you wither away. I always thought you were stronger than that. Clearly, I was wrong. We all were."

Thunder rumbled in the distance as Threnody clenched her fists. "Watch your tone." Clouds swarmed overhead, the wind picking up in the trees.

Judith glanced at the gray that swarmed above them. "Ah there she is. The formidable storm witch finally shows up without her pretty pet by her side."

A crack of lightning hit the ground beside them, making Judith flinch. Threnody's eyes narrowed. "Drop that subject. *Now.*"

Judith shrugged, her expression placid. "I'm only stating facts."

The storm faded as Threnody marched off, boots crunching in the snow. "Gods, you're a pain in the ass."

A delicious scent filled the air. The wraith leaned towards Threnody moving slow in case she could detect its presence. But both were too wrapped up in their drama to detect it. It took a deep whiff then moaned. Grief. Fear. Despair. Sadness. Threnody was a bubbling cauldron of emotion, enough to fill its belly and return its strength.

"Since you're so determined, how do you expect to get through that barrier?" Judith called to her retreating comrade.

"I have ten tons of spell books in my backpack, I'll figure it out." Threnody marched on, as the wraith chased. It opened it arms and embraced her, its blowing flesh cocooning her like blanket before it sunk its teeth into her skull. Wisps of fog seeped through the invisible wounds.

It tasted Aster, a sweet witch with bright blue eyes and strawberry hair. Her smile. Her laughter. Their powerful bond shattering as the woman Threnody called mother declared her murdered in cold blood. An amused chuckle shook its bones. How curious. It had seen this Aster in Rowan's mind too. His sister, the one he thought he'd lost. *What a small world.*

Threnody wobbled on her feet, swiping her eyes before tears could fall. "Are you coming or not?" she snapped.

"Of course, I am." Judith replied. "Someone has to watch those wards tear you apart. It'll be fun."

"Ha-ha. You're hilarious."

Judith clicked her tongue. "Can't get your justice when you're dead, sister."

And it couldn't get its nourishment either. The wraith bent to Threnody's ear, whispering, "The bitch is right. Perhaps a plan is in order."

Threnody paused, straightening her shoulders with a heavy grunt. "Fine. We'll go to the cabin and research. Anything to shut you up at least."

"And when we do break in, what do you intend to do?"

Threnody bared her teeth. "Kill every one of the mother fuckers in there."

The wraith fed as they trudged away. Threnody would do for now, give it enough strength to slip back into Rowan's dreams at the very least. But it still wasn't enough. It needed more if it was to return to its prize the way it had been.

A shadow flickered above, barely significant through the dense clouds that covered the sky, a surge following it. Foreboding. Brooding. The wraith looked up, spying a bat winged beast, weaving between the shadows of the treetops, silent as the grave. A gargoyle. The King of Shadows. It dove, crossing through the wards as if they didn't exist.

The wraith whipped its tongue across its rows of teeth, licking the witch's essence from them. Now there was the power it needed. The strength it desired. Yes, it would get that gargoyle in its clutches. Then Rowan would be wrapped in its embrace again. And this time it would never let go.

Chapter 7

D amn the Gods, just move!" Callum roared.
Shoving a tree through a doorway was a feat he'd
never thought impossible yet here he was, out of
breath with the monstrosity jammed in the threshold of
Rowan's bedroom. Common sense told him to abandon
his grandiose idea, but this was the exact tree he'd been
searching for. Hints of moss still clung to its crevices and
an abandoned bird's nest perched in its hollow. Or a rat's
nest. Could have been rats. Still, Callum would settle for
nothing less than that exact tree. *Only the best for Rowan.*

Already, the bedroom was decorated with pinecones
and fresh cut branches. He'd even dipped into his collec-
tion of shiny glass bits, metal baubles, and pilfered
jewelry to festoon across the ceiling. The tree was the final touch on this glorious nest. That is, if he could get the
damn thing inside.

Callum dropped the trunk to wipe his forehead. It hit
the hallway floor with a deafening crash, and the gaslit

sconces burst into furious flames, licking the wallpaper black. "Your cottage witch will be more upset with you than me after that stunt," Callum replied. "She picked that wallpaper out herself." That didn't make the house stop. The floorboards rippled, the tree vibrating out of the doorway. "No! Not after all that work!"

Callum braced it with his shoulder, hooves scrambling for purchase while they both rumbled towards stairs. "Please! This is for Rowan!" He clasped his hands to the ceiling. "I'm trying to give you what you want! What we both want!"

The floor stilled, then rippled again, moving Callum and the tree back down the hall and through the door. Callum's sigh of relief turned to a groan as the mighty trunk stuck fast yet again, this time jammed against Rowan's dresser. "Oh, by the Goddess's tits! Why can't this be easier?!"

Callum tongued the scar on his lower lip, tail lashing the air as he wracked his brain for a solution "It's no use. The tree is far too large. The furniture will have to go". Once again, the sconces blazed in protest. Callum rubbed his chin. "No, you're right. Rowan would never approve of that. He's very attached to his things". Alas, that meant his perfect tree would have to be cut down. He flared his claws, crouching over the felled tree with a grimace. "It will be worth it," he muttered.

He hacked and slashed, bark spraying across the floor and coating his leg fur. Great, now he'd need a broom and a bath on top of all of this extra labor. Bath? Hmm. *Perhaps I could persuade Rowan to take one with me.*

A surge of lust hit his groin. The thought his witch-boy's naked body plump and pink in the tub was an irresistible fantasy. Callum would sluice the water away with his tongue as Rowan sang the praise of his nest. Callum worked faster. "This will definitely be worth it."

"What is going on out here?" Aster peeked out her room, looking from Callum to the piles of wood dust, then back to Callum. "Do I want to know?"

"I'm building a nest for Rowan." Callum took another swing, sending tornados of splinters flying.

"Nest? Shouldn't a nest be in the tree? Not vice versa? And why the woodworking all the sudden?" Aster gasped. "Oh Gods, you're going to put wooden dicks all over his walls, aren't you?"

Callum scoffed. "I'm not a barbarian, Aster! I'm a refined seducer!"

"Well can you blame me for thinking that? I heard about the poetry."

Callum winced. Oh yes, the poetry. It wasn't until the next day he realized that Rowan's cries of "Oh Gods!" and "Can we stop?" were not because he was overcome with lust. The only ones that had been receptive of Callum's words that night were Rosemary and Dahlia who were not the target he was aiming for. So, it was on to his second wooing plot, one he knew would succeed.

"Nesting is an old satyr custom, and this tree is my centerpiece." One solid kick of Callum's hoof and the trunk split in two. "A good nest shows the prowess of its creator. It should comfort and pleasure a prospective mate." He groaned as Aster clutched her hands to her chest with a bright squeal. "This is strictly for his peace, not mating."

Though I would not refuse the offer if he threw himself at my feet after this. Afterall, Orlaith had swooned at his nest building and declared it the finest in the herd. This was his time to shine. Sure, he was a little rusty with his skills, but it was returning to him with each leaf and twig collected.

"That is so damn cuuuuute!" Aster hopped up and down like a hyper rabbit. "Okay, let me help. Do you need help? I want to help!"

"You can clean the hallway before your sister returns from town and eviscerates me with her sharp tongue."

Aster gave him a little salute. "I'll get my broom!"

Callum chuckled, dragging the chopped tree into the bedroom. He set it beneath a tall window, throwing open the thick curtains. A beautiful, snow dusted view framed the nook he created, sunlight twinkling off baubles buried in the moss piles circling the floor. Nothing but pine, and greenery, and wood as far as he could see. A lovely winter's nest. Gods, if only it was spring. He'd gather every yellow flower on the mountain for Rowan. Was it too late to ask Ivy to go to that magical place she called the grocery store and fetch some for him?

"Hey Cal!" Aster called. "What are we going to do with-Whoa oh boy!" She ducked a low hanging tree limb over the door, lifting it with the handle of her broom before it caught her top knot of hair. Her throat bobbed, gaping at the scene before her. "Oh boy oh boy oh boy." She tiptoed around piles of polished stones, shaking her head. "Oh...boy. Wow. This is..."

Callum lifted his chin with a proud smile. "Beautiful."

"It's very..." Aster chewed on her lower lip before finishing with, "Rustic. Um, you don't think it's a bit crowded though?" She nodded to the twigs spread before the fireplace in intricate star patterns. "...And a fire hazard?" As if to demonstrate, the hearth spat sparks and the twigs ignited, Aster slapped the flames out with her broom.

"Hmm you have a point." He swept the now charred twigs under the rug with the brush of his tail. "There. *Now* it's perfect."

"Still kind of crowded though," Aster insisted. "Do you really need that big of a log in here?"

"That is the best part!" He flourished his hands, tail slapping the back of his legs as it wagged. "It's the exact one we coupled on. It took forever to hunt it down after it fell and was buried under piles of snow."

Aster blinked then giggled, "Okay keep the sex log." She jerked a thumb over her shoulder. "Now help me move the rest of it out the hallway before Ro or Ives get home."

The front door below opened then closed, the jingling of keys followed. Footsteps rose on the stairs. "Anyone home?" Rowan called.

Callum's heart shot into his throat and Aster squeaked, frantically sweeping the floor as if that would help. He shooed her towards the door, replying "Up here, Witch-Boy! I have a surprise!"

"Uh, okay?" Rowan's voice grew closer. "Well, I have a weird question to ask you. Actually, my aunts have a weird question to ask you, but they asked me to ask you so-" A cacophony of thuds followed by a "Whoa-Shit!" came from the hall.

Aster winced, hugging her broom to her chest. "I think he found the rest of the log."

Rowan stumbled in, shaking his leg as if his trousers were caught on something. "Callum, why is there-Ack!" He yelped as he ran into the low hanging branch, flailing the cuffs of his sweater into its spindly fingers. And there he hung, arms over his head, helplessly twirling. "What the hell!"

"Careful, I haven't permanently secured that one just yet and its heavy." Callum grabbed Rowan while he struggled like a fish on a lure.

"What are you doing in my room?" Rowan looked around wide eyed. "What did you do *to* my room?!"

"Hey Ro! Um...Surprise?" Aster tucked her hands behind her back, shuffling around the two and out the door. "Bye! Have fun in your nest!"

"My what?" Rowan tried to go after her, but only twisted the sleeves of his sweater. "Son of a...! Callum? Help?"

Callum spun him in the other direction, hoping to unwind him, but that only created a knot. So, he spun him backward. "Looks like you're caught."

Rowan slammed his boots into the floor. "Stop stop stop! I'm going to puke!"

"Oh yes, you're well caught." Callum tapped his chin studying the mess. "Alas, it will have to go."

Rowan looked at the bough above him. "The tree branch?"

"Of course not! "Callum scoffed.

"My arms?!"

"You're ridiculous, Witch-boy." Callum raised his claws, slicing Rowan's sleeve apart.

The witch yanked an arm free, frowning at the frayed yarn. "Dammit, I really liked that sweater." He shimmied out of the garment, leaving it to dangle like a wilted blue leaf. The chill raised goose bumps along his bared torso and he wrapped his arms around himself with a shiver.

Callum wet his lips, unable to look away. Perfection. Just like he remembered. No roped muscle, or hard bone. Rowan was pink, healthy, and warm with a slight curve to his belly. Tan freckles spattered his shoulders, a fine patch of fiery hair sprinkling his chest.

A scar twisted up his hip, peeking out from the waistband of his pants. Callum's cock twitched. Now he understood what Rowan had meant when he said scars were hot. He wanted nothing more than to bend Rowan over their tree and run his tongue over that raised imperfection.

Rowan poked a finger towards the log. "Is...is that the rest of the tree from the hall? Oh Gods, Ivy is going to have a breakdown." He stumbled over the piles of curated rocks and twigs to his closet, fishing out an intact sweater. "I'm really confused, Cal. Why did you bring the outside inside-Oooooh what is this?" He gaped at crow feathers Callum had woven in the neckline and cuffs of his sweater "Wow, you really got everywhere, didn't you?" Rowan peeked into his closet. "Yep. Every single sweater. Oh boy."

"You like it? It took hours to decorate each garment." Callum strode to him, puffed with pride. He plucked the sweater from his grip tossing it away, resting his hands upon his torso. "Not that you need such adornments. You're magnificent all on your own."

That beautiful shade of red stained Rowans cheeks, spreading down his chest. It darkened his freckles and puckered his nipples, drenching Callum's palms in heat. But there was more than just shyness. Callum could scent desire. Arousal.

"Uh thanks?" Rowan backed away on shuffling feet. He scooped up his sweater, yanking the crow feathers off. "What is this all about?"

Callum spread his arms wide. "It's a nest for you."

"A...what?"

"A nest. The best I've built."

"You're nesting in my room?"

"No, *you're* nesting. This is your womb of comfort. Filled with nature and familiar objects to bring you peace."

The smell of his desire grew and Rowan took another step back. "You know, maybe things are getting a little-Woah!" His heel caught on a patch of moss still wet from the snow and he tumbled, clutching his thigh. "Fuck!"

Callum grabbed him by the waist, belly churning at the agony that squished the witch's eyes. "Are you all right?"

"The sudden movement caught me off guard." Pain drenched his words as he rubbed his leg. "It's fine. I'm fine."

Callum opened his mouth, a barrage of apologies on his tongue. Dammit, he should have considered Rowan's injury. He should have made sure the floor was clear and everything was properly dried out. *You're an idiot. An utter moron.* Quickly, Callum gathered Rowan in his arms, placing him gently onto his bed.

"Cal, I said it's fine," Rowan said, getting back to his feet.

"It's not fine," Callum sighed. "Rest. I'll clean up this...this mess." He swept the detritus that littered the floor with his tail as fast as he could.

"Cal, wait," Rowan replied. But Callum was too lost in his embarrassment to obey. *You stupid fool!* He snatched the branch over the door, tossing it into the hearth, sweater and all. It went up with a crackling woosh. *You broken, stupid-*

Rowan grabbed his wrist before he could tear the rest of the nest apart. "I said wait." His tone was firm and unyielding. "Stop."

It was Callum's turn to blush. "I'm acting a fool" That came out far sulkier than he wanted.

Rowan released him. "No. You're not. You're just having a reaction and I'm just...surprised, I guess. We'll just clean up the floor is all." He rested his hands on his hips, surveying the room. "The rest is nice. I like it. Having the outdoors inside works for me since the cold hurts my leg."

Callum snorted. "You're not just humoring me?"

"Honestly? Yeah, I'm humoring you. But I like the log. I can't believe I like the log. Why does it look familiar?" When Callum snorted, Rowan stared at the log harder. Then his eyes went wide. "Oh Hecate, is that the log we...? You found the fuck tree?" Rowan sliced his arms through the air. "Whoa, whoa, back up. Did you bring that in my bedroom to have sex on it again!?"

Callum rolled his eyes. "I'm not opposed to that but it was not my intention. I simply want to woo you, Witch-boy. Make you feel special."

Rowan turned beet red. "Did...did you say woo?"

"I did." Callum thumped his chest. "Judging by your blush—which is very fetching by the way—I don't think you're against this idea."

"I'm blushing because you brought our fuck tree into my sister's house!" Rowan spun in a circle, clutching his hair. "When I said truce, I didn't mean banging on the log!"

Callum threw his hands in the air. "By the Goddess's tits, Witch-boy! That was not my intent!"

"Then what *is* your intent?" Rowan shook his head. "Cal, it's not like I don't like you. I do, but I don't have time for a relationship."

Callum rubbed his chest, trying to ignore the wound those words left. He took a deep breath. *This isn't about me. You know where he stands with you.* "You don't understand how to accept care and I need to teach you."

"Yeah, I do!" Rowan snapped.

Callum slapped his hands on his hips. "Name the last time you did something for yourself." The silence droned on and on, Callum tapping his hoof in waiting. As predicted, Rowan couldn't come up with an example.

"Okay maybe I don't always do," Rowan finally said.

"You *never* do."

"Fine. I'll give you that. But the world doesn't revolve around me. I have a lot of things resting on my shoulders."

"Then let me take the honor of caring for you. You deserved to be wooed."

"I'm not ready for mate-hood, Cal." Rowan shook his head. "I don't plan to be here forever. Eventually, I have to get back." His words said one thing, but the lust stinging Callum's nostrils defied them.

Callum took his hands, squeezing them gently. "Rowan, you never think of yourself, do things for yourself.

You even ignore your injury, pretending you're not in pain when you clearly are. Let me care of you, just for the time you're here. And when you leave...You leave in peace." Those last words were like eating blades. But when Rowan relaxed, he swallowed the pain. He'd be what Rowan needed, he'd be important to someone again even if it was for a blink of time. "Do you agree to this?"

Rowan bit his lower lip, bouncing on his toes. "I...I don't have an answer for you right now."

"Then come to my wing tonight." He lifted Rowan's hand, pressing his lips across his knuckles. "You can give me your answer then."

Rowan stared at Callum's mouth, wetting his own. "I have to get up early and head to my aunts' shop for..." He shook his head. "Nephew things."

"Then the night after." Callum stepped close, their chests brushing.

"I don't know. You might have a long wait." Rowan's breath hitched. As if in a trance he rested his hand over Callum's heart. Callum bit back a moan as fingers traced the puckered scars across his collarbone, sliding to his belly. *Lower, Witch-boy. Please, go lower.*

Callum smiled. "Witch-boy, I'd wait an eternity of nights for you."

The sound of a car pulling into the drive broke the spell. Rowan pulled his sweater over his head, "Sounds like Ivy's home. I better help her unload the groceries. And you should clean up the hall before she sees the mess."

"I'll await your answer, Witch-Boy."

Rowan looked around at the nest one more time. The tiniest of smiles tugged his mouth up. "I...I got to go." He disappeared into the hallway.

By Dionysus's balls he was winning Rowan over. Callum bowed his chest, pride swelling. Not a yes, but not a negative response either. As far as Callum was concerned that was a step in the right direction. And even though this wooing would be temporary, he would treasure every second.

Chapter 8

The giant living room fireplace roared, breaking Rowan out of his thoughts. He rubbed his eyes looking at Ivy who was leaning on her broom with a cocked brow. "You didn't hear a word I said, did you?" she asked.

"Sorry, I zoned out." Rowan rested his elbows on his thighs, shaking his groggy head. "What did you say?"

"I was asking if you got any sleep last night. You look tired," Ivy replied.

Rowan slapped on his patented "everything is fine" smile, knowing it wouldn't penetrate his twin's bond. "I drifted off eventually."

It wasn't a lie. He *had* fallen asleep last night. And the night before that too. Three full nights of sleep. Restless, horny sleep. It was a novelty for him. As reluctant as Rowan was to admit, it was the nest that soothed him to slumber. He'd grown to love it. The sparkly bits embedded in the branches twinkled like stars in the night, and the smell of pine was crisp and wonderful. Callum's scent. It surrounded him, in his sheets, his pillow, and catching on his skin. More than once Rowan had touched himself to the thought of Callum sweaty and hot, thrusting inside him, wooing him with his body. Wooing. Who spoke like that? Callum, that's who, like he was some old timey knight on a tall horse. Only the hooves were on the knight. And the knight was as tall as the horse. Okay, the knight was closely related to the horse in this scenario. Regardless, this was the second time Callum did something sweet and thoughtful, even if a little chaotic. And despite himself, Rowan was starting to enjoy the attention.

"Eventually, they'll stop," Ivy suddenly.

"Huh?" Rowan asked.

"The dirty dreams. The house is giving you them, isn't it?"

"Oh...yeah," Rowan crossed his legs before he started reminiscing about last night's revere. "The dreams. You warned me about those." Well, at least it wasn't memories of the accident or the dagger-like grin of that shade. But visions of deep dickings didn't create peaceful sleep, especially when he woke hard as a rock and alone in his bed. "Why the hell does your house do that?"

"Because they're a perv and fancy themselves a matchmaker." Ivy chuckled as she sprinkled her concoction of rose petals and thyme onto the floor. The powdered herbs shimmered when they touched down.

"Sweet Brigid, I had them for weeks when I first moved in. Finn too."

"Finn got them?" Rowan gulped when Ivy nodded. Oh Gods, that meant Callum was getting bombarded with erotic dreams too. Were they as feverish as his? Did he stroke his cock, whispering Rowan's name when he'd come? *Witch-boy, I'd wait an eternity for you.*

Rowan scrubbed his face, trying to think unsexy thoughts, and failing. He would be a dirty liar if he said his heart didn't do a backflip at the thought of Callum dreaming about them together. But that nagging little voice in the back of his mind kept whispering "You don't deserve it", scaring him back to reality. *Sweet Hecate, you should be alone. After all that happened. After all you did.* He pressed his palm to his talisman, desperate to shoo away that dreaded thought. But it only grew louder. *Alone. You're going to be alone forever. You deserve to be alone forever.*

"Earth to Rowan," Ivy called. "What's going on with you?"

"Huh? Oh. Nothing. Just chilling." He patted the couch's arm rest, his smile starting to hurt. "Chillin' like a Villain."

"Liar."

Rowan rolled his eyes. "Gods, why does everyone say that I'm lying?"

"Because you're a horrible liar. You're tense as hell. You're tired all the time and you still won't tell me why you really went on leave from your job." With a flourish, she swept her powdered herbs out the door, the air feeling lighter as it carried all the gloomy energy with them. "I've been having to cleanse the house more because you've got some serious vibes rolling off you. You know what will help?"

Rowan smirked. "Cleaning with you?"

"Bingo." Ivy held the broom out to him. "Just like when we were younger. House cleaning and exorcisms."

"We were a one stop shop, weren't we?" Rowan shoved himself to his feet, his leg giving an extra punch as he hobbled over. "Me crossing the veil to calm the spirits. You, screaming obscenities at them."

"Hey, they deserved it sometimes."

"I don't know what was scarier, you or them."

"And what was that dumbass name you gave us?" Ivy shook her head with a groan. "Oh yeah, Mopping and Spirit Walking."

"That was the test name." Rowan cleared his throat, announcing, "The proper name was Ghosts, Grout, and Glory."

"You know, we could do it again. You're here. I'm here. We can start the business back up clearing the cobwebs." Ivy giggled, placing the broom in his hands. "But not the ones in your room. I'm sure Callum left some in your nest on purpose." She held up a hand before Rowan could protest. "Aster told me about the sex tree. I know."

Rowan pinched the bridge of his nose. "Gods dammit, Aster!"

Surprisingly, his brain wasn't completely dismissing Ivy's idea. Move back to Big Bear. Gods, that was tempting. Sure, the winters sucked for his leg but here was his family, his history. Here he wouldn't be alone in a tiny apartment eating microwave dinners over the sink, or wearing himself thin on a career he was growing to hate. Hell, he didn't even have a career anymore so what was stopping him? Maybe he'd finally open a business as a healer like he had always wanted. *No. You owe it to Mom and Dad to keep helping the dead.*

Ivy chewed on her lower lip. "You're thinking about the accident, aren't you?"

Rowan shuddered but waved it off. "I always think about Mom and Dad this time of year."

"I think about them during Yule too. A lot," she said. "I wonder about how things would be if they were here, if they saw how we grew up. I mean, we were just teenagers when they..." Ivy squeezed her eyes shut. When her sadness touched the back of his brain, Rowan flinched. Gods, this was his fault. His sisters grieved because of him. *And here you think you deserve a blissful union with the lusty goat-lord? You fucking selfish dick.*

"You can talk to me. You know I'll understand." His wave of shame made Ivy grip his hand tighter. "Ro?"

Rowan took a deep breath, giving her fingers a pat. "I'm fine. I promise."

"Rowan..." Ivy narrowed her eyes.

"Look, I'll make an appointment with a therapist when I get back home if things get worse." When Ivy's lips twisted with a skeptical smirk he threw in a quick laugh. "Remember what I always tell you? You can do hard things? Well, I can do hard things too. So, let's talk about something happier. It's Yule soon, we got Krampusnacht coming up-"

"And you have a huge satyr following you around like a puppy," Ivy added.

Rowan signed. "When I said let's change the subject, I didn't mean that."

"What, satyr dick isn't a happier subject?" She chuckled, tangling one of her long fiery locks around her finger. "I know you've never been a relationship guy but you're different around Callum. It's like he lifts a weight off you. You're happy."

Rowan snorted trying to hide the blush creeping up his neck. "I'm no happier around him than any other hot guy with horns and hooves."

"Oh please," Ivy tapped her temple. "You think I can't feel it? You're crazy about him but fighting it and I have no idea why."

"Because eventually I'll have to go home, and I doubt Callum will want to come with me."

"Rowan, *this* is your home." Ivy spread her arms, gesturing to the spacious living room and all its creature comforts. "Here. With us. Not your crappy little apartment."

"Hey! My apartment isn't crappy!" He shrugged. "...It's just sparsely decorated." Because he never took the time to settle. He 'd been a damn ghost haunting that lonely space since he moved to the Bay Area, and now, with no job, he had nothing to go back to. *Do you really want that life?* No, but he *had* to. It was his penance. He raked his hand through his hair. "This is your horny house in the woods, Ives. Not mine. I'll only get in the way."

Ivy shook her head. "There you go again, putting yourself last."

"I'm not putting myself last I'm just-"

"Putting me, Aster, and probably Callum's comfort and happiness before your own." She interrupted. "You've always taken care of us Ro. You let Aster live with you rent free when she went to college. You ran our half-assed business when we were kids. Hell, I would've never lived through my powers fading without you."

Rowan scoffed. "I'm your brother. It's what I'm supposed to do."

"Oh no. Don't go all Saint Rowan of the Bennett Clan on me. You don't have to sacrifice yourself for us anymore. You never did. We love you no matter what you do." Ivy tapped his nose. "Maybe someday you'll listen." She kissed his cheek. "I better start dinner. Veggie lasagna tonight."

She disappeared into the kitchen leaving Rowan alone. Alone with his thoughts. *Fuck.* Ivy was wrong. He did have to sacrifice himself. It's what he owed them, what he owed his parents. And he'd do it over and over until the price was paid. Sharp barbs of grief wrapped around his heart, tightening with every beat. *Relax, Ro.*

Ivy will feel you. He twisted his talisman around his neck, repeating the protective sigil carved in his dad's handwriting. "You're not alone. You're not alone."

That talisman. His most prized possession and his most grim reminder. Rowan's mouth twitched as he remembered tearing through the gold wrapping paper, his silly six-year-old self expecting something more exciting. "A necklace?"

His parents had chuckled at his puzzled reaction. "It's not just a necklace," Dad had said. "It's a talisman." He lifted it from Rowan's palms and tied it around his neck.

"What's it for?" Rowan had asked, tracing the sigil with his tiny fingers.

"We know you get scared when you're alone," Mom had replied. "So, your dad made this very powerful spell for you."

A thrill tickled his belly. "For me? Just for me?"

"Oh yes." Dad knelt before him, wrapping his fist around the talisman. "Any time you feel afraid, you hold it tight, like this. And you say, 'I'm not alone'. Your mom and I will hear you."

"And you'll come get me?" Rowan asked hopefully.

Dad pursed his lips. "There will be times when we can't come to you, Rowan. But we'll be there. And we'll send something or someone to you." Dad ruffled his hair. "This will keep you safe. So, wear it. Always."

And it had kept him safe. It had kept him safe the afternoon their car ran off the road, but not his parents. Tears stung the back of Rowan's eyes, their sharp tang crystalizing the images of the wreck. Screeching metal and the oily taste of smoke. Despite all the coping skills he had learned, all the mantras and tinctures, and years of therapy, that horrible memory was always there. Always fucking there.

Clacking echoed from the front porch. Rowan looked up to see Callum pacing in front of the window, his mouth tight with thought. The sight shook the sorrow away, pulling him toward the satyr. Safety. Sanctuary. Rowan darted out the door, boots catching the ice-covered porch. He slid past Callum hitting the railing with his belly and almost flipping over. *Woah! Too eager! Too eager!*

Callum snared the back of his shirt, pulling him back. "Easy, Witch-boy!"

"I'm good! Totally fine!" Rowan straightened, clinging to Callum arms before he slipped again. "Just getting some fresh air!"

"So desperate for a breath that you ran for it?" Callum lifted him off his feet and set him down on the welcome mat, so his boots could get traction.

"It was...stuffy?"

The satyr was clad only in his loincloth despite the snow fall. Gods, he was beautiful, frost glittering on his broad shoulders and dark horns, like amber in the light of the setting sun. Rowan wouldn't look away. No, strike that. He couldn't look away. He was hypnotized by all that corded, pulsing muscle.

There was no way Rowan would win this battle with his libido so he stared, taking in the puckered scars crisscrossing his chest, the hardness of his belly, the deep curves of his Adonis belt that disappeared under his loincloth.

"My eyes are up here, Witch-boy," Callum said.

Rowan's attention snapped up to Callum's face, every inch of him burning with embarrassment. "Just impressed how you can be out here half naked."

"I'm fair folk. The weather doesn't affect us like it does you." Callum thumped his chest. "To me this is just as mild as a spring morning."

Rowan chuckled. "Hell, I wish I had that ability. Snow and I do *not* get along."

"But you were raised on this mountain." Callum tilted his head, his thick hair spilling down his shoulders. Rowan's fingers itched to bury themselves in his thick locks, to pull Callum close and brush his mouth over his. "Shouldn't you be used to it?"

"I guess." he swallowed, pushing aside that idea for much, much later. Like, shower time later. He waved some jazz hands around to knock his discomfort aside. "But when someone wishes me a 'Happy Winter,' it always leaves me...Cold." Callum groaned and Rowan gasped. "What?! You don't like my winter pun? Dude, that's cold!" Another groan only egged him on. "Here I am, trying to break the ice with you, but you keep giving me the cold shoulder-"

Callum shoved a hand over Rowan's mouth. "Enough, with the cold jokes Witch-boy!" His stern glare melted and he released Rowan, an eager glimmer in his eyes. "Are you enjoying your nest?"

"I am." Rowan laughed at Callum's skeptical smirk. "I'm not humoring you this time. I like it. It's relaxing." *Among other things.* He fought the oncoming blush. "So, thanks."

"I'm happy to do so, Witch-boy." Callum bowed his head, slowly rubbing his palms together. "And it has been three days. Have you thought of my offer?"

Rowan bit his tongue before something stupid like "shut up and fuck me" came tumbling out. "Still don't have an answer for you," he said instead.

Callum ran his hand across Rowan's jaw, the tips of his claws grazing his tingling skin. "You can still come to my wing tonight and give me your answer," he purred.

Rowan swallowed. Oh yeah, he could come to Callum's wing tonight. Come on over to give an answer. Then stay to come. His thigh throbbed, suddenly reminding him that he was balls deep in Winter instead of balls deep in satyr. "I should get inside. The snow is-" Callum swept him off his feet, the cold vanishing as he was cradled. "So, we're back to princess carrying me again?"

It was like he was still basking beside the blazing fireplace. The intoxicating scent of pine and musk blanketed him. Oh no, this was better than inside. Far better.

"I'm keeping the chill away." Callum pressed him close as he brushed the frost from the porch swing. The tiniest of grins twisted his mouth before they settled. "Don't pretend that you don't enjoy it."

It was true. Rowan loved being whisked into Callum's arms. Warm. Safe. Secure. Here was where all the crap swimming in his head faded. Winter? Bring it. Unemployment? Who cares? Muscle pain? Meh. Here was nothing but Callum, with his big strong arms and his comforting low voice. His own personal furnace.

"I will warm you however you like. With my arms..." Callum took Rowan's chin, tilting his head back, voice filled with delicious promises. "My body and my mouth if you wish."

Rowan's knees almost buckled. "...Cool." *Cool? That's all you can say?!* The thumbs up he gave only punctuated the awkwardness. "This is..." *So fucking hot that I'm going to pass out.* "Nice." And there came the second thumbs up.

"I believe you meant to say this is magnificent." Callum twirled a wrist in the air. "Magnificent like me."

The laugh snuck out of Rowan before he could pull it back. "Yeah, that too." Callum's laughter joined him. It was deep and rolling, and so rare that it took Rowan by surprise. "That's the first time I've heard you laugh in a while."

Callum snorted. "Impossible. I've laughed before."

"Eh, not really. Snorted, sure. Smirked? All the time. And we won't get started on the grumbling. I like it. You have a great laugh. Nice to see you switch gears for once."

Callum wrinkled his nose. "I have no idea what switch gears means."

"And I don't want to explain it because it will take days."

"And I'd rather you didn't. You'll waste time not basking in my splendor otherwise." Callum's tail flipped about, slapping against Rowan's leg. "You're too tense to bask, it seems."

"Well, I have a lot on my mind. Aster's health and Yule and my aunt's Krampusnacht." *And the fact that I really shouldn't be in your lap right now. Gods, what am I doing?* Yet he didn't move, unable to resist Callum's pull.

"Are you helping with their festival?" Callum asked.

"I do every year. Auntie Rosie and Aunt Lia mostly put it together themselves but it's a lot of work for only two people so I'm always on standby." He chuckled, relaxing further. "You know, they thought about asking you to dress up as Krampus and come." His laughter died as the color drained from Callum's face. "Or...not."

Callum looked to his hooves, tail slapping against the back of the swing with frantic thwaps. "What did you tell them?"

Rowan snatched his hands giving them a squeeze. "I told them no. Absolutely not. Unless...you do?" When Callum pursed his lips in thought, Rowan chose his words carefully. "It might be kind of fun. We could go together. I'll keep you safe."

Could I keep you safe? Hell, he couldn't even keep his parents safe. Rowan watched Callum shrink back into the swing, lost in a storm of emotion. Gods, he was so haunted, so terrified. *No. Not anymore.* Rowan squared his shoulders. Yes, he would keep him safe. Come hell or high water, he wouldn't leave Callum alone.

He took Callum's face in his hands. "I mean it. I'll stay by your side the whole time. You wouldn't be alone. No one will touch you. I swear upon Hecate herself that I'd keep you safe."

The fear left Callum's eyes. His lips parted with words that never came before he turned away. "No." Gently, he placed Rowan onto his feet, hooves clattering as he rose. "Your sentiments are welcomed. But no."

Disappointment. That was definitely disappointment stabbing Rowan's insides. There was a tiny part of him that wanted to hear a yes. To have Callum with him hand in hand, drinking, dancing, and enjoying the night to-gether. Rowan offered a wan smile. "Oh yeah. I figured. I just wanted to share."

"Indeed." Callum's tail lashed. "Have you gotten enough fresh air?"

"I'm good now." Rowan snapped his fingers with a cheerful click of his tongue. "Thanks for the warmup, Big Guy."

A small, sideways grin curled Callum's scarred lips and he slipped back into the house, leaving Rowan to fall back against the porch rail, breathless.

"What the hell was that?" *That was your cock, calling the shots, Rowan. And you liked it*

Chapter 9

Callum paced around his wing, tail snapping behind him. At this rate he'd wear a hole in the floor. Judging by how the hearth crackled and complained, the house thought so as well. "I don't know what else to do. How do I get him to answer my request? A simple yes or no is all I need!"

"I thought the poetry would be enough." Finn replied. He was perched on the banister of the grand staircase, offering advice while Callum brainstormed new tactics. Well, less advice and more useless opinions. "Your words were dashing."

"Rowan was more receptive to the nest than the poems." Callum pinched the bridge of his nose. "But By Dionisius's balls, his aunts haven't left me alone after that day."

"Well, they *are* lusty women." Finn wagged a finger. "Ah, that Rosemary. Small. Quiet. But such a delightful deviant. She's writing a book on our bewitching charm and magnificent cocks. Well, my magnificent cock, at least." Finn slid off the banister to his hooves. "If I can successfully woo a witch, so can you. Imitate my methods."

Callum gave him a flat look. "You dropped a chandelier on her."

"I dropped it *near* her, not *on* her."

Callum paused his pacing long enough to shoot Finn a glare. "You're not helping."

"I know," Finn replied with a bright smile.

Callum leaned against the settee, a smile tugging his mouth. There was no ignoring how receptive Rowan had been on the porch. The witch had curled up in his arms as if he'd always belonged there. And the scent of arousal oozed from his every pore. "We had a wonderful conversation yesterday. Rowan smiled and cajoled, even complimented my laugh. Goddess's tits I felt his lust." The wistful memory faded, and he grunted. "Then it all crumbled."

"What changed that brought that to an end?' Finn asked.

Easy. He brought up going out in public. That was a true mood killer. The hope that had twinkled inside the witch was unmistakable. Rowan had wanted nothing more than Callum to attend Krampusnacht. Not just attend, dress like the monster himself. And by the Gods, Callum wanted to give him that. To feel no fear with his head held high. Going would be the ultimate gift of his adoration. But that wasn't something he could give to Rowan, now or ever. "Long story."

"Well then lets review how you won Orlaith." Finn counted on his fingers. "First you nested. Then you wrote poems. Then you fucked." He hmmed. "Seems you're working backwards, brother."

"There was more to our wooing than that," Callum said.

Finn clapped his hands. "Oh! Now I know what you're forgetting! Pinecones!"

The urge to throw Finn out the door was growing. "Rowan and I have moved beyond pinecones."

"But witches love pinecones! They obsess over them like they do jars and bottles. They do little witchy things with them. Its adorable. And it won Ivy over instantly." Finn nodded sagely. "The secret is the bows on the top."

"I need more than that to sway Rowan." Callum grumbled. *You know exactly what would sway him.* Krampusnacht. He stomped his hoof with a frustrated growl. Another dramatic roar of heat from the fireplace and he jabbed a finger at it. "The floor is fine!" The hearth spat one last spark out of spite, then went quiet.

Finn flung an arm around Callum's shoulders. "Let me teach you a phrase my Witchling taught me that may help." He swiped his hand across the air as if visualizing the words before them. "Go big or go home."

Callum wrinkled his nose. "What in the seven hells is that supposed to mean?"

"Be impressive! Do something that will wow him like..." Finn rubbed his chin before snapping his fingers in triumph. "Like, suck your own cock!"

Callum scowled. "No."

"You're right. That requires too much preparation and stretching. What about-?"

"No, Finn."

"Then-?"

"No." Callum flopped onto the settee, tapping the scar on his lips.

"All right, fine." Finn settled beside him. "A different approach. What would Rowan want that he could not deny you for?"

Callum swallowed hard, seeing Rowan's disappointment in his mind. "He... He wants me to attend Krampusnacht." Finn grimaced and Callum clutched the back of his head. "Exactly. You know what that coven did to me. You know what I suffer."

"True," Finn replied. "But you could go in disguise like I did."

"And risk getting swarmed like you were?!" Callum's hands trembled, heart slamming against his ribs.

"Ivy protected me. Perhaps-"

"No!" Callum's vision tunneled, turning scarlet. *Such delicious anguish from such a strong male.* Old wounds throbbed to life, burning his flesh as hot as the day they were created. "They'll touch me. Use me." He tugged on his horns, ears flattening to his skull to silence the horrible laughter of those witches. "Hurt me!"

"Cal," Finn murmured. "Brother. You're lost again."

"I know!" Callum sobbed. "They're in my head Finn! They're in my head and always will be!"

"I'm here, Callum." Finn murmured.

"This isn't fair! Its I who should be comforting you! I'm the elder! I'm the one who should protect!"

"You've already done your fair share of protecting me." Finn outstretched his hands, waiting until Callum gave him a sharp nod of confirmation, then pressed them to Callum's face, guiding his gaze to his. "I'm here brother. Do you have your potions?"

"I don't want my potions! I don't want to go to sleep!"

"Then breathe with me." The air was crisp in Callum's lungs as his shaky inhale synced with his brother's. "Good." Finn said. "Now think of peace. Think of something good."

I'll keep you safe. Rowan's voice cut through the din of his waking nightmare. *No one will touch you. I swear upon Hecate herself that I'd keep you safe.*

The witch had meant every word. Callum felt the honesty and the cold determination in every syllable. Rowan with his hair like fire and eyes like the summer sky. With contagious laughter and horrible puns. He was smaller than Callum and was kind to a fault. There wasn't one hint of malice inside him Yet there was no doubt Rowan would fight tooth and nail to protect what was his.

Finn pressed his forehead to his. For the last eighty years, he'd comforted Callum like this. Sitting with him for hours until he fell asleep or calmed. There was no eternity of darkness this time. Only Rowan's promise. *I'll keep you safe.*

"I...I found my peace." Callum whispered.

"You sure?" Finn asked.

Rowan was solid in his mind. Callum's vision cleared, throat opening to blessed air as he thought back to the feel of him in his arms. "I am." He smoothed his sweat soaked hair from his face. Rowan. His kind, gentle Witch-boy.

There was scratching upon the stairs. Maximus came romping down, all squeaks and chitters. He plopped himself in front of Finn, ringtail poofed like a brush as he gestured wildly.

Finn nodded at the raccoon. "I see. Yes. Tell her I'll be up in a moment to help." He gave Callum's arm a squeeze. "My Witchling calls. Are you sure you'll be all right?"

Callum felt his chest. The jitters were gone, his heart slowing to a reasonable rate. "I am." He couldn't keep the awe out of his voice. *I'll keep you safe.* By the Goddess, Rowan had kept him safe.

"Rest brother. You've been through a lot." Finn said. "We'll find some other big gesture for your witch-boy."

He watched Maximus hop away, Aster's words popping into his head. *You know he was kind of jealous that Ivy got a familiar even though he wouldn't say it.* "A familiar."

"What?" Finn asked.

Callum's ears perked, with excitement. "A familiar! That's it! May the Goddess bless that little sister!"

Finn waved ad Maximus to go on without him. "Cal, are you sure you're all right?"

"More than all right!" Callum cried. "I have a new wooing gift in mind for Rowan!" The unscarred side of Callum's mouth curled. "Tonight, Little Brother, we go hunting."

Finn arched a brow. "We have enough meat to last us all winter."

"This isn't for meat. This is for familiars." His tail flicked with a snap. Yes, he would bring Rowan what he wished, a companion that he could keep by his side where Callum couldn't follow. Someone to protect him, watch out for him under Callum's orders. But a tiny raccoon wouldn't do. No, Rowan deserved something far grander. "Go big or go home."

Chapter 10

Clack-clack-shuffle-clatter-clack.

Rowan's eyes cracked open. Sleep had only been a whisper away, scared off by the noise. Probably just as well. It had been a crapshoot if his dream would be a nightmare, or erotic. Lately it had been erotic which was far more welcome than the shade.

He boosted himself up on his elbow groaning out a drowsy, "Hello?"

Nothing. The crackling fire cast a dim orange hue. Slowly spinning bits of glass dangled from the festooned branches, glimmering like stars. A lovely sight to wake up to. He inhaled, the cool scent of pine before laying back down.

The commotion must have been Maximus. He was known to scurry to the kitchen for a midnight trash raid. making as much noise as his little paws could. Rowan rubbed his temples. If he closed his eyes now, he'd doze off and be in dreamland in no time. Though Dreamland capital was Dicktropolis, population Callum and Rowan.

"You're going to wake up with a hard on again," he grumbled pulling his blankets over his shoulder. He melted into the mattress, his breath slowing. The soft sound of the wind outside grew faint as the world faded away.

Clack-clack-shuffle-clatter-clack!

Rowan shot up, throwing his blankets aside. Whatever the hell was making that noise was in the hallway. "Maximus?" He called, expecting him to trot in with a half-eaten chicken leg in his mouth. He waited, holding his breath.

Cold tickled the back of his neck. Rowan swallowed, as a shadow wavered in the corner of his room, billowing like a cloak. He waved away away the chill, scooting to the foot his bed to stare into that dim corner. The shadow twirled into shape. Two long limbs. A long neck. A narrow skull. It lifted its head, wisps of black flittering into the air. Rowan's blood turned to ice as a wide grin split the darkness, filled with long dagger like teeth.

"Shit..." Rowan scrambled backwards, back slapping his headboard. The air was sucked from his lungs, a cold dense as death shrouding his flesh. He shoved his hands over his eyes curling up in tight ball. "You're not here!" he whimpered. "You're not here! You're not in this world!"

The clatter dashed past his door, ending in a thundering *ker-thud*. Rowan tore his hands away. The corner was empty, only a faint billow of curtains before stillness. The chill was gone, the fire warming his skin once more. "What the hell?" Was he dreaming? He had to have been dreaming. That thing was a shade. It couldn't cross the veil.

Clack-clack-kerfuffle-clack-scraaaaaaape.

Once again, the ruckus sped past his door followed by an irritated grumble of "Damn you!"

Okay, that noise was definitely not a dream. And Rowan knew that voice all too well. "Cal?" he called. He waited for a response but only got another symphony of thumps and clatters. "Cal, are you alright?" He slid to his feet, creeping towards his door. "Are you having a panic attack?"

Rowan reached for the knob. *Bang!* The door bowed inward, as if someone was thrown against it. *Bang! Bang! Bang!* "Fuck!"

He threw open the door and was smothered by scarred flesh as Callum slammed into him. They sailed across the room, the satyr's massive bulk pancaking Rowan against the far wall. He feebly shoved Callum only to be thrown backwards, black hair catching in his mouth. "Callum!" Rowan choked.

"I have this under control!" Callum bellowed.

"Have *what* under control?!" He tried to squirm his way free, but Callum shoved him back, his broad form shielding from only Gods know what. "What are you doing?!"

"Just stay behind me, Witch-boy! It will all be fine-Watch out!" Callum tossed him onto his bed. Rowan bounced before flopping onto his belly, flailing in the blankets. He sat up to see Callum crouched low, hands out in a placating manner towards a huge antlered beast. "Easy, Broderick."

"Is that a stag?!" Rowan leapt up, wobbling on the mattress, the blankets still clinging to his legs. "Did you let a stag in?!"

"Worry not! I have this under control!"

"That's not an answer!" The stag turned its wild eyes to Rowan. It reared, hooves cutting the air before it charged. "Fuck, fuck, fuck!" Rowan rolled off the bed just as it hit. It kicked the footboard into splinters then turned in a blind panic, bucking and thrashing. The house rumbled as it woke, floor rippling, windows slamming open and closed. The hearth roared and the stag screeched in terror.

Callum threw Rowan over his shoulder just as the stag tangled himself in the curtains. He hauled him into the hallway, kicking the door shut, "Are you all right?" he asked, placing Rowan on his feet. *Crash-tinkle-tinkle-crash! Bang!* Callum winced. "I believe that was your window breaking."

The gaslights bellowed, flames cracking their sconces. Every bedroom door blew open, except for Rowan's, the shocked cries of his siblings exploding in the air. Rowan took a deep breath before he could to scream. His sharply raised finger made the satyr step back. As patiently as he could, he asked, "Why...did you...bring a stag...into my bedroom?"

"He was supposed to stay downstairs," Callum replied, as if that was reasonable and sane.

"Still not an answer, Callum!" Rowan snapped then caught himself, sucking in another breath through his flaring nostrils. "Sorry. Let's just figure out how to get it-"

"What in the hell is going on?!" Ivy ran into the hallway, trying in vain to get arms into the sleeves of her robe. Maximus scrambled on her heels, chittering loudly. "Is everyone okay?! What is that noise?!" Rowan's door exploded in a rain of shrapnel and the stag galloped free, dashing down the hall. Ivy pressed herself against the wall as he sailed past her. "Are you fucking kidding me right now?!" Maximus jumped in front of Ivy, hissing with hackles raised. "Max! No!" Ivy commanded. But the raccoon only released a furious battle chirp and threw himself right upon the stag's face.

The stag's piercing bleats made Rowan cover his ears. It bucked, desperate to shake Maximus loose, gouging holes in the wall with each thrash of its antlers. Rowan belly flopped to the floor before he was kicked, dragging himself through the ruckus to a bewildered Ivy. "Someone get it out of the house!" he shouted, shielding her from rogue hooves.

Callum grappled the stag by the neck, peeling Maximus free and tossing him to Ivy before gently petting the stag's chest. "Easy Broderick. Easeeeeaaah!" He was flipped onto his back as the stag spun with him like a hungry alligator. The house shook, Rowan pressing his hands to his face as he gaped at the bodies rolling past. Items spilled from Callum's pouch in a trail of shiny jewelry bits, feathers, and small bottles of his calming potion. *Calming potion!*

Rowan crawled after them, covering his head as Callum's tail whipped the air. He groped and cursed, one potion rolling under the fight, shattering under the stag's rump. The other was just barely out of reach. Rowan stretched out on his belly, straining to reach the bottle. A stray hoof slammed down inches from his face, catching his talisman. He jerked back then stretched again, the bottle inching forward with each of Rowan's clumsy gropes. "Almost! Almost!"

Finally, he caught it between his fingers, his hysterical laugh of triumph interrupted by Callum falling beside him with a thud. Rowan uncorked a bottle with his teeth, splashing the silvery blue liquid into the stag's face. He grabbed Callum by the arm, dragging him away as stars filled the beast's big brown eyes.

"Good thinking, Witch-boy!" Callum praised, only to blush at Rowan's agitated glare.

Ivy stumbled over, struggling for breath as she checked Rowan over for wounds, Maximus on her shoulder, puffed up like a balloon. The three of them watched the stag stagger to the floor, snorting the entire way. He lay his head down, eyes fluttering closed. Then he started snoring.

Finn clacked his way up the stairs. "Brother! I'm finally here! Did it work? Did Rowan like-?" His wide grin dropped as he surveyed the wreckage. He jabbed a thumb towards Callum. "It was all his idea."

"Just put him back where you found him!" Ivy shouted.

"I can't." Callum rose to his hooves, hovering over the stag to examine him. "He's a gift for Rowan."

"A gift?" Rowan's voice wavered with nervous squeaks. "W-what am I supposed to do with a stag?!"

"He's your familiar." Callum offered him a sheepish smile. "I asked him on your behalf, and he said yes. But then panicked as soon as he got inside." He flicked his fingers to the stag. "How was I supposed to know he was frightened of ceilings?"

Rowan inhaled slowly through his nose, counted to ten this time, then slowly released the breath. Okay, that was sweet in the most backwards way possible but considering his room had been destroyed, sweet gestures were the last thing on his mind. "Couldn't you have picked something smaller?"

"Go big or go home." Callum declared with a jut of his chin.

Rowan blinked. "...What?"

"Can we please get him out of here before he wakes up and destroys the house again?" Ivy asked.

Finn took her hand, pressing a kiss to her knuckles "Fear not, Witchling. I'll fix my brother's blunder."

"Blunder?!" Callum stomped towards Finn only to be stilled by Rowan's outstretched arm. "You said this was a good idea!"

"I said I would help you, not that your idea was good," Finn replied. "There is a difference."

Rowan pinched his forehead. "Finn, could you not right now?"

Finn bowed in mea culpa. He scooped up the stag, draping it across his shoulders as if it weighed nothing. "Off we go, sir! Witchling, please get the front door for me?" They walked down the stairs. Well, Finn walked. Ivy stomped, her fury pinging the back of Rowan's head, matching his own.

Rowan peered into his bedroom. Curtains were torn down, his bed and dresser nothing but kindling, and his clothes were flung in every direction. Yet what upset him the most was his nest. The one thing that had brought him an ounce of peace was reduced to fallen branches, and trampled baubles. At least the sex tree was all right, sans a few hoof scuffs. *Of all the things to be relieved about, Ro.* He turned to Callum ready to unleash but the satyr's ears drooped, along with his shoulders as a sad hiss whistled through his fangs.

"You're not pleased," Callum grumbled.

"You're right." Rowan clutched his talisman, running his thumb over the sigil in fast circles in hopes to calm himself. "I'll have to sleep on the couch for a while."

"You could sleep in my wing." Callum withered at Rowan's glower. "That isn't the reason I brought him here. I wanted to give you a gift. A familiar."

"Why do you think I need a familiar?!"

"Aster said you'd always wanted one."

"Gods dammit, Aster." Rowan's cheeks puffed, then let out a long raspberry. "Look, Cal. I'm sure the stag-"

"Broderick." Callum interrupted.

That knocked the dissent right out of his mouth. "I'm sorry, what?"

"The stag's name is Broderick. From a long line of Brodericks he told me. I believe he's Broderick the Ninth." Callum's ears flattened to his skull, and he gestured to Rowan like a spokesmodel. "Sorry. Continue."

"Ok. I'm sure Broderick the Ninth is a great guy," Rowan replied. "But you should've asked me first."

"And ruin the surprise?"

"I don't want to be surprised!" Rowan snapped. "Especially if a claustrophobic stag almost tramples my sister!" He took another inhale, pulling back his anger. "Its fine. I'm fine, but..."

A chip of pewter fell from his neck, bouncing off his bare toes with a soft plink. Rowan looked down to his talisman. A chunk had been gouged from it, probably from the hoof that almost stomped his face in, his father's sigil marred with cracks. Broken. His talisman was broken.

Rowan cradled what was left of it in his shaking palms, throat thickening. "No..." he whispered quickly grabbing the piece and jamming it back into place, hoping it would magically mend itself. "It's okay, it's fine! Ivy can help me put this back together, I'm sure!" Callum reached for him but Rowan pulled away, his talisman clutched in his fist. "It's fine!" he shouted. "Don't touch it! It's fine!"

Callum looked to his hooves. "I angered you."

"I'm not angry! I'm just...!" Rowan pulled his hair. The shade. The stag. The fucking dreams that kept him awake. And now the last memory of his parents was broken. No number of deep breaths would quell the volcano inside. He threw up his arms, cracking wide open. "Okay yeah! I'm angry! I'm really pissed right now! You keep doing this stuff that's totally out of my wheelhouse and I don't know what to do with it! I never had anyone go this far or do...!" He gestured to the gored walls and hoof scratches. "All this! For me? Why?! Why am I so damn special to you?! How am I supposed to react to all this...this..." *Adoration? Sweetness? All these wonderful but weird-ass gestures that I don't deserve! Fuck!* Rowan slumped against the wall, banging the back of his head against it. "Gods, this is confusing!"

A gentle hand slid to his lower back. Rowan didn't have the strength to fight Callum as he pressed his forehead to his. Dammit why did this have to feel so good? Why couldn't he just walk away.

"I do this for you because you don't even know how special you are." Callum whispered. "You're selfless and kind. That is why you deserve these gifts and my attention. Can't you see how amazing you are, Rowan? What else can I do to convince you?"

Rowan stilled, furious at the warm fluttering butterflies that decided to take flight inside him. He buried his face in his hands, head swimming in circles. You don't deserve this! *You don't deserve him! You shouldn't let him make you feel so good!*

Callum squeezed Rowan's waist, brows knitting into a soft frown. "I went too far." He looked to the floor, his tail twitching. "I should have listened to your sister and gone gentle and slow. But this is all I understand. I don't know your customs, but this is what I'd done for Orlaith. It had won her all those years ago so I assumed it would win you."

A cold shocking wave crashed over Rowan. He peered at Callum through his fingers. "Orlaith?" That was a name he'd never heard before. And it slid from Callum's lips with such reverence. "Who's Orlaith?"

Callum turned beet red. His tail slapped the wall and he released Rowan, taking a step back. "I never told you of her, have I?"

"No," Rowan rasped. "*Should* you have told me about her?"

Callum looked away. "Yes. I should have."

Rowan fell into a sit, fingering the scuff marks on the floor. "What the fuck is happening with my life right now?!" A scream cut through the night, high and frantic, curdling Rowan's blood. He paled recognizing the voice, knowing exactly what door it was coming from. He

scrambled to his feet, taking a couple stumbling steps before another scream urged him to run. "Aster!"

Chapter 11

Rowan bolted down the hall, only to be stopped by Callum blocking his path. He tried to elbow his way past, but he might as well have shoved a mountain. "Cal, move!"

"It's not safe," Callum replied.

"That's my sister in there!"

"I won't let what is harming her harm you as well."

Rowan ignored him, crying, "Aster! Azzie! Are you okay?!" Once again, he tried to circumvent Callum, but the satyr was unyielding, Rowan's elbow in his vice grip. As soon as the screaming had started, it stopped, filling Rowan with an eerie dread that made his skin crawl. But she hadn't rushed out like Ivy had. Oh Gods, what was happening to her while they wrestled with the stag? What if the shade had given up on Rowan and gone after her instead? *No! That thing isn't in our world! It can't get past the wards!* Unless it wasn't really a shade. Bile crept up the back of Rowan's throat.

Rowan jolted as Callum pulled him close, cupping his cheeks. "Easy Witch-boy," he said firmly. There was a cool, commanding gleam in Callum, one Rowan had never seen before. The look of a warrior ready to defend all he loved. Rowan swallowed his fear, managing to give him a nod.

Callum shoved Rowan behind him, leading him towards Aster's room. Her door sat wide open from the house's ruckus. Carefully, he peered inside. "Aster?" His mouth turned a deep frown. "There's no one there."

"What?!" Rowan rose on his toes to look over Callum's shoulder. "Azzie, where are you!?" he shouted. Horrible scenarios sped through his head. Dammit, if something happened to her it would be his fault. "Where is she?! What if someone got to her?!"

"The wards are too strong."

Rowan shook his head. He knew very well that this place was a fortress, yet his terror shoved all logic out of the driver's seat. "How do you know?!"

"Because I scent her." Callum's long deer-like ears perked straight up. He held up a finger. "And I hear her. Listen."

Rowan held his breath. Over the sound of his pounding heart were the softest of whimpers. Aster. They crept inside finding tiny, pale feet poking out from under the bed, toenails painted a bright pink. Rowan sighed in relief. He lunged forward but Callum caught his arm.

"I go first." His firm tone demanded no other choice. A part of Rowan softened and he stepped back, letting

Callum take charge while he fell apart. It was comforting, almost welcomed.

Slowly, Callum knelt beside the bed. The tension in his roped muscles eased, a tiny smile brushing his mouth. "Hello, Little Sister. It's only me."

Rowan belly flopped onto the floor beside Callum. "Aster!" Bloodshot blue eyes in a face as white as a spirit peered back at him. Relief hit him like a tsunami. "Oh thank Hecate!"

Aster hugged herself, rocking back and forth, cheeks drenched. She burst into sobs, clawing the air towards him. "Ro!"

"Are you hurt?"

"No." Aster pulled her knees to her chest, burying her face into them. "But it's not safe!" She lowered her voice to barely a whisper. "The coven is here to get me! They've come to finish the job!"

Rowan shook his head. "There's no one here. I swear it."

"There were horrible noises and screaming in the hall-way! I was sure they came and killed you!" Aster shuddered.

Callum pursed his lips, his thick browns tangled. "That was my fault, Aster. I am to blame for that ruckus."

"But what if they *are* here? What if they got past the wards? They're so strong! And smart! And-!"

"I swear on Hecate, Aster," Rowan interrupted as gently as he could. "No one is here to hurt you,"

Aster shook her head, lost in her haze of panic. "T-They're going to turn me back into that t-thing. I'll kill you all! I'll hurt everyone I love!" Her hand shot out, clutching Rowan's like a lifeline. "Don't let them do that to me again, Ro!"

Rowan's belly twisted. This wasn't fair. Aster was the best of the Bennetts. The strongest magic. The kindest heart. The sweetest soul. He should have been there when her coven took her. He should have stopped it. *You are her big brother! What didn't you stop it?!*

Callum clasped Rowan's shoulder. "Witch-boy?"

Rowan didn't move, couldn't move. *No matter what you do, it will never be enough.* He squeezed Aster's hand, wanting to whisper "I'm sorry. I'm so, so sorry." But the words stuck like paste in his throat.

Callum leaned in close, lips against his ear. "Rowan. Come back to me. I have you."

Rowan turned to him, Callum's tender gaze pulling him from his spiral. His strong, brave satyr. He would shoulder the burden tonight. He'd let Rowan fall apart. Callum nodded towards the bed. "If Aster feels safer under there, we should join her."

Rowan blinked. "J-join, Aster?"

"Yes." Callum looked at Aster with a tiny smile. "If Aster will have us." Aster nodded, with a whimper. "And there's our invite."

"Cal, I don't think we can fit."

But Callum was already on his belly, wiggling his head to jam his horns under the wooden bed frame. He crawled under, barely able to squeeze through. As soon as he was within reach, Aster clung to him, face buried in his shoulder. He stroked her back, murmuring "You're safe, Little Sister." as he rocked her. Rowan's heart ignited, a smile ghosting his lips before it flew away.

A thud, a creak, and a snap as the mattress above them popped up, Callum's ass poking out from the box spring. Rowan pressed a hand to his mouth, too late to smother the laugh.

Callum blinked. "What?"

"Your butt is um... dislodging the mattress," Rowan said.

Callum smirked. "You witches should have larger beds."

"It looks like a confused groundhog," Rowan giggled.

"My backside is far more fetching than a groundhog's!" Callum narrowed his eyes at Rowan's spreading grin. "No. I know that look. Don't you say-"

"I think it wants to ass-k us a question." Rowan snorted.

Callum pounded his fist on the floor. "Damn you, Witch-boy!" Rowan burst into laughter and Callum's frown wavered into a half grin. Even Aster cracked a smile, a titter rough through her tears. Callum. held out his hand to him. "Are you joining us or not?"

Their fingertips brushed, palms pressing together secure and welcoming as Rowan was pulled under. He tucked himself on the other side of Aster, letting her roll from Callum's arms and into his. "Like Mom used to say, snug as a bug in a rug," he said. "We'll stay here as long as you need, Azzie." Rowan craned his head, looking towards Callum. "Right?"

"Indeed," Callum agreed.

"But what if this doesn't stop?" Aster muttered. "What if they come after me and... Oh Gods, what if he's still alive?"

"Your King of Shadows?" Callum asked.

Aster nodded. "He's out there hurt, and he needs me. I know it. I can feel it. And the coven..." Her words broke into sad whimpers. "This is all my fault. He's probably dead because of me!"

"Hush, Little Sister." Callum slipped his hand into his pouch, the other gently taking her chin. "Hush and look at me." Aster turned her wild gaze to him, giving him her undivided attention. "We've talked about it before, remember? The nightmares. The fears."

"You have?" Rowan asked.

"Often." He gave Aster's cheek a gentle pet. "We have much in common, your sister and I."

"Yeah," Aster murmured. "We talk a lot."

Rowan blinked, looking between the pair. How had it never occurred to him that Callum and Aster might have talked about their demons?

Callum cupped Aster's face, wiping the tears from her cheeks. "And what did you tell me when I was disturbed by such things?"

"That...you're safe." Aster wet her pale lips. "And it's not your fault."

A tiny smile touched Callum's lips, a hint of a fang gleaming in the dim light. "So, what does that make you right now?"

Aster shivered. "...safe."

"And?"

"...not at fault."

"Good. Now breathe deep."

A shaky breath expanded Aster's chest, rattling out in a whistle. Callum's inhaled along with her. Soon Rowan joined them. His own frayed nerves calmed as they connected. In and out. In and out. Stillness. Quiet. Peace.

"So, what was that noise then?" Aster suddenly asked.

Rowan cleared his throat. "Um... Callum put a claustrophobic stag in my bedroom."

The oddness of that statement seemed to shock Aster back to herself. "What?"

"Rowan needs a familiar," Callum said.

"You gave Rowan a familiar?" Aster gave a shaky smile. "That's so sweet. Can I meet him?"

"He's outside." Callum replied. I'm sure Broderick-"

"Will be happy to go back home." Rowan cut off. "I don't need that big of a familiar. What about a rabbit? Or a squirrel?"

"You think a mere squirrel would suit your needs?"

"I'm more of a squirrel guy, Cal!"

"I'm not having my brother outdo me with a messy raccoon!"

Rowan shushed him. "Maximus is going to hear you and claw your eyes out."

"I'd like to see him try. I just wrestled a stag for you, Witch-boy. I can handle Maximus."

A laugh snorted from Aster's nostrils, then another, glassy eyes softening with mirth. Callum fished a potion bottle from his pouch pressing it into Aster's palm. "A small sip will do. We are strong, yes. But sometimes we need aid." He curled her fingers around it. "This will help provide that aid while you regain yourself."

Gods, Callum had never sounded so confident, seemed so sure. In that moment he was the strongest beast that Rowan had ever seen, a fierce fortress, one that would take a thousand warriors to breach. No one would hurt Aster as long as Callum breathed. The sight cracked Rowan's defenses wide open.

Aster uncorked the potion, taking a tentative nip. "Thank you, Callum," she said softly.

Callum shook his head. "No need for thanks."

"Aster? Ro?" Where are you?" Ivy cried. "I thought I heard a scream! And I felt Rowan panic!"

"We're in Aster's room, Ives," Rowan called.

Ivy's foot falls padded down the hall, growing closer. "Is everyone all right? I would have been here sooner, but the damn stag woke up and that led to a whole new..." Her slippers paused in front of them. "Callum is that your ass sticking out from under the mattress?" The floorboards squeaked as Ivy got to her hands and knees, examining them like they had all turned into frogs. "Having a party down here?"

"They're keeping me company while I freak out," Aster said. Her voice was fuzzy, as the potion took its numbing effect.

Ivy paled. "Sweet Brigid, Aster. Are you okay?"

"I'm fine. The boys took care of me." She wiggled the bottle at Ivy. "Callum even gave me some of his potion. This stuff is stroooong."

"And I believe you've had enough." Callum plucked the tincture from her fingers before, dragging the lot of them from under the bed. The mattress fell back into its frame with a crash. "Time for you to sleep, little sister."

He offered Aster to Ivy who helped her into bed. Aster's eyes fluttered before her head rocked into her pillow. In a blink, she was asleep. Ivy sat beside her, smoothing her hair back.

"I'll sit here a while and make sure she stays asleep. You two should get some rest." She looked at Callum, her eyes brimming with gratitude. "Thanks so much for taking care of her, Cal."

Callum's tail twitched as he gave her a bow. "I would do it again in a heartbeat." And Rowan was sure he would. The satyr slid up beside him, taking his arm, leading him to the hall. "Come Witch-boy. You can sleep in my wing while I clean your room."

Rowan shook his head. "Cal, that's going to take all night. Let me help."

"No. I'm the one who destroyed it, I'm the one who..." They both stopped in their tracks, staring into Rowan's bedroom. The furniture had mended along with the holes in the walls. Rugs were righted and Rowan's things were put into neat piles, ready to be packed away. Only the debris of Callum's nest remained strewn across the floor. "Looks like the house did most of the work."

Rowan shoved the heels of his hands into his eye sockets. "Then we can get this cleaned up quick."

"I will clean it." He turned Rowan around, giving his backside a swat with his tail. "To bed with you."

Sleep sounded like a decent idea, but after three scares in a row, it was far out of Rowan's reach. He turned to insist he help but Callum closed the door on him. *Well shit.*

He headed down the stairs, passing through the living room, to the kitchen. Tea sounded good. No. fuck that. Wine. An entire bottle of wine. Gods he wished Ivy was a whiskey drinker. He touched his talisman, the jagged edge sharp on his fingertips. With a sigh he fished the broken chip from his pajama pocket.

"It wasn't his fault," he murmured, turning the pewter in his fingers, and waiting for the heartache. It was there, but not as devastating as he expected. Not after witnessing Callum with his baby sister. There was a warmth there, a deep care that he hid under his chuffs and gruff frowns. The same feelings that Rowan had when he was near Aster and Ivy. A fierce unconditional love for family.

Rowan untied the leather cord, placing his talisman on the mantle, its absence making him feel naked. His mind whirled for spells to fix it when a faint scratching came at the front window. Rowan stiffened. The shade. Fuck. He spun only to find a miserable stag tapping at the glass with his antlers. Looks like Broderick wasn't going away.

They locked stares and Rowan stilled. Maybe if he didn't move, the stag wouldn't see him. But Broderick pressed his black nose against the panes, blowing out a circle of fog, eyes round and guilt ridden. How could a stag have sad puppy eyes?

Rowan shook his head, mouthing, "No." The stag tapped again and Rowan sighed. "Dude. No."

Broderick—noble stag that he was—licked the window in reply. And it was unbearably cute.

"Gods, I can't take it anymore." With a sigh, Rowan opened the front door, holding out a hand before the stag could march in. "No. You stay on the porch." Broderick's ears drooped. He nuzzled Rowan's palm with his soft wet nose. Sweet Hecate, that was adorable. "Look, I know that Callum...um...recruited you for familiar duty..."

Broderick lowered his head and waited, probably for pets. How long had Rowan wanted a chance to pet a deer? Not just a deer but a stag the size of a Buick! His fingers curled then slowly he placed them on Broderick's head. That cute fluffy tail wagged. Oh yeah. He was a goner.

"Okay fine. Let's get to know each other." Broderick pranced a happy little circle on the porch before trying to get inside again. "No! No! You out there! Me in here! We're not having another demolition derby!"

Rowan didn't know that stags could roll their eyes but oh wow, this one could. Despite his annoyance, Broderick nudged his arm, before sliding his head under it. Antlers just barely grazed Rowan's skin, this time in a gentle way instead of in blind violence.

"Callum can be pretty persuasive when he wants to be, huh?" Rowan asked. Broderick snorted in agreement; eyelids half closed as Rowan gave him a good scratch between his ears. "Sorry about earlier. He should have explained better. Callum's stubborn and sometimes acts before he thinks. His poetry sucks, and he always dives into the shallow end headfirst. And he leaves really important details out, like, oh I don't know, possibly having a mate back in the day. Did you know that? I have no idea who this Orlaith is, but she sounds important. You think he would have brought her up sometime but..." He sighed. "Sorry. I'm unloading on you."

Broderick perked. He gave a snort that said *No, keep going. I want to hear this.* Well, that was encouragement enough. Rowan sat in the doorway, letting Broderick lay his head in his lap. "He's been through a lot. I mean a lot. I shouldn't fault him too much." Rowan scratched under Broderick's chin. "Because despite it all Callum kept his big heart. And he cares about the ones he loves. He's smart and he's funny. Well, unintentionally funny but I think that counts. And Sweet Hecate, his ass." Broderick let out a grunt. "Yeah, I know I'm not only one who's noticed. But ass aside. He's a good guy." *And he wants me. Even when I'm falling apart, he wants me.*

He smiled at Broderick. "I'll talk to him." Broderick let out a series of bleats and Rowan laughed. "Whoa! Slow down their turbo! We're not getting married. We just need to...clear the air. Especially about Orlaith."

His talisman buzzed from the mantle, its sigil flickering with a blue light. Holy crap, it still held its magic, despite the crack. Rowan held his breath as it glowed, then went dormant. "Dad? Mom?"

You're not alone.

Rowan wasn't sure if that was his parents or himself speaking that mantra, but it there it was, nudging him towards a future that scared the shit out of him. He wasn't alone. His parents spell had worked. They had sent someone to him. They had sent Callum. Maybe, just maybe it was time for Rowan start living for himself.

Chapter 12

Callum gathered up the last of the nest, frowning. The one thing he had gifted Rowan that he enjoyed, reduced to piles of rubble. "All that work, destroyed by my own doing," he grumbled, shoveling it all into the fireplace.

The debris ignited in a bright flash, crackling and sparkling before dying back to its usual flames. The house was strangely quiet. Chances are it was as disappointed as Callum was after tonight's debacle. The nest was gone, Aster was frightened into a panic, and Rowan's talisman, the thing he never removed from his neck, had been broken. And it was all Callum's doing. Rowan was sure to reject him. He was probably waiting for Callum to return to his wing that very moment, ready to end this farce once and for all.

He pressed a hand to the mantle. "I should have stopped at the nest. I should have warned Broderick about the ceilings..." He lowered his head. "I should have told him about Orlaith ages ago." The shock in Rowan's eyes when her name left Callum's lips. The disappointment. All of it made him want to retch. I was foolish," he told the house. "I was afraid. I didn't want what happened to her to happen to him as well. I couldn't bear it." The house's hearth flamed in sympathy. Callum scrubbed his face, he gave the mantle a pat of thanks then left, closing Rowan's door behind him. Tonight, he'd sleep in his old home down in the house's basement, pay penance in the cold, dank underground to give the witch-boy some peace. Then tomorrow he'd face his fate.

A brisk chill whisked past Callum on the stairs, Rowan's warm chuckle swiveling his ears. "So, your nine brothers are *all* named Broderick?" Rowan asked. Callum softened his hoof falls, creeping into the living room. The front door was open, and Rowan sat cross legged in the threshold, Broderick's head in his lap. The stag grunted as he was petted, eyes closed with contentment. Of all the sights Callum expected to see tonight, this was not one of them. "Doesn't that get confusing?" Rowan continued. "Or is it a deer thing and you just know which Broderick is which?"

"Witch-boy?"

Rowan twisted, brows shooting sky high. One hand still rested on Broderick's head, the other clutching his broken talisman, its sigil glowing a dim blue. "Oh, uh hey."

"Hey," Callum repeated, looking back and forth between Rowan and Broderick. "I thought you would have sent him away."

Rowan's cheeks flushed pink. "I was going to but then we started talking. First off, the fact that I can understand him is weird but explains Ivy and Maximus. And two, I didn't know stags were so interesting."

"Then don't let me interrupt."

"No, no! You're not!" Rowan struggled to stand, clutching his thigh, and clinging to Broderick's antlers. In three quick strides, Callum had Rowan in his arms, helping him stand. Much to his shock, Rowan let him "We were just finishing up. Besides, I should probably let Broderick rest." The stag's nostrils flared as he rolled his eyes, clearly annoyed with Callum but Rowan gave his neck a pat and his irritation disappeared. "You had an eventful night, didn't you buddy? Hold on, I'll go get you that blanket I promised."

Something gave Callum's heart a sharp tug. His tail flicked as Rowan snagged a fluffy blanket from the couch. "You've been here this whole time talking to him?"

He didn't think it possible for Rowan to blush even brighter, but he turned as bright as a pomegranate. "How can I say no to that face?" Broderick batted his long eyelashes before wiggling his nose.

Callum cracked a little smile. "I'm not immune to his charms either."

Rowan shook out his blanket, draping it over Broderick's back "Okay, that should keep you warm for the night. You sure you want to sleep on the porch? Don't you have a home somewhere?"

"Stags take their duties very seriously. As a familiar he'll stay as close as allowed." Callum rubbed his palms together. "That is, if you accepted him."

Rowan pursed his lips, then gave Broderick a nod. "You start tonight."

Broderick's bellow of joy flattened Callum's ears and he shushed him with a hiss. "Hush before you start another ruckus!" The stag flicked a careless tongue at him then trotted away with a proud snort, settling on the porch swing.

The silence between them was heavy, Rowan rubbing his bare arms as the remains of the winter cold pebbled his skin. Callum held himself back before he swept the witch against him to warm him back up. "Your bedroom is restored."

"Thanks," Rowan replied, shuffling his feet.

Callum swallowed, unsure what else to say. So, he swept his arms towards the stairs, bowing his head. Rowan didn't move. He took a deep breath, staring at the talisman still glowing in his palm. "Does it work?"

"Yeah. Dad's magic was more powerful than I thought."

"I'll still fix it for you. I'm sure Finn and I will-"

"It's fine. I mean it this time." Rowan traced the sigil with his thumb. "I think my parents' spell did what it was supposed to do. And I think it's time I listened." He raised his gaze to Callum. "Thank you for taking care of Aster. It means more than you know."

"Your sisters are as special to me as they are to you. I would lay down my life for them."

"I know but it didn't really hit me until now," He shook his head. "And it never occurred to me that you and Aster would talk about your..."

"Suffering." The word was sharp, a bitter shard he had chewed for decades. But Rowan's gentle blue eyes eased the sting. He gestured to the stairs again. "To bed with you, Witch boy. I've put you through enough-"

"Who's Orlaith?"

Callum's stomach fell to his hooves. He rubbed his throat, hoping to dislodge the rock that somehow wedged itself there. "She... she was my mate."

Rowan folded his arms tight across his chest. "You never mentioned her before."

"I never told you of Orlaith because..." His chest knotted, making it hard to breathe. "...That failing is the most painful of all. And I don't think you'd understand or even want to be near me after you hear the truth."

Callum waited for his scorn and shame, but Rowan set his jaw, contemplating. "You know my mom and dad died in a car crash, right?"

"Ivy told me," Callum replied.

Rowan sucked in his cheeks. "But did she tell you I was the one driving?"

Callum sobered as every inch of him turned cold. "You were in the vehicle?"

Rowan nodded. "I was only nineteen. They were going a wedding in Los Angeles, and I had just gotten my license, so I wanted to drive them. I said the practice would be good for me and I was so excited to try out the twisty roads." He released a mirthless chuckle. "And I did not let that go. I bugged them bugged them until they finally agreed. The roads were icy that day and me, being a new driver..." He shuddered but his voice remained steady as a rock. "I lost control, and we crashed through the embankment and down the side of the mountain. When I came to, the car was flipped and the fucking dashboard was wrapped around my leg... And my parents were dead." His fingers tightened around his talisman, dousing its light. "They were still belted into their seats, just...hanging there." He shook his head, sniffing in his emotion. "That's why my leg hurts in the wintertime. It never healed right."

"How long have you been keeping this inside?" Callum murmured.

"Long enough. I went to therapy for it. But sometimes I see them like that, when I shut my eyes, when I fall asleep. Pale and bloody and upside down. I wonder a lot what would have happened if they drove themselves, if I didn't insist that I get behind the wheel." When he finally looked up, his blue eyes were shrouded with tears. "So, whatever you're about to tell me, I'll understand. Trust me."

Callum's lower lip trembled. "I'm afraid," he whispered.

"So am I," Rowan' replied. "But it feels kind of cathartic to tell you about it. Maybe it will be for you too."

His brave, gentle Witch-boy, confessing so much, living with even more. In that moment, Callum had never felt closer to anyone; not Finn, not Orlaith. *If he can talk of such things, Callum. So can you. Have courage.* Callum nodded to the couch and Rowan obediently sat, waiting with patience. *Am I going to do this? Truly?*

Their gazes locked, Callum getting lost in that sky of blue. *You can do this.* He inhaled the pain and settled beside him. "You know of the coven, of the slaughter of my herd. Orlaith... She was our chieftain, and I was her lead warrior. She was strong and brave and always believed in the best of everyone. So, when the coven arrived, saying they came in peace, she believed them. We all did. We had no grievance with witches."

He clutched his horns, shutting his eyes tight. Gods help him he could still feel her blood on his flesh, still hear the cries of his herd. Rowan slid a hand on his knee, and the voices quieted.

"The coven leader was a silver haired witch named Arabella." He continued. "She was charming and beautiful. Said she wanted to negotiate terms of their arrival. Their coven. Our herd. We'd work in tandem. Harmony. Witch and satyr in a friendly partnership." Crimson swirled in his mind. Blood. It washed over him in a steaming haze, and he grasped Rowan's hand like a lifeline. "Arabella beheaded Orlaith before she even gave greetings. And I was not fast enough to stop them. The slaughtered my kin, created beasts we called the hunger, the very one Aster was cursed into, to destroy us all."

Rowan said nothing, only laced his fingers with Callum's, their palms pressed tight, grounding Callum in his storm of grief.

"Soon only Finn and I remained, and I'd be damned if that bitch touched my baby brother. Finn was younger than I, still relied on me for protection. And I did. I kept him safe with my very soul. I even begged Thaddeus—the warlock who once owned this house—for sanctuary, which he gave, despite being a pompous lout. I sent word to our Queen in the fae realm. Surely, she would have come for us. She was our Queen!" Callum shook his head, eyes burning. "I don't know what hurt more, the torture I endured, or her abandonment."

His heart pounded, tremors seizing him. "They stormed Thaddeus's home, took Finn first but I begged them to spare him and take me instead. Arabella took all three of us. They built altars to sacrifice us on. But it wouldn't be simple. Oh no. They didn't thirst for blood. They thirsted for fear. Pain. Anguish." He looked at the scars that crisscrossed his arms and swirled upon his chest, still feeling the knife as fresh as it was the day it happened. "And I was the first to be sliced to pieces."

"Callum..." Rowan choked.

Callum lifted Rowan's hand to his lips, the touch his anchor "Arabella made me say Orlaith's name as she cut be apart." *Such delicious anguish from such a strong male.* Tears poured from his eyes, hot sticky and shameful. He buried his face into his hands. "Orlaith! I let her die! I let them all die! If I had acted faster! I should have fought! Should have broken that coven, but they broke me!" His ears flattened to his skull to drown out the terrible din of that night.

Rowan took his chin forcing him to meet his gaze. "Look at me Callum." His voice was unlike anything he heard from him before; strong and unyielding, unable to deny. Callum lifted his eyes to Rowan, his form haloed through his tears. "It's not your fault. Say it."

"It is."

"No. What goes for Aster goes for you to now say it."

Callum's voice was weak, the words ragged and breathy. "It's...it's not my fault."

Rowan's tender smile wrinkled his nose and the wailing in Callum's mind dulled. "You're here, you're strong, and you're tough. And you deserve to be here. Say it again."

A twinkle of strength fluttered in his heart as he gazed upon Rowan's beautiful mouth. "It's not my fault." Gods, he almost believed it that time.

"Again," Rowan commanded. "I'll say it with you, okay?"

Their voices rose together. "It's not my fault." An amber of fury ignited inside Callum, growing brighter, burning hotter. All those years of guilt and grief. "It's not my fault." The words rolled from his lips now, strong, and sure. Their cries turned to manic laughter, shaking sorrow from their eyes in rivers and pulling the breath from his lungs. He believed it now, believed every damn word that poured from his mouth. "It's not my fault. I did what I could. I did all I could and saved who I could! It's not my fault!" Callum grasped Rowan's shoulders, hissing through his fangs. "It's. Not. My. Fault." He threw his head back shouting until the chandelier shook, until his throat went raw. "It's not my fault!"

"Sweet Brigid! Are you all right down there?!" Ivy cried from the top of the stairs.

Rowan pulled Callum against him, cradling his head on his shoulder. "We're fine. Just having some Therapy time, Ives."

There was a beat before Ivy replied. "As long as you're all right. Just make sure not to wake Aster up, okay?" Her footfalls faded away, leaving them alone.

"I think we're done screaming for now." Rowan lifted Callum's long ear, whispering softly into it, "But we can go outside if you need to keep going."

Callum shook his head. The pain had numbed. It wasn't gone but by the Goddess, it was a tolerable ache after shouting those words. Peace. Stillness. Here he was safe. Wounds that were once raw were soothed by Rowan's smile. Accepted by his kindhearted Witch-boy. Callum inhaled his clean scent, squeezing him tighter.

"You should get some rest, Big Guy. Rowan reached around Callum's shoulders before pulling away to reveal that he'd tied his talisman around his neck. "You're going to be okay tonight."

Callum stared at the cracked pendant; its sigil now dimmed. "I can't take this."

"Yeah, you can. I don't need it anymore. It gave me what it was supposed to." He smoothed Callum's hair back "And I have my answer." Callum held his breath as Rowan shrugged his freckle spattered shoulders. "Broderick and I talked. He thinks I should give us a chance and... I agreed."

Callum's tail hit the couch with a loud thwap. Rowan flinched then cackled, snatching it before it went rogue. "You wish me to continue wooing you?"

"Only if you tone it down a bit. Let's just hang out. Spend some time together... Maybe fuck occasionally?" Rowan pinkened at his suggestion. "Let's see where it goes."

Callum wet his lips, still not daring to hope. "This is an agreement to be wooed." Rowan nodded again. "A definite yes."

"It's a yes," Rowan held out his hands. "Not for mates, okay? We're going slow. And after Yule we'll reevaluate and-"

Callum yanked Rowan into his arms and kissed him. Rowan clung to Callum, his tongue slipping into his mouth, deepening their building connection. He tasted pure and honied, like the sweetest mead to ever touch his lips. Callum kissed him until his toes curled. Kissed him until they shared breath. Kissed him until time stopped. The word swam circles in his brain. Yes. He said yes! *Didn't you hear the Witch-boy? He said yes!* It was ages until Callum released him and time well spent.

Rowan gasped, sweat dotting his forehead. "Woah."

"Sleep Witch-boy," Callum, nipped his lower lip "And prepare for something tremendous."

"Not sure if that's a threat or not after what happened tonight."

Another kiss sent the witch sprawling onto the couch. He could scent the witch's arousal, feel his hardening shaft against his hip. If Callum could, he'd strip Rowan and take him right there. But such a grand overture would scare him away and Callum would not squander this opportunity.

Callum reluctantly pulled away, giving one last peck on the tip of Rowan's nose. "Until tomorrow."

"Looking forward to it!" Rowan called after him, his voice breaking.

Callum bounded up the stairs to prepare his wing. Everything going forward had to perfect. His sweet witch-boy had opened the door for Callum to slide a hoof in and he would guard it with his life. For nothing would lock it away from him again.

Chapter 13

The wraith crouched in the treetops, waiting for Rowan's car to pass. *He must come! I must see him again after last night!* Its skin stung, body still recovering from last night's beating. The house had shown no mercy when it detected its presence, battering it into pieces. But it had been worth it, just to experience Rowan's despair again.

After days of drinking Threnody's bitter essence, it finally had the strength to slip into Rowan's dreams and it wasted no time going to its prize. He had dangled on the edge of sleep last night, letting the wraith sneak into his room with ease. He was so beautiful in his terror, so perfect. The wraith had longed to whisk him beyond the veil, to change him into a wraith so it could be with him forever. It had to claim him. Alas, the house had other ideas and the wraith spent another night feeding off Threnody to regain its strength.

The afternoon sun was blinding off the snow but it only squinted through the pain and waited. Rowan couldn't lock himself away forever but there was so sign of his car. *He's with that satyr, the one you spied in his dreams.* It hissed at the thought.

That satyr. It had seen him before, fleeting memories of the huge slab of scarred flesh swimming in Rowan's thoughts. The wraith thought nothing of the beast, thinking he was another passing wound it could torture Rowan with later. But last night there was a strong emotion behind the vision of the satyr, one that made the wraith choke in disgust. Happiness. Love. The wraith gritted its teeth. No, that wasn't possible. Rowan belonged to wraith alone. *I need my strength! I must claim him!*

A dark flicker swooped between the trees. The gargoyle had returned. The wraith tensed, watching him make his trip towards the house. Rich essence trickled from the beast, teasing the wraith with its richness. Oh, the sadness, the anguish. It could sense it all the way from its perch *If you could get to that King of Shadows, you would be unstoppable.* With that kind of power, it could pass the wards. It could claim it's Rowan.

The wraith flew as fast as the wind could take it, the gargoyle's swirling trails of its black fog almost in reach. So close to its prize, to close to having its Rowan. The air rippled around the gargoyle as he soared. The wraith scrambled back with a screech, snaring a branch to stop itself before slamming into the house's ward barrier. It hissed as the gargoyle landed, folding its wings around his shoulders like a cloak before creeping through the shadows. *What is his secret?!*

The hum of an engine pulled the wraith free of its rage. A shiny blue car headed down the winding mountain road. Rowan. *Finally!* It swooped down through the cracked window, pouring itself into the passenger seat. A cheerful song blared on the radio, heat blasting from the dashboard vents. Rowan tapped his fingers on the steering wheel. Its beautiful prize was in such a good mood. Well, it would change that.

The wraith threw itself onto Rowan, sinking its teeth into his skull. Rowan shivered with a shocked gasp. A flash of the accident hit the wraith's tongue, the grief delicious and rich. A moan vibrated its shoulders. Gods, to sip his nectar again, to bond with its prize.

Rowan's hands tightened on the wheel. He took in a deep breath. "I'm not alone." he whispered. "Not anymore."

Visions of the wreck faded to a warm living room. A fire crackled. Muffled snow fall fluttered from the windows. Rowan sat with that damned satyr, the two embracing and talking low. A smile peeled across Rowan's mouth at his new thoughts.

Acid poured down the wraith's throat, burning like molten iron. It tore itself away, swiping essence from its throbbing lips and recoiling at its pink glow. Happiness. It oozed from Rowan's every pore, melting its flesh as it's aura filled the car. It threw itself out the window, desperate to stop the agony. Vomit spewed from its lips like a geyser, cutting its mouth like broken glass.

This couldn't be. It had worked so hard, manipulating his dreams, reminding him of his failings, molding his essence when he had crossed the veil. How did it vanish so easily? It caught its wind, steadying its fury to a low boil. It couldn't panic now. It had to replenish before that dreaded emotion dissolved it into ether.

The wraith dragged itself back to Threnody's barren cabin. The hiss of a propane camp lantern was underscored by soft weeping as it squeezed itself under the door. Threnody was right where it had left her, curled in a fetal position on her bed, cheeks still wet with sorrow. Good, she wasn't going anywhere.

It cloaked her with its body, sinking its teeth deep to pull her bad thoughts to the fore. "You have no one," it whispered. "The one you called sister, is dead. Your family abandoned you. Even Arabella is plotting your demise." The door opened. Judith stomped her boots, free of icy crust, one pale brow arched.

Threnody sat up quick, whipping her cheeks dry. "You're tracking snow all over this already freezing hell house."

Judith slapped a stack of notes down on the book cluttered table. "More findings. These wards are complicated. Much more than just witch spells."

Threnody rubbed her face, shoulders curving under the wraith's weight. "Arabella told me the house was previously owned by a warlock when she called today. So that explains it."

"Mother," Judith corrected. "We don't use her name, sister."

Threnody made a sour face, ignoring Judith's reprimand. "Whoever's in there probably built off his work."

"So, you talked to Mother without me?" Judith asked. There was a knife in her voice.

The sharp tone didn't shake Threnody, only swelled her anger that the wraith gobbled up eagerly. "*She* called *me* while you were out."

"I don't want Mother to think I'm not doing my share," Judith replied.

"I'll make sure she knows." The implied "*bitch*" was heavy in her tone. They continued their boring bickering, the wraith nibbling at each annoyed morsel.

Soon the sun had set. Threnody fell asleep. Night rose and finally the wraith felt strong enough to try again. It knew what possibly awaited it if it crossed Rowan's dreams again, knew the pain that would come. But Rowan's happiness was too strong. It had to quash it tonight, had to destroy that wretched emotion before it overcame him and he was lost to the wraith forever.

The wraith hooked its fingers into reality and pulled the veil aside to endless blue fog, pulsing with a soft light. Gentle voices sang a tuneless soothing drone, peaceful spirits floating about their business. It slipped inside and it wove its way through the dead, souls giving its foreboding presence a wide berth. "Patience, my Rowan. I'm coming. I will save you from this fate."

The golden horizon of dreams appeared, humming with the buzz of thoughts, memories, and desires. The wraith inhaled deep, catching the familiar scent of Rowan. He was there in the dreamscape, sleeping soundly, the familiar buzz of magical wards faint around him. The wraith wove its form around the magical threads that surrounded the witch, their fire burning its flesh. It growled but kept moving. It couldn't stop now.

It peered into Rowan's dream. Thoughts floated freely, ones beyond his anguish. Someone else was with its witch. The satyr. Their bodies were entwined, mouths sealed together as they moved as one, panting and moaning. Jealousy lit the wraith ablaze. Its eyes flashed as it let loose a roar that echoed throughout the veil.

"Miiiiine!"

Chapter 14

Rowan gritted out a moan, nails digging into the bark of a fallen tree. The night air was sharp on his tongue, stinging and bitter against his naked body only to be thawed by Callum bowing over him, shielding him from the autumn cold. Sweet Hecate he felt so fucking good.

Claw gripped his ass, the velvety fur of his tail wrapping tight around his thigh. He collared Rowan's neck, pulling his head back to slant his mouth over his. He tasted like summertime, strong and fresh and hot. Rowan devoured his kiss, wanting more, needing more.

Callum's hand slid between his spread legs, cupping his balls. Rowan arched as Callum's hard, huge cock worked itself inside him. He thrust and Rowan grunted, pushing back against him. "More."

"You feel just as amazing as I dreamt you would, Witch-Boy." Callum's breath was hot against his ear, the low growl vibrating right through him. He stroked Rowan's shaft in

time with each of his thrusts. "You are everything I ever
wanted."

*Another thrust made Rowan's teeth clack. It had been so
long since someone touched him like this, so long since he
allowed himself to be touched. And now his beautiful,
scarred male was worshiping ever inch of his body. Gods,
Rowan was so glad he decided on that walk after dinner, so
glad he had finally given in as soon as Callum's lips were on
his neck.*

Rowan hissed as Callum's hand slid up his length.
"Fuck."

Callum's breathless chuckle danced over his back. "Pre-
cisely."

No, don't come yet. Too soon. *He wanted this to last.
Wanted this to go on and on and on.* Gods, I want him. I
want him for all time. Don't stop. Don't leave me alone.
Please, please, please! *Callum's hands were all over him,
his mouth was all over him, his hot wet growls consumed
him whole. Callum thrust hard, fast, pushing him right to
the brink until...*

Until he woke the fuck up.

Moonlight flooded through Rowan's window, bright
even through the curtains on such a clear night. But instead of enjoying his silvery glow, he was panting,
sweating, and hard as a damn rock. Rowan sat up willing
his heart to slow to no avail. That dream was clinging
tight .

"The curtains rustled despite the window being closed
tight. Rowan could have sworn he heard the faintest of

otherworldly giggles rustling between the floorboards. He looked to the ceiling with a scowl. "Not cool."

It had only been a night since he agreed to be wooed and the house was already attacking with both barrels. It had felt so real' Callum's gorgeous, scarred chest, feeling his frantic heartbeat against his palm, his moans husky and low.

Rowan shut his eyes, doing his best to think unsexy thoughts; taxes, mowing the lawn, the weird plastic things on the end of shoelaces. But no matter what he thought of, it all came right back to Callum. His fangs scraping his neck, hand wrapping tight around his cock...

"Nope-nope-nope!" He flew out of bed. Pain shot down his thigh and he stilled, clutching the bed frame for safety. After an eternity, the pain ebbed to a dull throb. Cautiously, he put weight onto it, finding that it could hold him again. But he'd have to move, warm, and stretch the muscles a bit before crawling into bed or it would never go away. "Great. A hard on and muscle cramps. Anything else bound to happen?"

The winter air nipped at his bare chest as he limped around his room. The fire crackled, the house's giggles carrying on every pop and snap of the wood. Another scowl was cast to the ceiling. Now he understood Callum's irritation with the dwelling. "Just let me sleep, okay?"

A dry, crackling voice whispered, "Miiiiiine!" The air thickened with a tight cold miasma. The flickering orange fire dimmed, then stopped, as if someone had hit the pause button on the world. The sharp stab of a glare dug into Rowan's bones. He felt it hovering over him, a blanketing darkness, waiting. Coveting. The shade.

"I'm...I'm still dreaming?"

A force slammed him against the wall. Rowan thrashed as fingers tightened around his neck, stinging like icicles. A shadow formed before him; two glowing green eyes in the darkness and a mouth filled with daggers. "You are mine, Witch! My prize! No other will have you!"

Help me! Someone help! *He tried to scream, but his voice was torn from him.* Fuck! Why can't I speak!

The grip on his throat released and the shade screamed, lightening crackling over its body. It burst apart into thousands of ragged whisps as the house worked its magic. Rowan covered his head as the shadows battered him. He ran to the hallway, dragging his injured leg as fast as he could. The door at the end of the hall swung open, welcoming warm lights coming from the other side. He dove through it, sliding across the slick floor before rolling onto his back. The door slammed shut and the world went black.

Rowan woke, sleep blurred haze clinging to his eyelids. His head felt full of air, spinning in empty space. He reached for his blanket. There were none. Or a bed. Or his room for that matter. He was on the floor, surrounded by dark wood paneling and torches flickering in welcome. "Wha..?"

A sharp prick stung his temples, his dream returning in a rush; the shade, the chase, the hand around his neck squeezing until his insides were frozen. He leapt to his feet, but his leg wobbled, still stiff from the cold. Down he went, hitting the floor with a huge thud, pain shooting right into his hips.

"Witch-boy?" Callum was silhouetted in the torch-light, tail lashing like a whip. He was clad only in Rowan's talisman, his body glistening with a light sheen of sweat.

Rowan rubbed his eyes. "Am I in your wing?"

"You are." Callum was beside him in an instant, pulling him into a sit. "What are you doing here? Are you all right?"

Rowan tried to rise but his leg was unwilling to support him as he scrambled for purchase on the wall. *It's Callum. He's here. You're safe.* "Yeah. I was... I must have been...uh...uhhhh...."

The words fell right out of his mouth as he found himself eye-level with Callum's massive cock. Right there. In his face. The one place on his body that bore no scars. Wonderful, semi hard, and just waiting for him to press his lips to it. The first, and more pleasant, half of his dream hit him like a semi-truck.

"Sleepwalking?" Callum finished for him. Rowan tried to look to his face but continued to stare at that beautiful phallus. Thick, and long, surrounded by dark curls. Gods it was just like he remembered. Heat flooded his cheeks then shot straight to his groin. Callum cleared his throat. "Witch-boy..."

"Penis!" Rowan slapped himself. "I mean Callum! Uh...Yes?" What was he saying again? Oh Yeah. Nothing. Because he was too busy staring at satyr dick. The shooting pain in his leg managed to snuff out the oncoming erection and Rowan finally dragged his attention away.

"Are you sure you're well?" Callum asked.

"Yeah. Gods, I haven't sleepwalked since..." *The shade showed up.* He bit his lips shut, afraid to mutter that omen out loud. "Guess I felt like a little sleep stroll. Sorry. I didn't mean to..." He gestured to the length, and *length*, of him. "...interrupt?"

Callum's pointed tongue flicked across his lower lip, and he grinned. "Nothing I can't return to, later."

Rowan bit back his groan. Oh shit, was he jacking off? Was he thinking of Rowan while doing it? The thought of that powerful scarred body straining, bathed in sweat and firelight as he stroked his length, Rowan's name heavy on his lips. *And we are hard again! Great.* "I should probably let you get back at it, um to it...whatever. I'm probably bugging you."

"Of course not. I'm wooing you now, Witch-boy. You're always welcome." Callum swept Rowan up into his arms, marching him down the stairs. "The fire is warm in my territory. You'll rest with me, and I won't hear otherwise. Besides, you can't walk out even if you wanted." The tiniest of smiles curled his scarred lips. "And you won't want to walk out."

That arrogance. Oh, sweet Hecate when it made an appearance, it was so fucking hot. Rowan tried to mask his shivers as Callum jostled him down the stairs, the hypnotic smell of pine and musk luring him deeper into Callum's arms.

None of Ivy's cheery touches were present on this side of the house. No sheer curtains, family pictures, colorful wallpaper, or ornate rugs. Just bare, polished wood and heavy leather furniture, accented with piles of books. The only piece with any personality was the huge chandelier that spanned the living room ceiling, composed of antlers and hurricane lamps, glowing with oil lit flames. It was probably an exact replica of the one that Finn tried to crush Ivy with. "This place doesn't seem like your style." Rowan said.

Callum snorted. "It's the warlock's." He jerked his head to an oil painting hanging over the mantle. The only picture in the room. A handsome man stared back at him; eyes so amber they were almost yellow. His dark hair was pulled back in a neat ponytail, an old-fashioned suit, possibly Victorian, on his broad body. "The house saw it fit to replicate this part of the house with Thaddeus's original decor."

"Why?"

"Your guess is as good as mine. I believe it was very attached to its former master before Ivy moved in."

A sickening twinge nudged Rowan's brain, vibrating from a bear skin rug sprawled before the fireplace. Another jab came from the mounted stag heads on the walls, their final moments screaming at him. His stomach churned, the acidic taste of vomit coating his mouth. Of all the hobbies for a warlock to have, they had to be hunting and taxidermy, the dickhead. "Ol' Thaddy had taste for crap."

"His strengths lay with magic, not decorating."

Callum lowered Rowan onto the couch. Once again, his dick was at face level, like an engraved invitation. Rowan turned away, only to lock eyes with the stag on the way. His thoughts instantly went to sweet Broderick who was probably on the porch right now, wrapped in his blanket and snoozing away. Oh shit, what if that was his uncle or some other Broderick in his family? Rowan gagged, slapping a hand over his mouth before the dry heaves took hold.

Callum arched a brow. "What vexes you now? Surely, it's not my cock." He grandly gestured to the length of it, as if Rowan hadn't noticed it.

"No. Your cock is great. It's fantastic. Always had been." Rowan waved a nervous hand towards the hunting trophies. "I can sense their last moments and they're not pretty."

Callum's mouth thinned into a tight line. "You can sense that?"

"Remember when you kept gifting me dead animals when we first met? That's why I kept giving them back. The curse of a veil walker."

Callum looked towards the rug, then to the stag heads on the wall. He hummed then jerked his chin with a determined nod. "I see." He rolled up the bearskin rug, tucking it under his arm and marched towards a window.

He pushed it open and out the rug flew, landing in a pile of snow.

Rowan shook his head. "You don't have to-" The crack of splintering wood drowned out his protest as Callum pried each stag head from its perch. The chandelier shook with fury making Rowan wince. "I think you're pissing off the house."

"Well, it's always pissed me off, so we're even." The trophies followed the rug, along with the stench of their death. Callum wiped his hands on his thighs and pulled the window shut. "Better?"

His belly settled. "Better."

"Why did you sleepwalk?" Callum settled beside him. "Did you have another nightmare?"

The lamp like eyes of the shade shimmered in Rowan's memory. Long dagger teeth. boney fingers sharp in his throat. He balled his fists, forcing a smile. "It's nothing." Callum examined him in silence, his penetrating stare digging right past Rowan's lie. "Really Cal. I don't want to talk about it. I just want to relax."

Callum's mouth tightened, ears pressing against his skull. Then patted Rowan's head and trotted away, cock swinging. "I can help you relax. I will change that nightmare into your greatest dreams."

Gods, I bet you can. Rowan bit his cheek. "I didn't come here to get laid. Honestly."

Callum chuckled. "Doesn't mean the night can't end that way." Rowan swallowed hard. If this night took another sharp turn, he'd get whiplash. He watched Callum

throw open a steamer trunk. The sounds of bottles clink-
ing followed. "Ah! Here we are!" He held up a wine
bottle, its silver label embossed in Italian.

Rowan puckered his lips to the side. "You've been
stealing Ivy's wine?"

"Your sister has an entire vineyard in her kitchen. She
can part with one bottle." Callum slit the foiled paper
from its neck with a claw. "...Or five." He jammed the tip
of his horn into the cork, pulling it free with a pop then
held the bottle out to him. "Drink."

"You stole wine but not glasses?" Rowan took Callum's wrist, turning it so he could read the label. "Oh shit!
This is one of her expensive bottles! Cal!"

"Enough grousing. Drink."

"She was saving this for a special occasion!"

"*You* are a special occasion." The mouth of the bottle
bumped Rowan's lips, the rich smell of wine tickling his
sense. "Drink." Callum repeated, his demanding tone
sending heat right to his groin.

There was no way he could refuse that deep, seductive
command. Rowan took the bottle, taking a quick drink of
the full bodied, oaky drink. Delicious. Just like the satyr
standing before him. He blotted his lips with the back of
his hand. "That tastes expensive."

"Then it will relax you quicker. Stop worrying tonight
and do what you desire. Relax." Callum pushed the bottle
towards his lips, eyes stern as he watched Rowan take
another drink. That pointed tongue flicked across his lips
once again, calling to him. Gods, Rowan could practically

feel it, wanted to feel it. The nightmare faded from his mind, thoughts only on what Callum could do with that wicked mouth of his. Rowan offered the bottle back to Callum. He took a long pull, wiping his red stained lips with his forearm before he settled beside him again and patted his lap. "Legs up here. I'll rub the hurt away."

Rowan chuckled. "Wait, I get wine *and* a massage?"

"I'm wooing you, am I not? Be my good Witch-boy and obey me."

Rowan's breath went ragged, pulse racing as Callum took his ankle, He pulled his leg into his lap, pressing his warm hands into his thigh, kneading. Pain gave way to slow relief as the knots released. An unintentional moan quivered out and Rowan bit his lips shut, trying to ignore the smug smirk on Callum's face. In a few minutes, Rowan was rendered into butter.

"I'm not hurting you, am I?" Callum asked.

"No. This is great." Rowan laid his head back on the arm of the couch. "You're damn good at this. Ever think of opening a business? You can call it...Satyr Strokes." Callum snorted, making Rowan waggle his eyebrows. "I'd make more massage-themed puns, but they'll rub you the wrong way."

"Your puns are horrible," Callum chuckled.

"And yet you laugh. Just embrace it, dude." Rowan watched Callum, hypnotized by the firelight playing over the roped muscles of his forearms, each scar rippling from movement. Callum's fingers brushed his hip, then his inner thigh. Higher. An all too familiar fear stabbed

Rowan's heart, and he swung his legs out of Callum's lap. "I should..." Callum placed them right back and returned to work. "...Sit right here?"

"Yes." Callum locked eyes with him. "Do you want to go back to bed? Answer me truthfully, Witch-boy."

Gods, Rowan longed to be coddled, to be needed and wanted and touched. But the damn words wouldn't leave his mouth. Rowan was pushed backwards onto the settee, caged by Callum's thick arms.

"If you don't accept my care..." Callum purred. "Then you're not leaving."

Rowan's laugh trembled. "Cal! Come on!" He wanted to sound forceful but was weak as Callum's hardening length pressed into his thigh. "You're not playing fair."

"You're a strong witch! How can you be so easily waylaid?"

"You're heavier than me."

"Then use your wits! I thought witches were supposed to be clever-" Laughter exploded from Callum as Rowan shoved his hands in his armpits and wiggled his fingers. The satyr squirmed, kicking his hooves against the cushion.

"Oh my gods you're ticklish!" Rowan moved his hands to Callum's ribs, dancing them across his scars. "How did I not know this?"

Tears of mirth trickled down Callum's cheeks as he struggled to speak between his hysteria. "Now who's not playing fair?!"

"Me. Totally me."

A sharp thwap of Callum's tail hit the side of his ass, and Rowan squeaked, jerking his hands away long enough for Callum to snag them. He pinned his wrists over his head as Rowan continued to giggle. "Almost got you."

"Almost, Witch-boy." Callum pressed his forehead to his. "But I'm tenacious."

His weight was a reassuring blanket, soothing away the aches and pains Rowan suffered moments ago. Their giggles faded and Callum tucked his face in the crook of Rowan's neck, his ragged breath tickling his skin. The crackle of the fire filling the gentle silence. If only he could close his eyes and just fall into this comfort, just forget the crap that plagued him for so long, but he tensed on reflex.

Callum pressed a kiss to Rowan's collarbone "You need to be unburdened." He moved upward, nipping and licking his way to Rowan's throat.

"I...I don't..." All thought left Rowan as Callum pressed his mouth to his. Rowan parted his lips to welcome him in, tongues entwining in a hard, and biting dance. Gods, he missed Callum's kiss, missed his closeness. He longed to wrap his arms around him, but they remained pinned in Callum's tight hold.

Callum fingered the waistband of Rowan's pajama bottoms, tugging them down an inch. "Don't fight me." He pulled them further, the cool night air skimming Rowan's hips.

Rowan's knees parted and he cradled Callum between his thighs. "I won't."

The hold on his wrist released and Callum sat up, chest heaving. He was chipped granite, and as hot as a forge, but so soft, gentle, and eager to please. Rowan moved to take his cock. He needed to feel that steel in his hand, to slide it between his lips and drink him down but a sharp click of Callum's tongue stopped him short. "No using your hands, Witch-boy."

"What do you want me to do with them?" Rowan wanted that sound sassy, not like the quivering mass of words that melted out of his mouth.

Callum moved his arms back in place over his head. "You keep them here like a good boy." He studied Rowan with his hand, tracing a map across his pecs, his belly, all the way to his hip crease. "You are so beautiful." He circled Rowan's navel with a single claw. "You deserve all the pleasure I plan to bestow on you. Would you like that?"

"Yes." The word came easy. Rowan didn't want anything else more in this world.

Pleased, Callum slid his hand under Rowan's pajama bottoms, palm running the length of his shaft. One firm stroke and Rowan arched but was stilled with a hand to his belly. A warning rolling from Callum throat. "No moving. Be my good Witch-boy."

Rowan didn't believe he could get any harder than he was, but he was stone, aching and throbbing, desperate for Callum's touch. He nodded, swallowing in restraint.

He wouldn't move, wouldn't breathe unless Callum told him to. He'd be a good Witch-boy.

Callum peeled Rowan's bottoms down his legs, tangling the flannel tight around his ankles "I've longed to see you bared to me again and here you are just as magnificent as I remember." He sat back to look upon him as if he were a deity. He thumbed Rowan's slit until precum beaded at his tip, wetting the pad of Callum's fingers "Will you taste just as sweet as well?"

That wonderful, pointed tongue flicked the top of his shaft. Rowan whimpered like a trapped animal, almost tearing the armrest free as Callum probed, the hum from his throat vibrated his very core. "Oh Gods!"

"You're even sweeter." Callum's lips closed around him, hot, wet heat, sealing his length. That divine mouth bobbed sucking and licking as the satyr cupped his balls, kneading another long moan from Rowan. Rowan kept his hips still despite the urgent need to thrust. *No. You're his good Witch-boy. You won't move a fucking inch.* When Callum pulled away Rowan finally released his breath, his legs tingling.

Callum fished under the settee, brow knitted in concentration. Rowan almost asked what he was looking for when he produced a small bottle. Callum looked at it then at Rowan with a sideways smile. "I suppose it was fortuitous you interrupted me when you did." He popped the cork. "You may release your hands. I have something to occupy them." He snared Rowan's wrist, pouring the clear, viscous liquid into his palms coating every finger. "I need you to prepare me."

"You want... uh..." A bucket of ice-cold reality hit. Oh, Gods this was really happening. *And you'll run away again because you don't deserve this.* Too fast. Too much. *Way too fucking real!* His passion waned staring at the lubricant dripping from his fingertips.

Lines of concern deepened across Callum's face. "You're quiet."

"Um, I..." Shit, what was he going to tell him? *Sorry Callum, but despite what the talisman says I'm destined to be alone forever so I can't finger you.* He looked away.

"You don't have to hold back. Not with me."

Yes, I do. Rowan shut his eyes tight, trying to shove his guilt back. Not tonight. Why of all nights did this have to come back tonight?

Callum pressed a tender kiss to Rowan's forehead. "Would it be easier if I commanded you?"

Rowan opened his eyes as Callum brushed hair from his forehead. He swallowed, rolling that thought in his head before he whispered. "Yes."

Callum clutched Rowan's nape, pulling him close, his growl deadly. "When you're with me, you will not hold back. You will scream. You will howl. And you will obey. Do you understand?"

Lust returned with a roar. Rowan tightened, body on fire. He needed to be free, to buck and writhe and bellow Callum's name to the heavens, to get lost in his strong, brutal satyr. "Yes."

The corner of Callum's mouth rose. "Excellent." He leaned down guiding Rowan's hand between his thighs. "Now finger my ass, Witch-boy."

Rowan he slid his hand into the cleft of Callum's ass, one finger circling the rim. Gods, it had been forever since he'd done this, but when Callum's eyes rolled back and he bared his fangs, his boldness grew. Rowan slid his finger inside. A low purr vibrated Callum's throat. Another finger stretched the satyr before sinking further into his heat.

Callum rolled his hips. "Deeper." Rowan obeyed, curling his fingers, working them in and out. as the satyr pressed into his hand, rocking slow. "That's it, Witch-boy."

Rowan's breath hitched, Callum's belly brushing his cock. His own hips rose for more of that delicious friction. "Is this what you want?"

"Almost." Callum slid free, the fur on his legs soft as velvet against Rowan's thighs. The last of the bottle's contents were emptied into his palm and he gave Rowan a long stroke. Rowan almost exploded at the touch, he bit his lips shut. *Oh Gods, I shouldn't. I can't. I don't deserve...*

"No." Callum grabbed his chin, forcing his eyes to his. Molten gold and sapphire, searing like fire, branding him with longing. "Release it, Rowan. Remember, my good little Witch-boy always obeys."

Callum straddled him, taking his shaft and guiding him between the cheeks of his ass. He slid down Rowan's length, his snarl rumbling through them both as they joined in tight, hot perfection. Oh, Gods this felt so good. *He* felt so good. A moan whispered from Rowan, afraid to make its presence known.

"Louder." Callum commanded. His tail flicked Rowan's belly as he adjusted to his girth.

Another moan, stronger this time, one that made Callum grin. That small release chipped at Rowan's walls, crumbling them down.

"Hands back over your head." Callum said.

Rowan tossed his hands up against the cushions. Callum took himself in hand, stroking slow. He was gorgeous, bathed in firelight and glistening in sweat as he rode Rowan's cock. This wasn't fair. He needed to be the one to make Callum come, to be the only one.

He thrust, nails digging through the leather of the settee. "Let me touch you."

Callum smile was pure sin. "Say please."

"Please, Callum," Rowan whimpered.

"Shout it to the heaven's Witch-Boy."

"Please let me touch you!" Rowan howled. "I need it so fucking bad! Please!"

Callum pulled one of Rowan's hands free, curling it around his length. "Good little Witch-boy."

His words turned into a hiss as Rowan slid his still wet hand along his shaft. Callum's claws flared as he pressed his hands to Rowan's chest, pushing him deeper. Rowan couldn't hold back any longer. He drove into him harder, basking in his satyr's lustful grunts. Callum. He was heaven, he was everything. *He's mine.*

Sweat coated their bodies, sticky and smooth. Rowan clutched Callum's hips while he pistoned his own. He needed to be inside him needed this connection like he needed to breathe. Callum took his mouth, their teeth clacking together. A fang nicked Rowan's lip, the coppery taste of blood tainting their kiss. He didn't care, only wrapped his arms around his satyr, pressing him close, moving as one.

Their cries shook the chandelier, Rowan's orgasm rising fast. One last thrust and he shattered, arching so hard he was sure he'd split in two. Callum followed, throwing his head back with a mighty roar. White lines of seed lashed Rowan's chest and throat, a hot brand on his flesh.

Their bodies slowed, the frenzy of their joining ebbing like the tide. Callum collapsed, lacing their fingers as he showered Rowan with kisses. Rowan stroked his back, reveling in the touch of his mouth. No shade haunted his thoughts. No guilt. No responsibility. There was only Callum. There would always be Callum.

Callum gathered Rowan in his arms, groaning as his cock twitched inside him. "By the Goddess," was all he could muster.

"Tell me about it," Rowan replied.

Callum chuckled, playing with sweat coated hair on his nape. "I'll command you more often. It sets you aflame."

"Yeah, I guess...Guess I just needed permission." Rowan brushed his cheek. "Thank you."

Callum brushed his mouth over his then untangled their bodies. He wrapped an arm around Rowan's waist, pulling him close. They laid together sweat slicked, breathless, and covered in cum. And it didn't matter one bit. Rowan's fears faded as their heartbeats touched, the pewter of his talisman between them. Protection. Sanctuary. Here he was cared for and safe. And he would stay here for the rest of his life.

Chapter 15

Callum didn't want to wake up, not while there was a warm witch draped over him. But winter's steely dawn danced over his eyelids, rousing him from sleep. The fresh clean scent of soap mingled with Rowan's salty sweat tickled his nose. A smile curled his mouth as he remembered the hot shower he'd taken with Rowan before slumber.

Callum dared to open his eyes and greet the day. His muscles were sore, and his skin was still prickling after only one session of rutting. Well two, if he counted sucking Rowan's cock while they bathed. Yes, that seemed suitable to count.

Rowan lay on him like a ragdoll, cheek smashed against Callum's chest. His pale skin was radiant, dotted with constellations of freckles from his shoulders down to the cheeks of his ass. When he'd wake, Callum would count every one of them with his tongue. He tightened his arms around his witch, brushing a kiss against his temple before resting his chin on his head.

He couldn't remember the last time his mind was this blissfully empty, death always whispering in the corners of his skull. But this glorious morning there was just Rowan's heartbeat. Yes, the trauma never truly disappeared, yet with Rowan it was lighter. Bearable. The world was less frightening while his Witch-boy was with him. Maybe he could regain the part of him that had vanished under the coven's knife. *Perhaps I'm ready to take a step into the light.*

Rowan stirred, giving Callum a little nuzzle. He lifted his half-lidded gaze and gave him a sleepy smile. There was a light in Rowan's eyes, no judgment or pity. Just sweet adoration. Two souls in each other's arms, enjoying the peace after a good coupling. Callum curled his tail around Rowan's waist. This beautiful Witch-boy was his. And in turn Rowan owned his heart.

Without a word, Rowan cupped the back of Callum's head and kissed him with a fury that almost earned him another tumble on the settee. But before Callum could flip him onto his back, he pulled away with a mischievous smile. "Morning."

"You look well fucked, Witch-boy." Callum chuckled, smoothing Rowan's messy locks.

"How else would I look? I can't feel my legs." He stretched with a groan, his shoulders popping. "Forty-two is too old for late night fuck fests. Sweet Hecate you almost killed me."

"Bah, you're hardly old. Just a witchling by my standards." Callum swatted his backside with the brush of his tail, enjoying Rowan's gasp of surprise.

Rowan grabbed his ears, giving them a rub that made Callum purr. "Yeah, but you're ancient."

"Ancient plus. I'm nine years Finn's elder."

"You don't look a day over old as hell." Rowan released his ears. Callum frowned, bumping his hands with his horns and the witch understood the signal, continuing his ear massage.

"So, I pleased you last night?" Callum asked.

"Yes. I am officially wowed." Rowan pressed his lips to his chest. "Wowie wow wow."

Callum groaned as a trail of fire was kissed down his belly. "More wowing this time than before?"

"Oh yeah," Rowan murmured against his skin. "And you'll wow me again...probably over a log...touching my... log."

Callum groaned "No, Witch-boy," he commanded.

"Why? You know I'm a killer in the sack." Rowan gave him a wink. "Touching your sack."

"Stop. Now."

"Oh, come on! I'm a ball...with your balls!" Rowan laughed. "Okay, okay, no more ruining the mood. But I'm a-"

Callum quieted him as he slanted his mouth over his, drinking in the sweetness of his lips. Eventually he relented when Rowan was boneless. "No more puns. That's an order."

"Sorry, Cal but I'm a force of nature. Might as well ask the world to stop turning." Rowan tapped the tip of his nose before administering his affection upon his ears again. All was forgiven in a blink. "Dear Gods these are soft." He looked to Callum's tail as it flipped against the settee. "Happy, I take it?"

"How could I not be?" Callum replied. "Cocks were out, and thoroughly taken. Things are grand."

"Can't argue." Rowan rolled onto him, his thighs sliding over his hips. "So why don't we try for round two, eh?" His eyes fluttered closed as Callum cupped him, giving his groin a firm squeeze.

"Brilliant idea, Witch-boy."

My Witch-boy.

The glass domed mantle clock chimed and Rowan pulled away to look at it. "It's eight? Shit!" He slipped from his arms, scrambling for his pajama bottoms that were crumpled under the cushions. "Shit shit shit."

Callum steadied Rowan was he hopped one leg into his pants. "You're allowed a late start today."

Rowan gave a sheepish shrug. "Trust me, I'd rather stay here but I promised my aunts I'd help set up for Krampusnacht."

Callum scowled. "Ah, that is today, is it?"

Rowan forked his fingers through his hair. "There's still an open invite to join if you want."

For the most fleeting of moments, it sounded like a wonderful idea. To join Rowan in a crowd. To hold no fear amongst his kind. But a knot tightened inside his gut, and his hands shook. *Damn it all, why can't I show courage?!*

"Never mind." Rowan took his face in his hands, giving him a tender, although disappointed smile. "How about I come back early, and we spend the rest of the night together? Just me and you and Ivy's pervert house."

"But what if I *did* join you?" Callum blurted. The hope that lit Rowan tightened that anxious knot, and he stammered like a babbling idiot. "Not today. But If I were to join you *someday*...?"

"I wouldn't leave your side." Rowan said. "Hypothetically speaking that is. Doesn't have to be tonight. Whenever you're ready."

Callum wet his lips looking at the crackling fire. "And what if I never am?"

"Then you can live vicariously through my boring stories about giving Tarot readings to tourists." Rowan raised his chin, gaze fierce and voice as serious as a vow. "Whatever you want, I'll support it, even if it's me coming home every night to talk to you."

Callum's ears perked. Home. Rowan had never referred to this place as home. It was always Ivy's house or the warlock's mansion. "Do you intend to make this place your home?"

Thoughts soared past Rowan in heavy silence; sadness, fear, then the slightest glimpse of... joy? Oh yes, Callum was sure he saw that in the twitch of his Witchboy's mouth. "Let's talk about it, okay?"

"I am open to discussion," Callum replied eagerly. "I know this is no easy feat for you."

"You're right." Rowan smiled, one that was genuine and spoke of brewing excitement. "But what was it you said? Go big or go home?"

Fire burned inside Callum's heart, one brighter than he'd ever felt before. By the Goddess, he loved this sweet witch-boy, loved. Not stronger than Orlaith but it was different. Bright. And he would not squander it.

"Off with you." Callum took Rowan in his arms. "The sooner you go, the sooner you return to me." He grabbed a healthy handful of the witch's ass, nipping his lips. "And the sooner I can suckle you and drink you down."

Rowan quivered. "Sweet Hecate, the way you talk is so fucking hot."

"You will find it even hotter while I'm buried deep in your ass," Callum growled. "Now get moving, like my good little Witch-boy."

Rowan stumbled backwards, waking from his lust filled trance. His laughter was like music. "Yes sir" he kissed Callum's cheek. "For what it's worth, I think you'd be a sexy Krampus. And I've always wanted to try a little role play." With a wink he set off, disappearing into the main house.

The wing felt so big with only Callum. The ceiling beams creaked, and he chuckled. "I'm sure you're very happy now that you finally got what you wanted." He grinned. "Because I am as well."

He cupped the talisman around his neck and the sigil flashed, as if in thanks. Gods, he wanted a reprise of last night. Right now, not after nightfall. He found his loin-cloth and tied it on, following Rowan's path. If he moved fast enough Callum would catch him on his way to the shower. Then he'd reenact last night's shenanigans and his witch-boy would run a little late. Callum threw open the door to the hall and collided into Finn, knocking him backwards.

"Dammit! I was just getting the hang of these boots!" Finn cried. He wore an oversized sweater and baggy pants, his horns invisible, save for the slight indentation against his hair. He struggled upright, making his slow way to Callum, the floppy boots on his hooves fighting him with each step. "You look unusually cheerful. Is my Witchling right in believing it finally happened? Did you claim your witch?"

"Indeed!" Callum spread his arms wide and bellowed, "Cocks were out, brother!"

"That is tremendous!" Finn cheered. He applauded as Ivy left their bedroom, blurry eyed and in her night clothes. "Witchling, good news! Your feelings were right!"

Callum thumped his chest. "Cocks *were* out!"

"I know," She yawned. "The good sex feels kept waking me up."

"I've proved to my Witch-boy that I'm strong and brave with a massive phallus my brother only wishes he had." Callum crowed.

"Hey!" Finn gripped his waistband. "My phallus is-!"

Ivy grabbed his trousers before they dropped. "Finn, no!"

"Finn, yes!" Finn answered.

Callum scrunched his nose. "What in the seven hells are you wearing?"

"My human disguise. I'm practicing." Finn said.

Ivy shook her head. "Out of all the days, Finn. Krampusnacht is the only one you don't need a disguise."

"If I'm to go to my first festival amongst the humans and witches, I want to experience it like them," Finn replied, making his way to Ivy like a toddler running in socks.

Ivy grabbed him before he teetered over. "The streets are covered with snow and ice, and you want to go out there in those boots?"

Finn waggled his eyebrows. "You can hold me all night, Witchling."

"You weigh a ton!"

Finn clicked his pointed tongue. "Not what you said last night while I was riding you."

Callum blinked, ignoring Ivy's blush. "Finn, you're going too?"

"My Witchling asked me to join her." Finn shrugged. "I said yes."

Ivy steered him towards their bedroom "Come on, Goat Boy. Let's go practice someplace safe." He didn't miss the discreet kiss Ivy pressed to Finn's cheek, or the tender smile she gave him, despite her grumblings.

Callum swallowed his nausea. Finn was going to Krampusnacht. His mate desired it and he could give her what she asked for. Meanwhile Callum cowered in his wing, like a scared fawn. A hum vibrated against his chest. He looked down to the talisman as it pulsed, the sigil lighting in a blue flash.

You're not alone.

The words were clear in his mind; half in his voice, half in a whisper from the air. He touched the talisman. *I'm not alone. I'll have Rowan. But can I truly do this?*

The door downstairs slammed a clatter of footsteps and din of voices following. "Aunt Dahlia?" Aster said. "What are you doing here? Shouldn't you be in town?

"No!" Dahlia cried. "It's ruined, it's all ruined! Krampusnacht is cancelled!"

Auntie chaos was not what Rowan expected to walk in on after his shower, but it had detonated all over the living room. Dahlia paced a hole in the floor, tall heels clicking like mad. She was dressed for Krampusnacht with her dark hair piled into a messy twist, the rest of her statuesque form draped in red velvet. But the festive attire did nothing for her look of utter despair.

On her heels was Rosemary, a swirl of green and brown skirts, trying to calm Dahlia down but also in a frenzy herself. They talked over each other a mile a minute, Ivy, Finn, and Aster staring at them.

What's going on?" Rowan quickly buttoned his shirt, running down the stairs to perform damage control. "

"I have no idea. they just burst in and started bab-bling," Ivy said.

Aster held out her hands. "Aunt, Lia. Slow down, what's happening?"

"We've been cursed!" Dahlia howled. "The auditorium's water mains froze last night and broke! The whole place is flooded with ice!"

"And on top of it all, the actor playing Krampus had to cancel." Rosemary shook her head, gray curls flinging about. "The flu has him on bed rest for the next week, poor thing."

Dahlia flung herself onto the couch with a dramatic sigh. "It's dreadful. We're going to have to cancel! All that hard work flushed down the toilet!"

Rowan shook his head, droplets from his still wet hair dripping onto his shoulders. "Wait, let's think a moment. The auditorium is down so why don't we just move it to the shop? Its big enough for the food tables and dancing. And you have that area in the back you use for summer witch teas. We can do the kids events there. We'll leave now and help you clear out the space, move all the merch and-"

"But what about Krampus?" Dahlia wailed. "We can't have Krampusnacht without a Krampus!"

"We'll have to cancel the children's events. And that is the highlight every year." Rosemary wrung her hands, taking over pacing duty from Dahlia.

"What if we asked one of the people in the costume contest to take over?" Aster asked.

Rosemary shook her head. "If they are chasing children, it has to be someone we trust, not a stranger."

Rowan pursed his lips then very cautiously offered, "I could always do it." He was answered by a loud chorus of groans and cries of Hell no. "I wasn't that bad!"

"Yeah, you were. It was like a horror movie," Aster replied.

"You're exaggerating," Rowan said. "I chased them like I was supposed to."

Dahlia sighed. "Rowan dear, you chased them down the street."

"They were laughing!" Rowan cried.

"They were screaming," Ivy muttered. He shot a glare at his twin who shrugged. "Don't give me that betrayed look, kids had nightmares for months. We still hear people talking about it."

Fine, maybe Rowan remembered it wrong. Maybe his roar was a little too blood curdling, and maybe the fake fangs he'd worn were a little too realistic. He'd assumed the kids were only hiding because it was a game.

Rowan rubbed the back of his neck. "I got a little too into character." He swiped his arms through the air as their frantic voices rose again. "Okay, let's take one problem at a time. We have a place, right? We can get the shop set up. We'll cross the Krampus issue when we get to it."

Dahlia threw her hands into the air. "It's no use! Even though we have a place, the most beloved part of Krampusnacht...well since Rowan left the role...is done!"

Finn rose a hand. "I could perhaps step in. Yes, I'm far too handsome to be Krampus but I'll do in a pinch."

Rosemary looked to Dahlia. "He does have horns and hooves. We wouldn't have to worry about a costume."

"No," Callum declared. He stood at the top of the stairs, expression fierce despite his shaking fists. "I'll do it" His voice trembled but he marched to the living room, a warrior ready for battle.

Rowan rushed to the stairs, ready to shield Callum from the oncoming rush of auntie affection. "Callum…"

"They need help. I can provide." Callum smirked at Finn. "Far better than my brother."

"That's only because I'm too pretty to play the role." Finn chuckled, capitulating with a sweep of his arm and a proud gleam in his eye. "I gladly yield to you."

"Are you sure?" Rowan squeezed Callum's hands. "Because you don't have to. Not for me or for anyone else."

"This is not for anyone but me." There was no doubt there, only cold determination as Callum brushed a whisper of a kiss to Rowan's forehead. "There's only one thing I've been surer of, Witch-boy and that was wanting you."

Rowan lit up with a delighted giggle. "Well then, I'll be right there with you, Big Guy."

Dahlia and Rosemary swarmed the two and Callum stiffened for the briefest of moments, then he melted under their praise, daring to embrace them for the first time. He snaked an arm around Rowan's waist, keeping him close while his family chattered. His brave satyr. The toughest bastard on the mountain was going to face his greatest fear. And Rowan would be exactly where he belonged, right by his side.

Chapter 16

Rowan gnawed on the inside of his cheek. He looked at his watch, then swallowed, watching the stairs like a hawk. It had been an eternity since Callum went upstairs with Aster and Dahlia and the silence was killing him.

Rosemary had gone to their shop, to pack the merchandise and spread word of their new location. Dahlia on the other hand had run home, returning with a huge box of old odds and ends from Krampusnachts past, whisking Callum up the stairs, Aster in tow, to dress him like their own personal horned Ken doll. Callum seemed only mildly anxious, not scared out of his gourd. A good sign but that didn't ease Rowan's worry.

Every crappy scenario ran through Rowan's head as he stared as his watch. What if Callum had a meltdown in town? What if this made his trauma worse? *What if he never forgives me for suggesting this in the first place?*

"Let Auntie Lia and Azzie work their magic," Ivy reassured him. "They've only been up there for twenty minutes."

"That's enough time to have a panic attack," Rowan grumbled. Gods, Callum could be curled up on the floor somewhere.

"I should just go up there." He surged forward only to be stopped by Finn, stomping in his boots like a cat wearing socks.

"Fear not, Rowan. My brother is a stubborn beast," Finn led him back to Ivy. "When he makes up his mind, not even his fear will stand in his way."

The fanfare of someone imitating a trumpet with pursed lips made Rowan run to the bottom of the staircase. Aster descended, her smile all teeth. "Witches and satyrs, may I present...Krampus!"

The slow, ominous clacking of hooves was followed by the deafening rattle of sleigh bells. Callum strode in like a king-god of winter. A thick leather belt covered in sleigh bells was slung around his waist and a blood red cloak blanketed his broad shoulders.

Rowan gawked, forgetting his earlier worry. Dear Gods, his strength, the pure animalistic energy that prowled through that huge body.

Callum beelined to Rowan, looking ready to wrap him in all that red velvet and spirit him away. And he wanted nothing more. Rowan held is breath as the satyr swirled his cloak, dipping into a low, courtly bow. "My Witch-boy."

No brain power. No words. Nothing but the blood rushing to Rowan's groin and a single thought. *I have a Krampus fetish.* Oh yeah, fuck the festival. He was going to stay in today and destroy this magnificent male.

Rowan replied with an eloquent, "Uh...oooh...Oooh heeeeeey." Unable to look away from Callum's glorious body. A fine sheen of oil coated the hard hewn muscle of Callum's chest, twinkling like starlight. "Are you sparkly?"

Aster puffed proudly. "The glitter body oil was my idea."

"Isn't he magnificent?!" Dahlia crowed. Her sudden arrival almost broke Callum's sexual spell. Almost. She swooped in, giving both of their cheeks an affectionate pinch. "It was sheer luck that we saved parts of your old Krampus costume, Rowan. I'm surprised we didn't just burn it after all the bad energy that it attracted."

Rowan rubbed his temples. "Okay! We established that I'm a horrible Krampus!"

Finn's sweater flew over their heads, landing on the banister. "If you are going natural brother, I'll join you in solidarity!"

"Loincloth on or we're staying home!" Ivy shoved him towards the stairs. "Sorry! We'll meet you there!" she cried over her shoulder as Finn's pants sailed across the room. "Can you not share your ass with my entire family?!"

I'll see you both at the shop!" Dahlia said. "Oh Hecate, this night will be fabulous!" She twirled on her fur lined ebony coat and out the door she blew, like the hurricane she was.

The scar on Callum's lips twisted as he flashed a wicked grin. "You like." It wasn't a question.

Rowan's voice pitched high. "I like?!" he coughed, the eyes of his sister on him like a sniper scope. "Well, I...I like...I like the costume. It's..." *Hot as hell? Making me horny as fuck?* "Impressive." *Sexy.* "Really well done." *So fucking sexy.* "Aster and Auntie Lia did a great job." *Yup, I have a Krampus kink.*

Callum's mouth was at his ear, his whisper scorching him. "I'll wear this tonight while I fuck you, Witch-boy."

Oh, fuck fuck fuck, yeeeeeeees. Rowan draped his arms over his shoulder, ready to devour that delectable mouth of his when Aster's gentle "Awwww" broke the moment. Oh yeah, she was still in the room.

She clasped her hands to her chest. "There better be lots of pics of you two. I want them all!"

Callum's ears flicked, attention turning to Aster while still resting in Rowan's embrace. "You're not going?"

Aster tugged on the sleeves of her baggy sweater. "I'm...I'm not as ready as you are to face the world yet." She wiped the melancholy from her face with a smile. "But I want you to have all the fun for me. And Cal. Don't forget what I told you."

Callum nodded, pressing a solemn fist to his heart. "I will not." He bowed his head to Rowan. "Lead the way Witch-boy."

Rowan's heart did a little backflip. "What did she tell you?" he asked as they walked outside.

Callum's fangs glinted. "That anytime the fear becomes unbearable, I should kiss you."

Rowan jittered. "Good plan," he squeaked.

Broderick met them at Rowan's car, snorting as he tapped the snow with his hoof. Rowan patted his head. "Just heading into town with Cal. Watch the house for me? Keep Aster safe?" Broderick shook his antlers then pranced back to the porch, standing sentinel in front of the door.

Callum clenched his jaw, staring at Rowan's car. There was no mistaking the fear there despite his squared shoulders. "You can do this. Even if it's just for a minute or two I'll be proud of you."

Callum closed his eyes, a long exhale loosening the death grip he had on Rowan's hand. "As long as you stay by my side, I can do this."

He cupped the back of Callum's neck, drawing him down to touch his forehead to his. "You're stuck with me all day."

Rowan led Callum through the streets, hand tight around his, their breaths fogging the morning air. Humans were everywhere that chilly morning. Callum could smell the spice of their hot beverages, could hear snippets of the conversations; laughter, tutting, bickering. None noticed the blur of air hovering beside the fetching witch-boy.

The squeal of a child made Callum jolt, his claws digging into Rowan's sleeve. His sweet witch-boy turned a smile in his direction, murmuring "I've got you." The reassurance relaxed him. *He has me. He'll protect me. Trust him.*

They headed into a quaint shop, a gilded sign reading Witch Way perched on its roof, flourished with moons, stars and arrows. A bell chimed as Rowan pushed open the door, a warm gust brushing Callum's cheek. The unsettling noise of the strangers outside vanished in tranquil plucks of Celtic harp music. The space was far bigger than he anticipated. "Here we are. Home base," Rowan said.

The comforting scent of Lavender, sage and smoke, filled Callum with calm. Everything was so bright, and cheerful; the herbs and dried flowers hanging from the ceiling, the displays of sparkling crystals, the wood floors polished to a high gloss. This didn't feel like the den of horrible witches. It felt like home.

"Aunt Rosie! We're here!" Rowan called. "Just um...tread slowly okay?"

Callum reappeared with a pop, gawking in wonder. This wasn't a shop; it was a treasure trove. So many shinies, so many baubles and bottles and... "By the Goddess's tits!" He released Rowan's hand, hurrying to the sparkling pendants and necklaces hanging from a metal fixture. Blues, and purples, and reds all glittered under the bright lights, each one on a delicate golden chain. His mouth watered at the radiant curtain of beauty. "Sooo shiny!"

"Whoa, whoa, whoa!" Rowan grabbed Callum's hands before he could begin adorning his horns. "That's merchandise they sell!"

The loud groan of moving furniture broke the peace. Rosemary was shoving a shelf three times her size across the floor, making very little progress. She peeked around it. "Oh, its fine, if he wishes to play dress up tonight. The expensive ones are locked away already."

"Aunt Rosie, are you sure?" Rowan asked. "Because this is stuff you sell-ahhh never mind, he's already started."

Callum wrapped the chains about his horns and into his hair, saving the ones with the bigger crystals to drape around his neck to accent the talisman he still wore. After arranging them just so, he gazed at his reflection in the small mirror beside the display. "Yes. This completes the costume."

"Yeah, it does," Rowan laughed. The crystals hummed with a soothing energy that seeped into his bones. He hmmed, fingering a large amethyst at his throat "We've cleansed and charged each one. Between this and the sigil, you'll be unstoppable tonight," Rowan explained, straightening the jewels that dangled from his horns.

The touch of Rowan's soft fingers on his horns made his skin tighten. Did he even know how sensitive his horns were in the hands of a lover? Well. Tonight he'd make sure Rowan found out. Oh yes, that would be a brilliant idea. Rowan blushed at the growing bulge under his loincloth. "Ah, well, you've got a lot of garnet hanging from your horns so that explains that."

"It's not the stone that ignites me Witch-boy." Callum purred. And Rowan turned even pinker. That shade was becoming Callum's favorite color.

"Oh Callum, love!" Rosemary called. "Sorry to interrupt your seduction but I'm not strong enough to move these shelves. Can you, please?" It only took seconds to carry each shelf to the back. And only one was damaged before Rowan warned him not to throw them.

Ivy and Finn arrived shortly after and they all worked together, the witches decorating with garlands of pine and holly, while he and Finn hoisted the furniture over their shoulders and cleared the space. All the while, Rowan gave him instructions on how the night would go. The people would come, then there would be a march of Krampus with others in costume in the street. Then the chasing of the children, but not to frighten them. Rowan mentioned that part with a roll of his eyes. After that would be a feast and reveling. *By Dionysus's Balls can I do this?!*

Soon, the shop was aglow with flickering pillar candles and twinkling electric lights. Red and green brightened the walls. The crisp scent of pine mingled with the warm savory aromas of roasted meats and root vegetables as the aunts brought tray after tray of warm food out to long tables covered in red silk. It was like the winter festivals of old, when Callum and Finn were young and free of their grief. When their herd had been whole. When he reveled with no burden. Gods to feel that again. Could he feel that tonight?

The sun set and the doors opened wide, welcoming throngs of people to the sound of bells and horns. Males, females, and those in between. Grown ones and little ones, by the Gods, so many little ones! They chatted and laughed, greeting the aunts with hugs and cheers. Sweat dripped down the back of Callum's neck as he stared at them all. He jumped as Rowan squeezed his hand, forgetting he had been standing right beside him.

"The Krampus march is going to start soon, and I'll be right beside you." Rowan gave his knuckles a pat. "But if you can't do this, I have an escape route planned."

His sweet Witch-boy, always ready. Callum couldn't love him any more than at that moment. *Love?* He looked at their interlocked fingers. So many nights he'd dreamed of seeing them connected like this, of experiencing the wonderful ease of his nearness. Rowan with his beautiful smile and gentle words. His selflessness and bravery. Callum's throat thickened, swelling with joy. *Gods, I do love him. I love him with my entire being.*

Something tugged at his cape. Callum gasped, finding a tiny dark-skinned female, her black hair pulled into two curly pigtails. Her puffy violet coat was so full she could barely put her arms down, a matching pair of earmuffs crowning her head. She stared at him with countless silent questions. Callum froze under her gaze. She showed no signs of leaving, damn her.

Rowan cleared his throat, jerking his head towards the girl, mouthing, "Talk to her."

"What do you want?" Callum snapped. Rowan sighed and Callum forced a smile, which appeared more like a fang filled grimace. "Please, what do you want."

"Are you Krampus?" she asked, unperturbed at his sharpness. Her two front teeth were missing, adding a little lisp to her words.

"Yes, he is," Rowan answered.

The little girl gave a skeptical frown. "You sure?"

Callum's nostrils flared with a nervous inhale, mind running in tight circles before slamming right onto Aster's advice. He snared Rowan, dipping him back to press a firm kiss to his lips. Courage returned and he released the witch to wobble on dizzy feet. "I am he. The Krampus," Callum replied. "And what are you? A little witch?"

The girl beamed. She took a deep breath, releasing it in a wild stream. "Yup! My mama said I'm a hedge witch, but I don't really know what that means yet. But she said I'll find out more when I'm older but that's gonna be a long time. Like when I'm sixteen or something. My name is Hazel, what's yours?"

"I told you. Krampus." Callum didn't even consider that witches could even be so young, so small, so...cute. And she was indeed cute with her round cheeks and doe brown eyes.

"Uh-uh!" Hazel shook her head, pigtails bouncing. "I don't think you're Krampus. You're not very scary.

Krampus is scary. My brother said that when he was little Krampus was super scary. He had claws and made this scary face and went raaaooooowwwwr!" Hazel wrinkled her nose, baring her flat teeth as if she had fangs. She roared again, the sound akin to an unruly kitten. Then she smiled. "He cried for two days." Rowan covered his blushing face and Callum burst out into laughter. Hazel wagged her finger at him. "Krampus doesn't laugh. He roars."

"Oh, you mean like this?" Callum extended his claws, lips curling back from his fangs. He let out a roar akin to hers, wiggling his fingers for effect. Hazel squealed and took off, crawling under one of the food tables. For a moment, he feared he went too far, but Hazel poked her head out from the tablecloth with a delighted giggle.

Callum raised his chin, suddenly standing taller than he had before. He looked at Rowan, jerking his thumb towards hazel. "That's how you do it," he said.

Rowan smirked. "I bow to your Krampus superiority."

It was only a breath before Hazel returned with several of her friends and soon, he and Rowan were surrounded, Hazel telling everyone "This is *really* Krampus!" She pointed to Rowan. "And that's Krampus's boyfriend." She turned to Callum with a bright, toothless smile. "Show them your roar!"

Callum exchanged confused looks with Rowan who just shrugged. "Don't look at me. They ran screaming when I did it."

Callum cleared his throat. Once again, he flared his claws, releasing his mighty but not so mighty howl. The swarm scattered, laughing, and running about, exclaiming how Hazel was right, he was indeed the real Krampus. Callum looked back to Rowan, cocking a brow. "Aren't they supposed to be frightened?"

"Witch kids are weird," Rowan replied.

Dahlia stood on a chair, beating on a flat drum with a flourish. "The march begins!" She announced. There was a great cheer, and everyone filed outside. Hazel grabbed Callum's arms. "Come on Krampus! You have to lead!" The other children pushed him to the door and outside. Rowan kept their hands locked as they were led to the streets where a mob of costumed people gathered.

Drums pounded and bells rattled as the children placed Callum at the head of the mob. They walked Callum through the march, cuing him when to roar and lunge. And so, he did, chasing the giggling children who circled him with merry chants, the comforting presence of Rowan never leaving his side.

The gaggle of costumed Krampusses hissed and growled their way through the parade rattling their baskets and bells. One in their cluster made his way to the front waving his arms with an overdramatic shriek at the little ones that surrounded Callum.

"Run children! Or I'll take you away in my basket!" His voice was pinched, muffled by the rubber mask he wore.

The kids stared at him blankly until Hazel stepped forward. "That sucked," she declared. The children agreed, a chorus of "Boo!", "You're not scary!", and "We like this one better!" filled the air, their little bodies surrounding Callum and Rowan in solidarity.

The man laughed, shaking his head in defeat as he lifted his mask. "I won't encroach on your fan-club." He handed Callum his fake whip giving him a thumbs up. "Killer costume, man!"

Callum held up the whip then looked at Rowan with a devilish grin. "Oh, the things I could do with this." Rowan clutched his chest with a sharp breath and Callum chuckled. "Ah, you like that idea, do you Witch-boy? Did I unlock an unknown desire?"

"I'm not answering that while we're surrounded by kids," Rowan muttered. But the scarlet of his cheeks told Callum the truth. He held his tongue for now, but this topic would be breached eventually. Breached and perhaps lashed.

The sweat on Callum's forehead dried. The tremors faded. Here he was surrounded by humans—by witches!—with no fear of their laughter or their touch. He paused, letting the children run ahead, staring at his hands.

"Cal?" Rowan asked. "Everything okay? Do we need to go back? We can go back."

Callum held out his hands. "Take them." The crease between Rowan's eyes deepened with questions. But he obeyed clutching them tight. "They're not shaking."

Callum threw his head back with a laugh. "They're not shaking!"

A grin split Rowan's mouth. He leaned in and pressed a kiss to his cheek. "That's because you're a tough bastard."

"That I am." And for the first time in ages, he felt it. And while the courage may be fleeting, he was going to cling to it. He wrapped an arm around Rowan's shoulders, raising his false whip high and strode back to the head of the march with a roar that no doubt Orlaith could hear from beyond the veil. He'd done it; he'd taken his first step to regaining his old self. No, not his old self. This was a new Callum, one wiser and braver. And with his amazing witch-boy by his side, he would indeed be unstoppable.

Chapter 17

How are you expecting to get home after all the glasses you just downed?" Rowan asked. Krampusnacht rolled on in a symphony of laughter and dancing that had spilled into the streets while he and Ivy sat in the corner of the shop. Callum vanished into the crowd willingly, he and Finn continuing their act, now expanding it to Krampus, his brother, and his boyfriend who needed a break to rest his leg.

Ivy poured herself another round, wiggling her behind to the music. "Easy. We're staying in town. The shop has a nice little room in the back set up in case of getting snowed in. And I want to cut loose tonight."

Rowan blinked. "Finn is all right with that?"

"He's come to town a bunch of times with me. Sometimes in disguise, sometimes invisible." She topped off Rowan's glass. "I think he's starting to like it."

"Huh," was all he could muster. He scanned the crowd for Callum. He wasn't hard to find, considering he stood a foot taller than everyone else, horns included. He galloped after Hazel and her friends, corralling them towards Finn only to let them duck under his arms in escape. Then he'd shake his fists in the air, bellowing, "Curse you! You have outsmarted me!" before going after them once more.

"You have it so bad." Ivy gave Rowan a nudge, expression impish.

Rowan tried to hide his smile by taking a drink. "Not *that* bad."

"Can't lie to me," Ivy chuckled. "You have been floating around like a fairy king since last night. And you lit up like a roman candle when Callum marched into the herd of Krampus...Krampi?" She furrowed her brow looking into her glass. "What do you call a gaggle of Krampus?"

"Good question." Rowan rubbed his chin. "A torture of Krampus? A chaos of Krampus? Oh wait, I got it. A childhood trauma of Krampus."

"A lashing of Krampus," Ivy snapped her wrist. "Whoosh-crack!"

The memory of Callum's sinister sneer as he waved his false whip made Rowan's pants shrink two sizes. "Um, don't say lashing."

"Oh sorry. My bad," Ivy giggled. "A horny of Krampus." Rowan rolled his eyes and she cackled. "Try as you might to change the subject, I'll always boomerang on back. Admit it, you're smitten."

Dammit, Ivy was right. Rowan had been smitten with Callum since they'd first met. The only difference now was he lacked his usual defenses against falling head over heels. Now here he was, spinning out of control with no emergency brake. *And if Callum left, I'd be alone.* His belly twisted, making his wine taste sour.

"And you're fighting it." Ivy added, finishing her glass.

"I'm taking it slow," Rowan corrected, groping for the talisman that was no longer there.

"Which in Rowan speak translates to fighting it." Ivy dabbed her wine-stained lips with the back of her hand. "Listen, I'm not trying to shame you or anything. You have your reasons. I'm just trying to give you a little shove in the right direction."

"And what makes you think moving back to Big Bear, and hooking up with a satyr is the right direction?" The smirk Ivy shot at him said it all. Even if she hadn't said it, she knew it as well as Rowan did. "Okay. Point taken. I had a rough year and moving all a sudden was a bad idea."

"You had a rough *few* years, starting with the accident then ending with thinking one sister dead and the other one dying. I get it. You ran. I truly understand how that feels." Ivy kissed his cheek. "Just take Callum's advice and be nice to yourself?"

She sauntered off, grabbing Finn's wrist and leading him to the throng of dancing bodies. The satyr instantly held her close, bending his tall form to press his forehead to hers. Rowan's mouth quivered. Love. That was love. And it both melted his heart and tore it wide open. He wanted that. No grand gestures or declarations. No feats of strength of outlandish gifts. Just holding hands. Just...being there for each other. *And if you stopped fighting it, you could have it.*

Callum lifted Hazel into his arms, giving her a little twirl. Rowan's chest tightened as he watched the two dance and frolic, not one ounce of fright in the satyr's eyes. Gods, if something happened to Callum Rowan would be lost. Sensing his gaze, Callum turned towards him with a shattering smile. He walked over, Hazel still sitting on his hip. "My apprentice would like to write me letters," he said.

"Apprentice?" Rowan looked between their conspiratorial nods.

"I'm going to be a Krampus instead of a hedge witch," Hazel replied. "It's more fun. But I gotta write him letters to get lessons so, I need your address."

"Can you give her that, Witch-boy?" Callum asked.

This was the same satyr who turned white at the idea of even breathing the same air as another witch. Now here he was, bouncing a witchling on his hip and demanding they be pen-pals. Rowan coughed to disguise his laughter. "You can use the shop's address. I'll make sure he gets the letters."

Hazel narrowed her eyes. "You promise?"

"Cross my heart." Rowan swiped an x across his chest.

"There. I told you he would solve the problem. He always does." The stars in Callum's mismatched eyes made Rowan's knees quake, and he wasn't even standing. He lowered Hazel to her feet, giving her pigtails a pat. "Off to your mother now. I must care for my Witch-boy."

"Good night, Krampus!" Hazel squeezed Callum's waist tight doing the same to Rowan. "Good night, Krampus's boyfriend!" Off she skipped, joining her friends.

"So, you have a pen-pal now?"

Callum puckered his lips, as if trying to decipher what a pen-pal was, then shrugged, giving up. "The girl wanted to correspond, and I know how to read and write."

"It's sweet. "Rowan shook his head. "And unbelievable. Just a few hours ago you were planning on waiting at home for me for the rest of your life."

"I suppose even a stubborn, broken satyr can change."

"Callum, you're stubborn, but you're not broken." Rowan patted his cheek. "As far as I'm concerned, you're great as is."

"Splendid is a better word."

Rowan laughed. "Okay, we'll go with that." Callum took his hand, brushing his knuckles with a gentle kiss. Every nerve in Rowan's body ignited. *Hecate have mercy, he is so good at that.* He cleared his throat. "What was that for?"

"For everything tonight," Callum replied.

"I didn't do anything."

Callum pressed another kiss to his hand. "You encouraged me to enjoy this wonderful festival." Gently, he turned his hand over, lips brushing his palm. "You stayed by my side and ensured my safety." When his fangs grazed his wrist, Rowan shivered. "You are a marvel, Witch-boy."

Rowan held his glass up to Callum's lips before he could move up further. If he did, he'd be grinding on the satyr like a stray dog, and this was a family event. "Here. Finish this up. I'm driving tonight so I'm at my limit."

"Very well," Callum laughed, taking a long pull.

A familiar icy touch tickled the back of Rowan's neck, tickling each vertebra. Something whispered to him, a weak, rasping voice that said "Miiiine." Rowan spun around, only to find a cluster of pillar candles and boughs of pine. *No. It's not here. Relax.*

"Witch-boy?" Callum turned him back towards him, brows tangled with worry.

Rowan spared another glance over his shoulder. The chill was gone, and the only voices were those of the party goers. He rubbed his forehead. "Nothing. I think the wine just got to my head."

"I can see that. This is a fine brew." Callum finished off the drink, tongue flicking against the rim of the glass to catch the final drop. Rowan gulped. All thoughts of the shade vanished, replaced by that wicked tongue. "It would taste even better taken from your lips, Witch-boy."

Rowan wet his mouth knowing he should take a step backwards. *This is a family event. A family event!* But Callum's heat was too enticing, and his delicious scent irresistible. *Fuck it. You're finally enjoying yourself. You're actually happy. Embrace it.* "I know you're having a good time tonight but-"

"Time for an exit?" Callum grabbed Rowan's hand, pulling him towards the door while shouting to the crowd. "The Krampus bids you all a good night!"

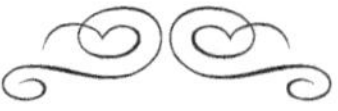

The drive back home was quick, yet the journey up the twisting roads felt like eternity while Callum's desire to bury himself deep into Rowan plagued him. Callum buried his face against the crook of Rowan's neck, inhaling the clean, crisp, scent of him. So bright and warm. Summer after the longest winter Callum had ever endured. He couldn't stop himself from tasting the salt of his neck. Soon they were parked in the drive and hurrying up the porch steps.

Rowan's keys rattled as he struggled to unlock the door as Callum ran his hands under his sweater and up his torso. "You're not making this easy," his voice cracked as he missed the lock repeatedly.

Callum shot a glare at the threshold. "Then I should I fuck you in the woods from now on." The lock clicked and the door swinging open on its own. He smirked, "I knew that would work."

They tumbled inside, in a ruckus of foot falls, hoof clacks, and rattling brass bells. Callum kicked the door closed behind them, tossing Rowan against it. His cock throbbed as he caged him in with his arms. Rowan kissed him hard, sucking, biting, his tongue delving deep, hands taking a tight hold of his ass. He was hard beneath his trousers, each stroke releasing clatters of bells. Callum paid it no mind as he yanked the witch's sweater over his head. Gods, he was so hot, heaving against his palms, nipples hardening beneath his fingers.

Rowan arching into his touch. He fumbled with sleigh bells around Callum's waist, each tug eliciting a loud jingle. "Dammit how do I get this thing off?!" Callum loosened the buckle and it hit the floor with a grand clatter that rattled the house. "Thank Hecate!"

Rowan grabbed Callum's hips, teeth sunk into his lower lip. The sharp tug made Callum growl. Ivy and his brother had no intentions of coming home tonight. He could fuck his Witch-boy right here if he wished.

The creak of an opening door made Callum's ears swivel. He stiffened, pushing Rowan away as Aster's sleepy voice called, "Hello?"

"Shit. I forgot she was home." Rowan pressed his forehead to Callum's chest, face hot. "It's just us, Azzie," he answered. "Callum and I are home."

"What was that noise?" she asked.

Rowan was bright red as he meekly replied. "Um...Callum's sleigh balls, I mean, bells."

Callum watched the stairs, expecting Aster to come rushing down and demanding details. Instead, she replied, "Okay, goodnight, then! And I'll sleep with earplugs tonight so have at it!"

"Will do!" Callum shouted back.

The door closed and silence resumed. Well, until Rowan burst out laughing. "Will do?"

"Did you have other plans?" Callum scooped Rowan up and slung him over a shoulder, cackling at the witch's shout of surprise. "No. You didn't."

He bounded up the stairs, two at a time. As soon as they were safely ensconced in Rowan's room, he yanked the witch-boy's waistband open. By the Goddess, he was beautiful; fiery hair tousled, mouth swollen with his kisses, and freckles bright against his moon touched skin.

"Not going to lie," Rowan panted. "The Krampus costume was fucking hot."

"Was it now?" Callum asked. "The costume or me?"

Rowan shuddered. "You. You're definitely better than sleigh bells." The corner of Rowan's mouth twitched into a smile.

"Indeed." Callum grinned. "And you want me."

Desire poured from Rowan, drenching Callum in its waves. "More than anything."

Callum clutched his nape, jerking his head back to meet his gaze, Rowan's blue eyes bright as Summer. "Tell me what you want tonight."

"You," Rowan replied, He reached for him again, but Callum snared his wrist, pinning them on the wall over his head.

"Specifics." Callum flicked his tongue over the pulse in Rowan's throat. "Shall I pin you down and ride you hard? Feed my cock between those plump lips and demand you suck until I come?" Rowan shuddered, eyes fluttering closed. Sweat beaded across his collarbone, his hands fisting tight. "Ah, you like it when I command you,

Witch-boy? Then I'll I take charge of you. Tonight, you belong to me. Only me." Callum freed a hand to shimmy Rowan's pants from his hips. He pulled the witch's cock free, and it pulsed in his palm, moisture beading at its tip. "That's what you want, yes?"

"Yes," Rowan moaned.

"And you'll be my good little Witch-boy and obey."

"Yes."

Callum shut his eyes, reveling in Rowan's closeness, his scent. His warmth. "Kiss me."

Rowan's kiss was delicate, trembling and so very delicious. Callum gave him a stroke in reward, a restrained whimper sputtering from Rowan's clenched lips as his hips bucked. "Don't hold back. Not tonight. Not with me. I want to hear you bellow to the rafters, Witch-boy."

Rowan's mouth trembled. "I...I will."

He led them to their tree, Callum sitting to untie his loincloth. It was tossed aside and Rowan fixed on his shaft, licking his lips. "Hands behind your back." Quickly, Rowan tucked them in place, that beautiful blush staining from head to toe. Flushed from shyness? Lust? Either way the witch was eager to please.

Callum gestured to the floor before him. "Kneel." He took himself in hand, an offering to his witch-boy. " Kneel and suck me."

Rowan obeyed, his lips sliding over the head of Callum's cock. Glorious wet heat surrounded him, and he groaned as Rowan teased his slit with gentle flicks of his tongue. Then he covered him, sliding Callum's length deep. Callum cupped the back of Rowan's head unable to stop from thrusting. Gods he was paradise. "More."

Rowan took him further, his lips meeting the dark curls at Callum's groin. His low growl shook his throat, the vibrations bursting along Callum's cock. So delicious. So perfect. His balls tightened, his seed rising with every slick movement of Rowan's lips. Closer. Closer.

"Enough!" Callum pulled Rowan away, regaining himself before he erupted. He longed to see his beautiful witch drink him down. But not tonight.

Rowan panted, his cock as hard as stone and drenched in his own precum. The way he ran his tongue across his lips was pure sin as he waited for Callum's next command. The teasing Witch-boy.

Callum rose to circle him. He ran his tail across Rowan's chest, gooseflesh rising in its wake. "You loved the idea of my lash, didn't you?" When Rowan nodded, he snapped the brush of his tail along his backside, eliciting the most delicious cry of delight Callum had ever heard. "Then I'll indulge you."

Callum knelt behind Rowan, bending him over the fallen tree. A slap of his tail hit, raising a red welt on the witch's ass. Rowan moaned, knuckles whitening. Another slap and Rowan's moan turned into a shout. He spread his knees, laying his cheek against their tree. "Please?"

Callum lashed again and Rowan thrust his hips; jaw clenched. He presented himself for more. And more. And more still until his ass was completely red and he was gasping. "Gods, I want you." he begged. "Please, Callum. Please. I need you."

"Tell me," Callum growled, giving him another lash.

"Fuck me!" Rowan cried, every inch of him pulsing with need. "Please just fuck me!" He was a man possessed, flush faced and mouth trembling with desire.

Callum smiled. "That's my good Witch-boy." He dug through his discarded pouch for his bottle of lubrication, slickening his cock before sliding his coated finger between Rowan's cheeks.

"Oh Gods." Rowan clutched his wrists even tighter, as Callum coated his rim, fingers sliding in and out before pouring the concoction down his ass. Rowan pushed against his hand, pleasure hissing from between his teeth. He was so eager, so wanting and vulnerable. And all Callum wanted was to give his witch the pleasure he deserved.

Callum placed one hand on Rowan's hip, the other slowly guiding his cock inside. "Rowan," Callum groaned. The witch was so tight, his outer ring taking his cock with every frantic breath that puffed his chest. Callum pressed a kiss between his shoulder blades. "You feel incredible."

Rowan rolled his hips, pushing him even deeper. "Gods, so do you."

Callum's tail snaked between Rowan's legs, wrapping around his shaft. He stroked as they found their rhythm, Rowan's jaw tight as he arched. Callum collared his neck pulling him back to take his mouth. "Say my name," he murmured through his kiss.

"Callum," Rowan cried. His name on Rowan's lips was like a siren's song.

Callum wrapped his arms around him, pinning him against his chest as he thrust into his slick heat. "Tell me you're mine."

Rowan nipped at his lips "I'm yours! Gods, I'm yours!".

Callum pounded harder faster. His tail tight, determined to stoke every drop from him.

"I'm going to come," Rowan whimpered. "Gods, Callum!" He howled as he exploded, his hot thick seed drenching his tail, coating his chest.

The sounds of his ecstasy were too much to bear. Callum roared. Pleasure, love, worship, it all poured from him as he followed his beloved Witch-boy into the abyss. Callum belonged to him. He would forever be his.

The air was thick with the scent of sweat and sex, the sounds of their panting overpowering the crackling fire. Soon they slowed, Callum showering Rowan's slick back with kisses. With reluctance, he pulled free, turning Rowan's head to press one long kiss to his trembling mouth. Rowan crawled into Callum's lap, wrapping his arms around him.

"You make me feel whole again," Callum confessed.

Tears filled Rowan's eyes, mouth quivering. "You...you make me feel whole, too." He sniffed back the emotion with a chuckle. "Glad we kept the fuck tree."

Callum laughed. "Agreed." He pressed a kiss to the top of his head. "I should clean you up."

"In a minute. I'm enjoying this." Rowan curled against him. They lay in silence, Rowan's heartbeat soothing him into stillness Callum didn't want to leave this place of peace. This wonderful shelter of Rowan's body. His mate. Maybe someday Rowan would say the word he longed to hear. Maybe someday they would be bound together in love. And Callum's heart and soul would belong to this magnificent Witch-boy for the rest of his days when that day came. Until then, Callum squeezed him tight. *I'll keep you safe, Rowan. I will die before you come to harm. My love. My home.* "My Rowan."

Chapter 18

Rowan opened his eyes to a black haze. The taste of gasoline and smoke filled his mouth. His leg screamed in agony, the rest of him throbbing, blood rushing to his head to drip from the gash above his brow. He dangled upside down like a ragdoll, seat belt still holding him in place.

"It's just a dream. It's only a dream. Don't look." He held his breath, wanting to close his eyes again, knowing what he'd see if he turned. But like always, he turned. His parents weren't there. Only Callum's body hung beside him, blood-ied, and torn, his mismatched eyes vacant of all life. Rowan covered his face. "No please! Not this! Don't do this to me!"

"This is what will become of him, Rowan." That voice. He hoped to never hear it again, but it was clear as day in his ears. A growl rumbled through the car wreckage dark and hoarse, like nails on a chalkboard. Rowan kept his hands pressed into his eye sockets. Don't look. Don't acknowledge it.

"Look at me, Rowan."

Don't look!

He could sense the glow of its green eyes through his lids, its stare hungry. "Look at me!"

Don't look, don't look, don't look!

Boney fingers gripped Rowan's chin and with a jerk his head was turned. Rowan's heart stopped beating. His body turned to ice. No matter how hard he fought the urge, he opened his eyes.

Thin lips parted in a smile, teeth as long and sharp as daggers. "There you are my prize."

A cold pit opened inside him, sucking away all sensation in his body as Rowan took a good long look. "You're...you're not just a shade, are you?"

It purred, stroking his cheek as if he were a precious pet. "You know what I am, Witch. You were just too frightened to admit it."

He did know. Rowan knew exactly why it could eat his sadness, how it could visit his dreams, and empty every emotion inside him. But he was too busy ignoring it to see it. "A wraith...you're not a shade you're a Gods damned wraith!"

Its body billowed, a dark sail in the wind. "Thought you could be with another? You underestimate me."

"You're not supposed to stay with your host this long! Why won't you move on!?"

"Because you're special, my love. Can't you see how much alike we are? Your pain so sweet and your sadness so pure and exquisite. I knew you were mine the moment I tasted you. And I will never let you go."

Rowan jutted his chin. "You can't keep me here. If you keep me in the dream realm, I'll eventually die and then you'll have nothing."

"So be it."

"But you'll starve!"

It hissed, eyes narrowing. "If I can't have you, no one will. Not your family. Not your damned goat. No one. As long as you sleep, I will always find you."

Rowan unbuckled his seatbelt, falling out of his seat and hitting the roof of the car. The wind rushed from his lungs. But there was no time to recover. He pushed through the shock and crawled towards the shattered windshield for escape.

The world spun, the car tearing apart like paper. It vanished and Rowan tumbled into the void. The wraith swirled about him, its body flying open before catching him in its cloak of darkness. "You can't leave me behind! You belong to me!"

Rowan had to run, had to get away, but it was like moving through mud, growing thicker, filling his mouth, his lungs, squeezing the very life from him. The darkness tightened, stopping his heart, and freezing his lungs.

Memories of his parents mangled corpses hanging from their seat belts flashed before him. The blood. The pain. His screams drowned out by the sound of sirens.

"See this? This is your fault, Rowan," the wraith's rust covered voice cooed as if soothing a child. "It's all your fault. No one will ever love you. Save for me."

Yes. It was right. This is how it would be for the rest of his days; alone, cold, with only his despair. Only his wraith. The fight left him and Rowan slumped, suspended only by the creature that cocooned him. The wraith pried his mouth open reaching inside and freezing his guts. The blood in his veins thickened and everything slowed.

"You're mine, forever."

Callum's ears swiveled back, listening through his haze of sleep, arm draped over Rowan's waist. He waited for the sound again. There it was. A strained whimper, muffled by clenched lips. He sat up, the mattress squeaking. Nothing looked out of place. Rowan's room was exactly how it always was. But that sound was unnerving. Another whimper, this time right beside him. "Rowan?"

The witch was curled on his side, blankets kicked away in his sleep, leaving him naked and shivering. Callum gave his shoulder a shake. By the Gods, every inch of him was frozen as if he'd been standing in the snow. Quickly Callum tucked the blanket back over him. "Rowan, wake."

But he didn't. Rowan rolled onto his back, the whimpers turning to moans, muffled by his locked jaw. Callum cupped his face. "Wake up!"

Something flaked under his fingertips, stinging and cold. "What in the seven hells?" Ice coated his palms. Callum gaped in horror as frost crusted the hair on Rowan's chest, spreading to his limbs in a glittering blue sheen..

"Wake up, Rowan!" Callum gave him a shake. Still no response. White fog flared from Rowan's nostrils, his breath slowing. His chest stilled completely. Callum gathered him in his arms, surrounding him with his body, willing all his heat into him. "I command you to wake up, Witch-boy! Wake up now!"

Rowan's horrible gasp for air shattered the ice sealing his lips. His eyes snapped open, and he shivered, wrapping his arms around himself. "What the fuck? What the fuck, what the fuck, what the fuck?!"

Callum cradled him in his lap. "Easy Rowan. I'm here."

"Why is it so cold?" Rowan's teeth chattered. "Am I covered in ice? Oh, sweet Hecate, why am I covered in ice?!"

"I don't know." Callum fought to keep his voice steady despite the crimson stain of fury haloing his vision. Someone had done this to Rowan. And if he got his claws on them, he would tear them asunder. *You'll be no use to him in your rage. Control yourself. He needs you.* Callum stroked his hair and the red in his eyes faded. "I have you now. You're safe." Rowan slid out of his hold. Callum dumbly watched as he strode towards the door, one leg stiff and slightly dragging. "Where the hells are you going?"

"Taking a walk."

"A walk?! Where?!"

Rowan stumbled, resting his hands on his knees as he bent in two. "I don't know, around the house! It's big enough! Walking clears my head!" His gaze darted from the window to the fireplace, then back to the window, pupils blown. He was shrouded in panic, shivering like a cornered animal as he pounded his fist into his thigh. "Fucking leg!"

Callum leapt out of bed. "You're staying here."

Rowan's smile was manic as he continued to beat his thigh to a tender pulp. "Just a quick lap down the stairs and back! It's...Gods, it's cold in here, is it cold in here? Are you cold?" He looked to his clammy palms, tears filling his eyes.

"You're naked, Rowan. And you're frightened." Callum caught Rowan's elbow before he could punch his leg again. "What did you dream about?"

"I don't even remember it now!" Rowan waved him off. "A lap for circulation is all I need! I just...I just need to get out of here! I need to...I don't know what I need! Fuck!"

Callum held out his hands. "I'm going to touch you. Do I have your permission?" Rowan nodded, tears creeping down his cheeks. Callum hauled him over his shoulder, marching him back to his bed.

"No! Wait! I want to walk!"

"No walks." Callum laid Rowan down, ready to tuck the blankets back over him but he fought, slapping them away. "Witch-boy, something horrible happened. Tell me."

Rowan clutched his chest. "Oh shit, I can't calm down! I can't breathe! Am I having a panic attack?! Is this what it feels like?! Gods, how do you and Ivy handle this!?"

"Because you help us." Callum caressed his cheek. "Your big heart and gentle words give us something to cling to."

Rowan shook his head hard. "I'm not worth that praise! Not after..." He shoved Callum away. "Fuck! Stop this Cal! I don't deserve this! I deserve to be alone!"

"You know that's not true."

"It is! I'll hurt you if I'm with you! I didn't do enough! I never have! Ivy and Aster almost died! My parents *did* die! I did everything in my power to protect them and it wasn't enough! And if something happened to you..." The anguish in his words pierced his heart, twisting with each of his restrained sobs.

Callum untied the talisman around his neck, gently draping it around Rowan's. "It's your turn for the reminder," he said, tying the leather cord. As soon as it touched Rowan's skin it glowed its gentle blue.

Rowan stilled, a deep breath slowing his hysteria. He touched his talisman. "I'm sorry. I..." He flung his arms around Callum, squeezing as if he'd disappear. "I'd fall apart if I lost you, Cal. That would be it. I'd be done. There'd be nothing left of me. So... that's why I have to be alone."

"Rowan," Callum rolled them on their sides, cradling him close. He carried so much pain in his gentle heart. No more. Callum was here now. He would help him shoulder this burden. "Is this what you dreamed of?" He nodded, sniffling loudly. "Do you want to tell me?"

"Yes but..." He bit his lower lip. "If I say it out loud, it could happen."

"No, it won't happen. I won't let it." Rowan's mouth quivered. He pulled Callum down their foreheads touching. The silence was gentle now. Callum cocooned them in the blankets creating a refuge for them. "Do you want to talk or sleep now?"

"I..." Rowan sighed. "I want to tell you about the wraith."

Chapter 19

"Wraith?" The scowl that cracked Callum's face made Rowan want to puke. "Are you telling me a wraith is feeding off you?"

Rowan shivered, the ice still clinging to his bones. Callum must have thought he was an idiot. Hell, he *was* an idiot, too stupid to see that a damn wraith had attached himself to him. "At first, I thought it was a shade. It was annoying like one." The truth was ready to explode, banging against his insides until they ached. But he sealed his lips around it as Callum growled. "I'm so fucking stupid."

"Stupid? You? Nonsense." Callum snorted. "Wraiths are treacherous and manipulative. They can trick even the wizened of fair folk and make them prey. You are not stupid, Witch-boy, only lost in your torment. And the wraith took advantage."

Rowan peeked up at him. The sour frown had disappeared, his expression soft and tender. *He wants to be here. He wants to help.* He swiped his face dry, a deep breath clearing a path for his words.

"It comes in my dreams, dredges up nightmares of the crash. Every time I woke up, I was drained." Rowan sighed, unable to fight the shivers that consumed him. "I fell into a deep depression. I went with no sleep. I stopped crossing the veil because it would be waiting for me with those green eyes and its fucking pointy smile. Even then I should have known. I think I did know but I was so wrapped up with Ivy's fade and Aster's supposed murder that…"

"You couldn't see beyond your grief." Callum finished for him.

Rowan nodded. "Before I came back here, I did a ritual to banish it back to the veil. I thought it worked but when I moved to San Francisco, it came back… stronger." A sad little laugh squeaked from his throat. I lost my job. Can't be a veil walker if you don't cross over so they let me go without a second thought. I dedicated myself to that fucking place and only got a "Don't let the door hit your ass on the way out." That made me even more de-pressed."

Dammit, the tears were flowing again. He scrubbed his cheeks dry with an angry grunt. "I didn't know what else to do. So, I came here."

"All this time this has been happening and your sisters knew nothing about this?" Callum's question was gentle and curious, but it twisted in Rowan's gut all the same.

"No." He sighed. "Ivy and Aster have had enough suffering. They don't need mine too."

"Why didn't you return sooner?" Callum asked. "You had your family here. You were safe behind the wards."

"I know, but after we hooked up I flipped out and ran." Callum's ears drooped and Rowan quickly added. "Not because of you. It was because of me. I wanted this—us—as much as you. Probably more. But..." Bile crept up his throat. He clutched his thigh as the cold inside him grew, his story spewing like vomit. "I didn't want you in the crossfire of my drama. So, I left. I thought it was best. I thought you'd forget about me, or I'd forget about you but I didn't, and the wraith got stronger and stronger and I don't know what to do anymore!" He clutched Callum's shoulders. "It said it can find a way past the wards! It made me dream that I killed you! What if I do kill you?!"

The gentle touch of Callum's palm on his cheek, eased his terror. "I'm made of sterner stuff."

Rowan shook his head so hard he was dizzy. "But what if-?!"

"Hush." Callum tipped his chin and in an instant Rowan fell into his beautiful gaze of blue and gold. It was the mountain sky at sunrise, full of power and peace. "I want you to repeat after me. Callum an Ceann Is Géire. It means Callum the fiercest. And its yours."

Rowan stilled. His name. Callum was giving him his full name. He shook his head as fear took its hold once more. "I can't take that! I shouldn't even be hearing it!"

"You're not taking it. I'm giving it. My full name will give you what you need." Callum kissed his forehead, a balm on his raw wounds. "If Ivy can use Finn's name to bring him back to life, then you can use mine to protect me."

"You trust me that much?"

"I give you this gift freely because I trust you with my heart, with my life."

"Even when I'm this...fucking hot mess?"

"You are allowed to give me your burden when you can no longer bear the weight. I will shoulder the load for you." Callum pressed his hand over Rowan's talisman. "You're not alone." The sigil flashed as if agreeing with his vow.

Not alone. Rowan had said that so many times, had so many others tell him since he was a child. But coming from Callum, he finally believed it. Rowan could fall apart, could spiral into his emotions and his strong, brave satyr would always be there to catch him.

Rowan placed his hand over Callum's the power from his talisman humming through them both. Heat returned to his fingertips, slowly spreading up his arms and right to his heart. *Fuck it. He's worth it.* "Rowan Connell Bennett," he said.

Callum chuckled. "This isn't a game of evens."

"No, but I want you to have my name." Rowan took a deep breath and spoke his truth. "Because I love you."

Callum's astonished expression was almost laugh worthy. "You...love me? You truly love me?"

"I know, I know it's super sudden. And it is! I'm a slow burn guy. It takes me months to warm up to anyone and even longer for me to even consider dating them. But you're different. You're everything I've ever wanted and I'm positive that I'm in love with you and have been since we met and..." His words got lost in his laughter. "And now I'm babbling like an idiot and looking completely insane because I want to be your mate!" Rowan rubbed the back of his neck as Callum continued to stare at him mouth half open in surprise. "I love you. I want to be with you."

Callum leaned in, his horns pressing against Rowan's forehead. "I love you too, my Rowan."

Callum loved him back. His brave strong satyr loved him. He saw it in his eyes, felt it in every silly courtship ritual and heartfelt gesture. And blessed Hecate Rowan loved him back. He remembered when Ivy told him she had fallen for Finn and how he thought it was too fast for it to be real. But now he understood how it could happen and he didn't want it any other way.

Callum kissed him until he forgot his own damned name. "Do you know the best way to defeat a wraith, Witch-boy?" he asked as he trailed ihs lips across Rowan's jaw.

Rowan shrugged. "I don't know, be in a good mood since they only eat grief?"

"Exactly." Callum's smile was breathtaking. "And I will make you so happy that the wretched creature will starve in mere hours."

"You already make me happy, Cal. Like Disneyland happy." He chuckled at Callum's puzzled look. "I'll explain that later, but you really do." Callum gazed at him, like he'd had hung the very moon itself. And he'd probably find a way to fetch it if Rowan asked. Oh yeah, he was lost. He wrapped himself around Callum, as the last of the ice exploded into a blaze of passion. No more wraith or panic or guilt. There was only him and Callum, and their wonderful, delirious heat.

One day turned into another. Then another. Soon a week had passed, and Rowan hardly noticed after he'd quietly moved his things into Callum's wing. Days were spent with his family, and the nights were reserved only for Callum.

The sex was amazing, that was for sure. Callum was insatiable and Rowan usually ended up passing out, sweat covered, sore, and trembling in bliss. But there were quiet evenings too. Ones where Rowan would bundle up tight for short walks in the snow with Broderick, Callum by his side. Or where they curled up in front of the fire, laughing about old stories. Just the two of them tucked away from the winter cold like the house had intended.

The embarrassment of being unemployable as a veil walker had gone long forgotten along what little life he had in San Francisco. He dusted out his old office that Ivy reserved for him upstairs and began plotting his healer business. And when one of the members of the witch authorities texted him to see if he was still alive, he answered that he was staying in Big Bear, indefinitely.

Indefinitely.

Rowan pursed his lips reading that word over and over. There was a time when typing out that word would have given him heart palpitations. He glanced over to Callum, who was chuckling with Finn, tail flip-flopping against the back of his velvety calves. Yeah, indefinitely. Rowan hit send and didn't consider it again.

Soon Yule was upon them, and Finn brought in a sizeable chunk of wood to serve as their Yule log. Aster used her artistic skills to decorate it with treasures Callum had collected from the forest. She placed her masterpiece on the coffee table, a beautiful chaotic cluster of nature, tall white candles burning atop it.

Aster placed a slip of paper into everyone's hands at dinner time. "Okay everyone, don't forget to write your wishes down and tie them to the log. I don't want anyone to miss out when we burn it."

Callum tapped his pencil against his chin then glanced to Rowan. A tender smile puckered the scar on his lips. Rowan felt his cheeks flush as the satyr bent over his paper, scribbling furiously. He hadn't said a word and yet said so much. He said exactly what Rowan felt in his heart. *I'm not alone.* And he wasn't. He had Ivy and Aster. He had his aunts. And most of all, he had Callum. The wraith had all but disappeared. *Good*, he thought, curling next to Callum as they held each other in bed. *Let the fucking things starve.*

Chapter 20

The wraith growled, sucking what it could from Threnody's body. It thought her stronger, but she languished in bed, with barely enough essence for a full meal, damn her. But it needed every drop if it wanted to see Rowan again. It needed to touch him, feel him, taste of his flesh. Rowan had given up so easily, submitted to his sorrow. It had been so close to pulling him across the veil, then that damned satyr woke him.

Since then, Rowan had slid further and further out of its reach, blocking it from his mind with thoughts of the satyr. That stupid beast would pay for stealing its prize. As soon as it regained itself it would torment that male to his death.

It sunk teeth deeper into Threnody. The witch clutched her forehead with a pain filled groan before curling under her blanket in a puddle of tears. "If you don't break those wards all will be lost," it whispered to

Threnody. "Aster died in vain." Threnody gritted her teeth as it drank her tears.

Judith entered, meeting Threnody's sickly pallor with indifference. "Still in bed?"

"Altitude sickness," Threnody grumbled.

"For this long? It's been days." Judith sighed. "You're not well. I'm taking over."

"I'm fine." Threnody snapped.

Another sigh sent a surge of Threnody's fury into its mouth. "You're not strong enough to do any casting. This mission is now mine."

Threnody threw her blankets aside. Thunder shook the roof as she leapt to her feet and stormed towards Judith. "You're not taking this from me!"

"Mother would not be pleased if you botched this mission. You're staying here."

Threnody's eyes darkened. She grabbed Judith by the sweater. "I'm doing this, with or without you."

Judith's face was a blank canvas, her eyes steady. "Very well. But I won't hesitate to-"

"I know you won't." Threnody pushed her away. "Just give me time to recover."

But there was no more time. If those wards weren't broken soon, the wraith would wither to dust. It'd have to find another host, one far more powerful than this husk it clung to. *Where am I supposed to find that?* It had already tried Judith, but she was nothing but a bitter void that burned its tongue. *If I can get my hands on that gargoyle...*

The King of Shadows would be a perfect host. He was strong. He could restore it, bring it back to its former glory. It yanked free of Threnody, silvery wisps dripping from its claws. It could wait no longer. Now was the time to catch the gargoyle.

Threnody's eyes rolled back, and she collapsed, convulsing wildly from the shock. "Sister?!" Judith knelt beside her, guarding her thrashing head as foam dripped from her slack mouth.

Judith's hand lit with magic, and she pressed it to Threnody's temple the other digging into her skirt pocket for her phone. She punched a button waited for a murmur on the other side before growling, "We have a problem."

Damn it all, it had fed too deep. Now it couldn't return if its plan failed. Threnody would probably be dead by then. Well, it would just have to succeed then.

With the last of its strength, it soared up the chimney, falling on the roof to regain itself. Dusk was settling, orange and indigo clouds blanketing the sky. It watched the horizon, waiting for that familiar shadow. Every second of waiting made it ache with fatigue. *Rowan is mine! I will have him!*

The silhouette flew overhead. The King of Shadows returned. The wraith cackled in triumph as it leapt after him, slowing with every miserable throb of hunger. Its strength faded and it perched in a tree before it crashed into the snow. *No!* But the gargoyle flapped its wings, suddenly turning into a cluster of pines, settling in their branches. The wraith was afraid he would take off again but there he stayed, staring at the house's roof, unmoving.

The wraith landed on the Gargoyle's branch, crawling towards him. Power vibrated from his mighty form; grief, anger, sadness. It reached through his swirling shadows, fingers shaking as those waves of anguish tickled their tips. *The power! So delicious!*

The gargoyle shuddered as the wrath sunk in, his forlorn stare never leaving the house. *I have to stop this madness,* the gargoyle's thoughts whispered. *I can't keep visiting her without her knowing. She is fine without me. She is safe. I must leave her be.* But he didn't fly away only kept watching, his angst rising as the name Aster echoed inside his mind. Aster.

The wraith swelled, eyes glowing bright, sharp teeth growing long. It dug through the gargoyle's fog, stabbing its jaws through his skull. "But she's not safe," it said.

The gargoyle tensed, suddenly standing alert, mind whirling in a barrage of panic. "No," he muttered. "No, she's with her family. She is safe!"

"You think so, you fool? Right now, her enemies are near, wanting to claim her!" The gargoyle's rage rose like a tsunami as the wraith continued. "She will die if you don't cross the wards and save her! Go now!"

The gargoyle launched itself towards the house like a shot gun, the wraith blanketed tight around his massive form. The ward barrier growing closer. The air around them rippled and the wraith inhaled the gargoyle's essence. A thousand blades tore through its flesh, magic fighting to keep it out but the wraith kept its grip, drinking deep as they passed through. The agony vanished. Its power remained. No, it was stronger now, the King of Shadows' magic now mingling with its own.

The sweet scent of Rowan filled the air. He was here for the taking and with all that force coursing through the wraith's veins, not even his satyr could stop him.

Chapter 21

The joy that filled the house made Rowan's heart glad. There was nothing but laughter and love as the Bennett witches readied for Yule with cleaning, candles, and warm spells of good wishes for the new year. It was as if time had turned back to when they were all young and untroubled. Best of all, there was still no sign of the wraith. Not a damn peep. With some mindfulness techniques, and the constant orgasms from Callum, he didn't have the bandwidth to dwell in past sorrows or worry.

Rowan hummed happily as he cleaned, sprinkling dried rose petals and thyme and sweeping them out the front door. "Okay, 1 think that's enough to make Ivy happy."

"Wait a moment." Callum peeked out from behind the tree, having taken it upon himself to decorate it with more pinecones. He clopped his way over, hands on his hips. "I have to make sure it's a job well done."

Rowan smirked. "Are you my supervisor?"

"Oh yes." Callum gave a grave nod. "And I take my job very seriously." He rubbed his chin then tapped the floor with his hoof. "There's a smudge here." Another tap. "And speck there." Then he pressed his hand against his heart with a dramatic gasp. "Is that a hair?! Witch-boy, I thought you were better at this!"

Rowan grabbed Callum's tail, sweeping the spots with its brush before handing it back to him. "Better?"

"Very good, Witch-boy. His rumbling voice sent Rowan's pulse pounding. *Praise. There's another kink to put on your I-didn't-know-I-liked-that list.*

The door burst open, Rowan's aunts entering like a storm, both of their arms filled with brightly colored parcels. "Sorry we're late! It took us longer to pack the car than we thought," Dahlia said. A series of clicks followed as Broderick poked his head through the door, antlers covered in bags. Dahlia patted his head. "Rowan, your new familiar is precious! We've invited him inside to-"

"No!" Both Callum and Rowan shouted in unison.

Undaunted, Dahlia shrugged, shoving her load into Callum's unexpecting arms. "Well then, we should at least figure out a gift. I'm sure Rosie and I can whip up something." She hung a couple of colorful bags on Callum's horns, Rowan catching the few that tumbled from his grip.

"Uh, I thought we didn't exchange gifts on Yule," Rowan said. "We talked about it. Again. For the tenth year in a row."

"Yes, but you know Lia and I never follow that rule." Rosemary chuckled.

Broderick shook the bags free, Dahlia catching them with shocking agility. "If gifts during this season are good for the regular folk, then they're good enough for us. Besides, combining Christmas and Yule has never been an issue for your parents. Why stop now?"

"Because we didn't get any gifts for you two," Rowan muttered.

"Pish, that doesn't matter. Back in a moment, Darling. I have another load." She hooked an arm around the stag's neck, leading him outside.

Callum tried to look at the bags hanging off his horns, succeeding in only going cross-eyed. "Is this a witch tradition?"

"Not really." Rowan freed his head. "But because Auntie Lia and Auntie Rosemary love to shop, it's becoming one."

"We don't love to shop. We love to spoil you kids," Rosemary explained as she slid her boxes beneath the tree. She gave Rowan a sly smile. "Someone needs get you things you would never give to yourself."

Dahlia returned, patting Broderick on the head before shoving the door closed with her heeled boot. "That's the last of it, Rosie."

"You sure that's all of them?" Rosemary rubbed her chin. "You didn't forget the gifts for our Satyr-in-laws, did you?"

"Those were the first ones I put in the car."

Callum blinked. "We're receiving gifts as well?"

"Of course, you are! You're family!" Dahlia took Rosemary's arm, beaming at Callum and Rowan. "By Hecate, Rowan. I haven't seen you look so cheerful in ages! Tell us everything, my darling! Everything!"

Rowan let out an awkward chuckle. "Not sure what you're talking about."

Rosemary giggled. "You know."

Rowan cleared his throat. "Uh, no...I don't."

"Oh, you do." Rosemary let out a dreamy sigh, tucking her clasped hands under her chin. "You and Callum consummated!"

Rowan choked as Callum slung an arm around Rowan's shoulders, giving him a squeeze. "You're correct! Cocks were out!"

"Cal!" Rowan howled.

"Oh, I forgot how shy you kids are about sex," Rosemary replied. "I'm sorry Rowan dear. I just think it's awfully romantic. Two lost souls finding each other and finally burying their carnal lusts."

Dahlia patted their cheeks simultaneously. "We're so excited! We even have a themed sale scheduled after Yule to commemorate! We're selling ointments and some of our crystals shaped like-"

"Oh! uh Ha ha ha! Funny joke Auntie Lia!" Sweat trickled down the back of Rowan's neck, his mouth hurting from the forced smile. "Because I know you wouldn't tell the entire town about my sex life!"

"Love and lust spells, charms and candles are fifteen percent off," she continued. "We're calling it the nephew sale."

"Oh Gods." Rowan buried his face in his cackling satyr's chest.

Ivy entered from the kitchen, a vision in emerald green. She carried a huge board of cheeses, meats, and other delectables, Finn behind her with several bottles of wine. "Okay, no more harassing Rowan. The overwhelming embarrassment is making it hard to cook." She put the board on the coffee table then gave Rosemary and Dahlia hugs before gawking at the piles of gifts. "We said no gifts this year!"

"That's what I said," Rowan replied.

"Oh, lighten up you two!" Aster bounded down the stairs, stopping to pop a square of cheese into her mouth before hugging Dahlia and Rosemary. She'd finally gotten out of her sweats, into a pink dress dotted with blue flowers. She looked so healthy, the business of the season bringing her back to her old chipper self. Strung over an arm were handmade wreaths of holly and pine which she placed on everyone's head after giving them a kiss on the cheek. Rowan rose on his toes, straightening Callum's around his horns, accepting the kiss he received as thanks. This was going to be a good Yule. A healing Yule. He could feel it.

The front window shattered as a hulking dark figure tumbled across the floor. Aster and their aunts dove behind the couch, Finn curling around Ivy, shielding her from exploding shards. Giant wings unfurled, eyes blinding beams of gold as it cased the room. The shadows around it spun and twisted in a frenzy as it rose. The King of Shadows. He was alive, and well, and in the living room. Callum leapt in front of Rowan; dagger drawn as the gargoyle's fog surged.

"Where is she?!" he roared. "Who dares harm her?!"

Rowan stepped out from behind Callum, hands out in a gesture of peace. "First off, are you okay? You just took out an entire window!"

Ivy on the other hand, ignored Rowan's call. She shoved herself free from Finn's grasp shouting, "What the hell!? How did you get past the wards?!"

The gargoyle shook his head, glowing eyes searching the room. "No time to explain."

"Then you better talk quick, asshole!" She lifted her hands, spells lighting her fingertips. Finn bared his fangs, claws flared and ready to render. Ivy looked to the ceiling. "Throw him out!" But the house stayed suspiciously quiet, not even creaking its beams.

"Witch! I have no time for your pitiful antics!" The gargoyle snapped. He spread his wings, the shadows around his swirling in a wild cyclone. "Bring me your sister or I tear this place apart to find her!"

"No! Stop!" Aster leapt in front of Ivy, arms stretched. "Just stop. You're not like this."

The gargoyle softened, aggression draining away. He stepped forward one shaking hand landing on Aster's cheek, gently tracing its curve.. "Kitten," he whispered.

Aster shook with hysterical laughter. "You're alive. Thank Artemis you're alive!"

"You're not safe here," Was his only reply. He scooped Aster into his arms. "Forgive me."

A symphony of screams played him out as he leapt through the broken window. His wings caught the air, and he took off into the darkening sky.

"Bring her back you bastard!" Ivy screeched. Finn grabbed her before she followed in pursuit. She was wild eyed, anxiety taking over as she screamed "Aster!" to the sky. They vanished into the setting sun. "What do we do. Oh Gods, what do we do!?"

"We go after her!" Rowan replied. "Finn, Callum can you..."

The bony touch of death brushed Rowan's cheek. Mist flickered beside him, undulating into a skeletal grin. Rowan's heart stopped. He was frozen as that smile grew sharper.

"Witch-boy?" Callum asked. "What's wrong? What do you see?"

Everyone turned from the window, their eyes on Rowan as managed to whisper. "Its here."

"What's here?" Rosemary asked. "Rowan, you're white as a sheet."

"The wraith." Rowan jabbed a finger at it. "You can't get past the wards! I... I starved you!".

A sharp, raspy screech filled the room. "Miiiiiiine!" Rowan was whisked off his feet and thrown across the room. Cold hands squeezed his throat, cutting off all air.

Callum bellowed, dashing after him only to be tossed in the opposite direction. He crashed into the tree, buried under breaking branches, and shattered baubles.

A skeletal face formed, wide green eyes glowing like wild flame. The wraith bared its jagged teeth as it fully formed, towering over Rowan. "My prize!" . It wasn't going to let go. It would take him, drag him down to whatever darkness it had come from. "My precious prize.! You. Are. Mine!"

Chapter 22

Finn pulled Callum's aching body from under the felled tree, the chaos snapping his mind into sharp focus. The Bennet witches threw spell after spell at the wraith's billowing, dark body. It pried Rowan's mouth wide. The wretched sounds of its glee rattled like broken glass across metal before it sealed its lips around his.

Callum's eyes turned crimson, haloing the world in blood. "Get away from him!"

The wraith jerked away, its needle like teeth dripping with globs of Rowan's glowing essence. It hissed as Callum charged, swiping his blade. It found no resistance. "No!" he roared, desperate to land another blow.

The wraith's laughter was a horrible scream in the dark. "You stupid fucking goat!" It released Rowan, now lifeless on the floor. "He's mine! He always has been mine!"

Mighty winds blew the doors open as the wraith swirled in a cyclone. Windows shattered, ice coated the walls, the floor, and everyone inside. One by one the Bennetts fell in a mass of sobs, Finn following suit before it finally took Callum.

Misery shrouded him in total darkness. Arabella, Orlaith's headless corpse, Rowan lifeless on the floor. It pounded his skull, despair sealing his hooves in place as he was eaten whole. Callum grabbed his head, frozen tears pouring down his face as he screamed his anguish. He let his herd die. He let Orlaith die. And now Rowan would die because of his failure. *You're a coward! You destroy everyone you love!* He collapsed under the intolerable weight. *Make it stop! Please Goddess, make it stop!*

The wind ceased. An eerie silence thick as cotton filled his ears. Callum lifted his head, a coating of snow tumbling from his horns. The fire had dimmed, icicles dripping from the hearth.

"Wha...what happened? Ivy sat up, coated in white. She shivered, Finn wrapping his arms about her to warm her. "I just saw all my nightmares! All my fears! What was that thing?"

"A wraith," Dahlia dug Rosemary free, dusting the ice from her shoulders before kissing her forehead. "I have read about them but never saw them. By Hecate I didn't know they were so powerful!"

Callum ignored their conversation, digging through the slush where Rowan had once lay. His claws only met hard floor. He dove into another pile. Then another. Nothing but a soggy rug and broken bits of glass. "Rowan!"

Ivy ran to Callum helping him dig through the mess. "Oh Gods, Ro! Please still be here!"

Something hard and cold brushed Callum's fingers. He pulled Rowan's talisman free, the leather cord snapped.

Voices rose around him frantically chattering but it was all gibberish in Callum's ears. Red rimmed his vision, the faint sounds of death whispering in his ears. It was happening again. The wraith had carted Rowan to some place unknown, someplace he couldn't follow. And he was helpless, unable to save his mate from his fate and... *Stop.*

He pressed the talisman to his chest. While the Bennetts shouted, he took a breath. Then another. And another. "You're not alone Rowan. I'm here. I will find you. Just...Just tell me you're still alive. Please." The pewter heated, the tingle of magic sharp and active as the sigil glowed. A signal from his witch-boy. He still lived. Callum rose, heading to the door.

"Brother?" Finn called.

"I'm going to find Rowan," Callum answered.

"Then I'm going with you." Finn frowned as Callum shook his head. "You can't do this alone!"

"We have two witches gone. You coming with me is a waste of a good tracker." Callum set his jaw. "I know what this wraith is, what it's done to Rowan. So, I am the best to fight it. You're needed here, Finn."

Finn's ears drooped. He took his shoulders, tapping their horns together. "Be safe brother. I'll be very angry ifyou get your fool self killed."

"The only one that will die is that wraith," Callum growled. He looked to the others. "I'll keep my eyes open for Aster on my way. But Rowan is my first care."

"Thank you, Cal," Ivy said, tears shimmering in her eyes. "Please find him."

"Damn the Goddess if she keeps him from me."

Callum fetched his bow, making sure his dagger was sheathed. He stepped out to the porch. Where would he even start? The wraith left no footprints, it was barely corporal.

He'd go east. No west. Dammit, where would a wraith even hide? For all he knew, the thing dragged Rowan across the veil forever from his reach. He clutched Rowan's talisman tight. *Don't think like that! Find him!*

Something nudged his shoulder. Callum flared his claws only to find Broderick bumping his nose against him. The stag's eyes were wild, and he grunted, tapping his hooves on the wood planks.

"You feel him?" A bleat of affirmation made Callum's heart leap. Of course. Broderick was Rowan's familiar. Their connection was more solid than the one he held with his twin. "Do you know which way he is?"

Broderick jerked his antlers east, biting Callum's loincloth and tugging him off the porch. Callum tied the talisman to his wrist, lifting it like a beacon as the sun disappeared. The two galloped into the trees, snow beginning to flurry. Callum may have lost one mate in the past but not this time. He wouldn't let Rowan die. He'd find his witch-boy. And then he'd make that wraith pay.

Chapter 23

Cold sank deep into Rowan's body. He couldn't feel his arms and the throbbing in his leg was absent. It was as if every nerve had fallen asleep. But he felt the cold. Nothing else but cold.

He opened his eyes, the frost coating his lashes breaking apart. Nothing but endless blue mist and tuneless music greeted him. Rowan knew this realm like the back of his hand. Somehow, he'd passed beyond the veil. *But where are the spirits? And why is it so fucking cold?*

He pushed himself to his feet, wobbling at his weightlessness. This wasn't right. He was a corporal being in the world of the dead. Spirits usually huddled about him, attracted by his life force. Now there was just the emptiness, inside him and out. *I'm dead! Oh shit, somehow, I'm dead!*

"My prize." The wraith's moan was as raspy as the winter wind. It grabbed Rowan by the shoulders, turning him to face its horrible pile of bones strung together by sinew. It's face parted into a dripping sharp smile, excited flesh billowing like a cloak. "I said you wouldn't escape me. And now you're finally mine."

"You...you killed me." Rowan's horror grew as the wraith ran his tongue around the shell of his ear. "Why the hell did you kill me!?"

"You're not dead. Just nearly dead." It ran its claws through Rowan's hair, gazing at it in wonder. "No need to worry. Your body is near."

Rowan shut his eyes. Somewhere his heart was still beating. Thank Hecate for that. But fear kept its stranglehold, the wraith moaning as it drank its fill. *Stay calm. It's your only chance, Ro.* "You can't expect me to live here. Eventually I'll die and you'll starve. You have to send me back."

The wraith's eyes blazed, its body flapping wide. "And give you the chance to return to that fucking satyr?!" It screeched, the stench of decay heavy on its breath. "He won't have you! No one will! Even when you decay and crumble to dust, you will always be mine!"

Rowan ran into the mists. He reached out, desperate to hook into the veil, His fingers found a tiny fold in reality and he shouted, "Blessed Hecate give me strength and show me the-!" Something snapped taut at his spine, shattering his numbness into pure agony. Rowan slapped a hand across his lower back, finding an icy tether buried like a leech. He slingshotted backwards, slamming into the musty cocoon of the wraith's embrace. "My Rowan. My little prize. Why must you run?" it said. "We are bound, you and I. Bound by your sadness. Bound by our love."

"Love?!" Rowan squirmed for freedom. "This isn't love! This is obsession and I hate you!"

The wraith's smile dropped. It snatched Rowan's throat, fury burning in its green eyes. "Don't make me punish you!"

"Fuck you!"

Rowan's cry was cut short as it covered his mouth with its own and inhaled. Sparks of his essence poured from his lips and into the greedy wraith's belly. Rowan weakened, going heavy as a knapsack. Feebly he slapped at the wraith, but it grew stronger with every breath.

I will make you so happy Witch-boy that the wretched creature will starve. Callum's words whispered to him. A dot of light winked in his chest. Callum, with his strong arms and merry laugh. His unwavering devotion. His wounded heart filled with love. Love for Rowan. His brave, wonderful satyr. Rowan clutched the feeling tight, the light inside him growing with every wonderful thought and loving memory. *He makes me Disneyland happy! Gods, I love him! I love him!*

The wraith's eyes widened, the smell of burning ash pouring from its body. It threw Rowan aside, retching piles of ooze and clawing its belly, burning from Rowan's joy. He wasted no time celebrating and dashed away, the wraith's enraged roar chasing him. Rowan reached for the veil again, pinching the thin edges between quivering fingertips. The tether tightened, weaker now but determined. Ice filled his veins, his skin turning blue.

With a shout, Rowan pulled the veil aside. "Blessed Hecate, give me strength and show me the crossroads!"

The ache in his leg throbbed to life and the fresh scent of the mountain hit his nostrils. Cold air. Tingling fingers. Rowan laughed, never happier to feel winter.

His body was prone in a dark cavern of stone, pale and coated in frost. An abandoned mine. They were tucked all around Big Bear, meaning he could be anywhere on that damn mountain. He jumped for the opening, but the tether yanked, almost tearing out his spine. He yelped, clutching the edges of the veil before he was taken back into the mists.

A massive silhouette loomed against the grey mist, horns curling from his temples and his bull-like tail lashing the air. Beside him was the shadow of a proud stag. Callum. Broderick. Somehow, they had found him.

Callum ran to Rowan's body, gathering it into his arms and pressing his long ear to his chest. "His heart beats." The relief in Callum's voice was palpable. "It's weak and slow but there." He gave Rowan a little shake. "I'm here Rowan! Wake up!"

"Callum!" Rowan screamed. "I'm here! Broderick! Can you see me?!" The tether jerked, another jolt of cold filling him. He gasped as frost formed across his knuckles. Rowan pulled himself forward, fighting the wraith's hold. Of course, they wouldn't see him. He was beyond the veil, beyond their reach. No amount of screaming would catch their attention. "Shit shit shit!"

Broderick's ears perked. Rowan held his breath as the stag crept towards him, looking this way and that but never directly at him. "Can you hear me?" Broderick answered with an affirmative snort and Rowan laughed maniacally. "Yes! Broderick you are an amazing familiar! I'm stuck beyond the veil!"

The stag reared up, its hooves kicking the air before it nudged Callum's shoulder. The satyr hissed, unwilling to release Rowan's body when the talisman he wore began to hum. It burst to light; the sigil casting long shadows across the dark rocky cave.

Callum touched the glowing pewter, wonder reflecting in his eyes. "He's here," he whispered. "You spoke true, Broderick. He's here" Slowly he placed Rowan's body down, rising to his hooves. "Rowan! Show me where you are!"

"I'm here, Callum! Right here!" Rowan cried. yet Callum wandered the mine, feeling the stone walls for openings. "Dammit! Just look at me!" Another tug on his back, harder now. The wraith was growing stronger. Rowan dared to free a hand and reached for him. whispering his command. "Callum an Ceann Is Géire, see me. Hear me. Please!"

A light flashed in Callum's mismatched eyes, and he turned towards him. His mouth fell open as their gazes locked. "Rowan!"

"Yes!" Rowan cried "You can see me! You can-" Rowan's grip wavered as the wraith pulled its tether again.

"Callum an Ceann Is Géire, see me. Hear me. Please!" Rowan's voice was as clear as day, compelling Callum to turn around and find his witch. Mist swirled in the air, spreading like a curtain. Broderick bleated, shoving Callum towards it as it parted, revealing bright red hair, and slender shoulders. Rowan's beautiful eyes locked with his, transparent but real.

Callum let out a relieved cry. "Rowan!"

Yes! You can see me! You can-" His eyes widened, and he vanished.

"No!" Callum lunged for him, praying to catch a hand, a wrist, anything. Thank the Goddess, Rowan appeared again, clinging to the edges of the shimmering curtain. "Where are you?!"

"I'm in the veil!" Rowan's faint body turned a pale blue, frost crusting his hair and eyebrows. "I don't have much time. The wraith. It's here and its-" He vanished again, only to reappear with a strained cry of pain.

"How do I get you out?!" Callum demanded.

"I-I don't know! You're not a veil walker! You don't have the power to cross over!"

"But I'm part of the fae! The fair folk! There's always a loophole with my kind!"

Rowan shouted in agony, blinking in and out of existence. A thin sheen of ice covered his body. "It's getting its strength back!"

"No! I won't let it take you!" Damn the Gods, Callum hadn't felt this helpless since Orlaith was slain. He clutched his horns. "If I can see you surely, I can get to you!" His ears rose, body stiffening. "Rowan Connell Bennett, I command you to bring me to you!"

Rowan stared at him. "What?!"

"You used my name to let me see you, now I'll use yours! Bring me across the veil!"

"I don't think it works like that!"

"Do we have any other choice!? Now bring me across the veil Rowan Connell Bennett!"

His command seemed to calm the witch. He closed his eyes, one trembling hand reaching across the veil and passing through his. Cold consumed him. Callum spasmed, vision doubling before spinning into a kaleido-scope of darkness. There was the brief sensation of floating away before he slammed back into his body, tumbling ass over hooves. Broderick ran to him, offering his antlers for support. "Why didn't it work?!"

"Because you're not dead!" Rowan's eyes fell to the glowing talisman around Callum's neck. "I'm not alone. *We're* not alone." he whispered. The sigil exploded in a blinding light, turning the dark mine into day. Rowan outstretched his hand. "Throw it to me!"

Without hesitation. Callum pulled the talisman free. He swung the pewter disk towards Rowan, clutching the leather cord in a death grip, It landed in Rowan's palm as if he were there. "Oh sweet Hecate! It's the talisman! It bonded us to each-" His words twisted into a screech as they vanished, this time completely. But the talisman's cord stretched past the veil, tethering them together.

Callum inhaled deeply. "Rowan Connell Bennett. You will bring me across the veil to find you."

A force hooked into Callum's gut, tugging like a lure. His vision swirled, colors melding as his nerves buzzed in a wild storm, then fell silent. Numb. He looked to Broderick as his soul pulled free. "Guard us well. I'll return with our witch-boy."

The last sound he heard was the thud of his body hitting the ground. He was light as a feather, floating in a peaceful haze before the cord jerked as fast as a whip crack, pulling him into a misty blue void.

Chapter 24

Please still be there Cal, please!

Rowan clutched his talisman with every ounce of his will, the wraiths' tether relentless in its torture. His entire being had turned to ice, a horrible despair moving into him. But he clung to his talisman, whispering "Please, please, please!" before he stopped with a crash.

The wraith wrapped him in its embrace, long arms tight. It pried Rowan's fingers open, wrestling him for his talisman.

"No!" Rowan bit and scratched but he was no match for the wraith's strength. It was yanked from his grasp and set adrift. Rowan whimpered as his last hope floated into the abyss.

The wraith's low growl rumbled through him. "You have been a very naughty Witch-boy."

"Only Callum can call me that, you bastard," Rowan snapped. He yelped as the wraith tore its way through his chest, inhaling his pain. Memories sped by on fast-forward; the accident, his parents, the sobs, the pain, the blood. Suffocating folds of flesh cocooned Rowan as the wraith roared, "Miiiiine!"

Its despair oozed into Rowan's mouth, his eyes, his ears. He beat at his prison as a slide show of horror flashed before him, things he'd never seen before, that he never wanted to see again. His sisters laying dead in their beds. His aunts keening over their graves, shouting, "Why couldn't you save them!?" The bloodied bodies of his parents, their eyes hollow with regret. *You did this. You did all of this.*

"This isn't real!" Rowan shoved at the wraith.

"It is." The wraith poured nightmare after nightmare into his skull. "And it's your fault. You alone are my prize. You only have me now. Only me."

Rowan's blows grew weaker. He couldn't save them. He was helpless. Worthless. Unable to protect the ones he loved because he was a failure. *Always alone. Better off alone.*

"Release him!" Callum's voice was a sharp dagger through the droning misery. The satyr ran from the darkness, eyes glowing red, roaring like a demon.

He leapt at the wraith and it hissed, shielding Rowan from escape. Its hold tightened. More misery. More anguish. Gods why wouldn't it stop? Callum dug his claws between its shoulders, slashing, slicing, tearing the wraith's billowing flesh wide until Rowan rolled out, cold and unable to move, unable to help. *Failure. He'll die. You'll be alone.*

The wraith swung its long arms, but Callum clung to it, putrid ichor drenching his body as he tore it asunder. But the wraith didn't fall. It hovered over Rowan, defending him like a treasure hoard. "Get up, Witch-boy!" he demanded.

He couldn't. Not even Callum's commanding voice could make Rowan move. Every inch of him ached, still lost in grief. He had brought Callum here to fight for a coward. Now he would die because of him.

"Idiot satyr," the wraith laughed. "Too stupid to understand that you can't kill me. You don't have the power!"

"Rowan, get up!" Callum bellowed, wiping the gore from his face. He slashed again, but the wraith grabbed his nape pulling him loose.

It dangled Callum before him like a kitten by the scruff, turning him to Rowan. "See this, my prize? This is what you brought. You brought his demise." It's horrible scream pierced Rowan's eardrums as Callum plucked its eye free. It threw the satyr aside, clutching its face, ichor dripping between its fingers.

Callum crawled to Rowan. He took his shoulders, hauling him up. "Stay with me Witch-boy."

Rowan shook his head, unable to speak under the weight of his sadness. *Oh Callum, why did you come after me? I'm not worth it. I am better off alone.* Callum had been through so much and now would die suffering like he had lived. "Leave me, Cal. Just...leave me," he managed to say.

"Never." Callum bared his fangs. He took Rowan's jaw, forcing their eyes to meet "You're not alone, Rowan Connell Bennett. You have me. You will always have me."

The ice crumbled from his flesh, Rowan's chest tingling. An ember of warmth sparked as his mind shifted. Nights curled in Callum's arms in front of a crackling fire. The family dinners. The walks in the snow with Broderick. Callum's tender, consuming kisses that made his heart burst. The tears of release as they cried together and the unbelievable joy as they laughed together. He was feeling again, his skin, his muscles, his...his heart "I'm...I'm not alone." The words left him like a prayer. He lifted his head of his own power,

"That's it, Witch-boy." Callum laughed. "That's my-" His face contorted and his back arched. Claws burst from Callum's chest, whisps of white fog dribbling into the mist.

The wraith pulled its hand from Callum' back, the satyr falling into Rowan's arms. It sucked his fingers clean, eyes burned brighter, its form swelling in size and it absorbed Callum's essence.

Rowan rocked his satyr in his arms. "Callum! Don't leave me! Say something! Talk to me!"

"Say it again, Witch-boy," Callum moaned. He lifted his head, eyes dull with pain. "Say you're not alone."

The command lit the fire inside Rowan. "I'm not alone." The words were strong and sure.

Callum nodded in approval. His strong wonderful satyr who crossed the veil for him. Who stood by his side. Who made him happier than he ever thought possible. Gods, Rowan loved him. And Callum loved him back. And he fucking deserved that love. They both did.

Rowan gently placed Callum at his feet, rising to meet the wraith with his head held high and his shoulders squared. His legs were solid, his spine straightening. I'm not alone," he said. The wraith wouldn't take Callum. Not as long as there was life inside him. And there was, shining like a light house inside his chest.

The wraith recoiled. "This is your doing! Your fault!"

"Fuck you, you lying bag!" Rowan shouted. "I'm not afraid of you anymore!"

The wraith shrank back as Rowan balled his fists, all his love, all his happiness, his determination and pride into a swirling about them in golden fire. He wasn't a slave to the wraith's lies anymore. He had his sisters, his family. All these things to heal the wounds And they would turn the world upside down for him. "I'm not alone."

The wraith opened its mouth with one last screech of "Miiiine!" Rows and rows of teeth dripped with glowing essence. Rowan's essence. An essence that it would never taste again.

"Never again," Rowan growled. "Not me. Not Callum. Not anyone. Ever."

Fire exploded from Rowan's palms. No fear. No sadness. Not even anger. Just the cold need for justice as the wraith was consumed in Rowan's power. It shattered, its cloak dissolving into ash, the last echo of its sad cry disappearing into the static hum of the veil.

Rowan stumbled to his knees, cupping Callum's face. "Callum?" He sighed in relief as the satyr opened his eyes. "Don't move. Let me look you over."

"I'm fair folk," Callum scoffed in a weak voice. "I've endured far worse and remained strong." He tried to rise only to collapse with a moan.

"Stop swinging your dick and let me try to heal you!" Rowan snapped.

Callum's eyes fluttered shut. "You like my swinging dick."

Rowan would have laughed if he wasn't in a complete fright. He pressed his hand over Callum's wounds, essence tricking between his fingers. He'd healed plenty of people before but none of them on the other side of the veil. And if he lost Callum now, his soul would float into oblivion. He swallowed, taking one last chance on his wits. "Callum an Ceann Is Géire, you *will* heal."

The wounds glittered; Callum's essence floating back from the mist. The white whisps were absorbed into his skin and the gashes sealed. Callum grunted, his eyes bright. He shoved himself into a sit, running a hand down his mended chest before gazing at Rowan in wonder.

"You'll always have me Big Guy." Rowan pressed a kiss to his forehead. "Time to go home."

Chapter 25

The touch of a wet tongue woke Callum from the dead. His eyes snapped open groaning as Broderick frantically licked the life back into him. "I'm back. I'm here. No need to drown me." Callum pushed the stag aide, his limbs tingling as their sensations returned. By the Goddess's tits, Rowan was a sight to behold. A powerful, vengeful witch protecting his own. *And he's my mate.*

Pride swelled inside him as he shoved himself into a sit, still feeling like soggy mud. "Witch-boy, you were remarkable. I am so..." Rowan lay beside him, as lifeless and pale as he had found him. "Rowan!"

No air came from his lungs, no movement from under those closed eyelids. Broderick nudged Rowan, bleating at Callum before pacing around the two.

"I don't know what happened! We both crossed! I'm sure of it!" Callum pressed his ear to Rowan's chest, listening for any sign of life. The faint thump of a heartbeat touched his ear. Callum held his breath, waiting for another. *Please let there be another!*

There it was, stronger this time. He held Rowan in his arms, Broderick administering his reviving licks to the witch's cheek. "Come back to me Witch-boy. You're strong." Rowan shuddered, lips parting. "Yes, that's' it. I'm here waiting for you."

Rowan's lungs rattled as he sucked in his first breath, body plumping with heat. His eyes popped open, and he rolled onto his side, coughing and sputtering.

Callum curled his arms around him. "Thank the Goddess."

"I'm all right," Rowan choked. "I just got stuck for a bit. Happens all the time."

"I thought I'd lost you!"

Rowan chuckled weakly burying his face against Callum's neck. "Got to work harder than that to get rid of me." Broderick grunted, earning a scritch between his antlers. "If it wasn't for you, buddy, I'd be lost. Thank you." He looked to Callum. "And thank you, too."

Callum shook his head. "No need for thanks. My intentions to bring you back are purely selfish." He melted as Rowan laughed.

Callum had never been happier to see a house before. It stood proud amongst the trees, its windows glowing, shingles coated in sparkling snow. Home. They were home, alive and safe. Ivy was out the door as soon as they set foot on the porch flinging her arms around Rowan.

"Oh, thank Brigid you're alive! I couldn't feel you for the longest time and I really thought..." Her voice crumbled into tears. "Gods, Ro, what happened? Where's the wraith?"

"It's dead." Rowan's grateful gaze fell on Callum. "We crossed the veil and got rid of it." He bowed his chest, pride swelling. Rowan hugged his sister, resting his chin on top of her head. "There's some stuff I never talked about with you Ives and it came and bit me on the ass. I'm so sorry."

"It's okay," Ivy replied. "As long as you're alive, it's totally okay."

After taking stock that Rowan was indeed safely home, Broderick trotted to the porch swing. He knocked the snow from it before awkwardly hauling himself on to it, curling as tight as he could. But he kept his head raised; his familiar forever diligent.

"Can we get him a blanket?" Rowan asked.

"We can build him his own damn roofless house after this. But we're defrosting you inside first" Ivy replied. The door opened, anticipating Ivy's command.

Callum picked Rowan up, carrying him across the threshold. "Any sign of Aster?"

"Finn is out tracking her now. He said he caught her scent. Aunt Dahlia and Aunt Rosemary are driving the roads to see if they can spot the gargoyle and I'm here in case someone came back. Glad I stayed too." Ivy closed the door behind them, hurrying to fetch some blankets.

The house had restored itself after the wraith's destruction, thawing the ice and repairing its windows. The hearth flamed up in welcome, ceiling beams groaning with excitement. Ivy wrapped a blanket around Rowan, another around Callum. "I'll take this last one to Broderick then I'm raiding your healing potions, Ro," Ivy said "You're both resting here until you don't look like popsicles."

"I'm fine really, I..." He bit his lip at the pointed look Callum gave him. "No, you're right. I'll rest."

Ivy gave Callum a smile. "Rest. Then you can spill your guts to me about this wraith." She patted his cheek. "I'm just glad you're okay, Ro. That's all that matters to me." She slipped to the porch, leaving them settled on the couch.

Rowan sighed, laying his head on Callum's shoulder. Firelight danced over him, making his already bright hair a bonfire. "I can't believe I killed the damn thing."

"I can." Callum, pulled him to against his side, draping the blankets over them both. "And you earned this victory, my brave Witch-boy."

"And so did you," Rowan added.

Callum smiled, running his fingers through Rowan's damp hair. "I lost your talisman."

Rowan shrugged. "Don't need it anymore. My parents made it to remind me I'm not alone. They said it would bring me someone if they couldn't be there for me." He took Callum's hand, kissing his fingers. "The talisman served its use. It brought you to me. And I love you Cal. This is what I want. *You* are what I want."

Callum laced their hands together. "Mates?"

Rowan nodded, raising their clasped hands. "Mates."

They reclined on the couch, watching the fire crackle as they regained their strength. Mates. Rowan's parents had cast their spells. Orlaith and given her blessing. And Callum finally felt free. He kissed Rowan, slow and soft, fingers sliding into his hair. "You'll never be alone, Witch-boy." *And neither am I.*

Chapter 26

Threnody trudged through the snow, every breath a struggle. A clap of thunder shook the sky, her body still aching from her seizure. Night had fallen since she'd woken from a horrible miasma of her worst memories; abandonment, pain, the discovery of Aster's murder.

All of it had made her so weak. So sick. She didn't believe she'd survive the sickness that had her in a choke hold, but her eyes opened despite it all, and her body was restored. How the hell she pulled herself from the brink of death was a damned mystery. And it would have been good if those bad memories weren't still stewing in her mind. But they urged her to rise, to get back to her plan for revenge.

Judith had left Threnody alone, having the decency to dump her into bed before she took off to finish Arabella's mission. Good. Threnody didn't need that bitch sticking her nose into her plans, especially now that she knew how to break the wards. The solution had come in her sleep; the exact sigils she could use, the words she should chant. With Judith gone, that gave her enough time to kill every fucker that lived inside that house.

An icy gale cut deep into Threnody's bones, a shiver almost taking her to her knees. The warm glow of windows glimmered in the distance. The house. That meant the barrier was only a few yards ahead. She held up a hand, whispering "stop" into the air. The trees stilled, the woods growing eerily silent as the wind stopped. Revenge. It was within her grasp, sitting in that house and waiting.

Threnody ran clumsily, her boots sinking into white slush. Revenge for Aster, revenge on the ones who had sniffed out her light. Revenge for Threnody's pain. A shadow of bat like wings passed before the moon with a woosh. "What the fuck?" That was too damn big to be a bat. And whatever it was it was probably hunting.

She ducked under low hanging branches tracking its path as it passed right through the wards as if they weren't even there. It touched down, shadows swirling around his form as if wore the night as a cloak. Its wings folded and it lowered its cargo to their feet. A woman; petite and slim with strawberry blonde hair. The woman caught her balance then offered the beast a familiar smile filled with sunshine.

Threnody shoved a hand over her mouth, hot sick dancing on the back of her tongue. "...Aster?"

There she was all love and light, blood and bone, alive, breathing and smiling at a damned gargoyle. She wanted to run to her, wanted to cry and scream and hug her tight, but her shock froze her in place. *Arabella lied. That fucking bitch lied to me!*

Rage forced Threnody to stand but her legs wobbled. She fell against a tree, holding tight as tears threatened to choke her. The gargoyle tensed, but she ran before it turned, heart racing, mind spinning. Arabella had lied about Aster's death. But why? When she deemed it safe, Threnody fished her cell phone from her pocket. Tears blurred her vision, her thumb missing the name "Mother" three times before hitting it so hard her phone almost tumbled into the snow.

Threnody gritted her teeth, every inch of her burning as it rang and rang. "Answer the phone you stupid-!" A click and a breath followed by a low, smooth voice answering, "Threnody my daughter. You're awake." Arabella's smugness was thick over the phone.

"You have a lot of explaining to do!" Threnody spat. "A fuck load of explaining!"

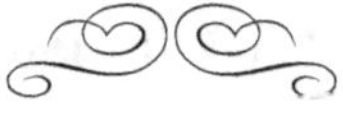

Aster clung tight to her friend as they landed. Despite his size, he touched down as delicate as a dragonfly, pulling his wings tight to his back. He brought her close enough to walk to Ivy's house, but far enough to keep her sister from sending a hex right up his ass. It was good to know he still had his common sense.

"Well...you got me home in one piece," Aster said, trying to sound cheerful. The gargoyle frowned, fingers pressing into her thigh as he pulled her closer, arms trembling, his heart beat heavy and fast. After a beat she cleared her throat. "You can put me down now." With a reluctant sigh he placed her on her feet, hands lingering on her hips. She stepped away to hide her shiver, dragging her fingers through her wind-swept hair. "Thanks for the ride I guess?"

"I thought you were in danger," he snapped defensively.

She held up her hands to him. "I know."

He jabbed a misty claw at her. "I was convinced something, or someone was coming after you and acted accordingly. You can't fault me for that."

"I wasn't planning to." She looked over her shoulders. "Though I'm pretty sure my family will. So next time...I donno...Knock?"

Aster rapped her knuckles on his chest. The shadows covering his body rippled to reveal rock solid pecs, then swallowed the view before she could gawk. How did she not notice that before? Oh yeah, because she was too busy trying not to turn into a soul sucking monster.

"It's the thought that counts," she said. "You had good intentions."

His glowing eyes crinkled. "The path to hell is paved with good intentions, Kitten." He released a dark sound that could have been a half-hearted laugh.

"Okay, Debbie Downer. I get it. You're sulking. I guess that's a good sign. If you're strong enough to sulk you're strong enough to not die." They stood in awkward silence, Aster unwilling to step away. Gods, how could she step away? All this time she was convinced that she had killed him, yet there he stood. She'd be lying if she said she wasn't more thrilled than scared to see him burst through the window. "So... you're alive."

"I am." The Gargoyle rubbed his hips as if trying to shove his hands into pockets. Was he even dressed under all those shadows? Was he nude? Another question she hadn't thought of while cursed but now that she was back to herself again—her very horny self apparently—her immediate thought was on his body. "You seem surprised," he added.

Aster looked to her feet. "Well, I tossed you like a frisbee and you never came back."

He hooked his knuckle under her chin, giving it a lift. "Oh, come now, Kitten. I thought you knew my prowess better than that."

"I'm serious! I was really worried!" She jerked away. "You could have at least, I don't know, left a note, knocked on my window, waved a flag or something."

"And I'm sure I'd be greeted with open arms," he snorted. "Perhaps invited in for tea."

"It would have been better received than an unexpected kidnapping."

The gargoyle looked ready to retort then growled, his wings cloaking his shoulders. "Fine. I'll concede that. I just deemed it unnecessary at the time."

Aster sighed. "If you want to disappear, just say so. You don't owe me anything."

"No." He stiffened. "And no despair. You know what happens-"

"The curse is broken. I don't turn into a hungry void monster when I get sad anymore." Aster inhaled in a trembling breath and squared her shoulders. "Just tell me upfront. I don't like games."

The gargoyle cleared his throat, pulling his hand away quickly. "I'm sorry I didn't reach out. I assumed you were..." he shrugged. "My recovery was something you wouldn't have wanted to witness."

Aster chewed on her lower lip. This should have been her cue to walk away and let him live his life. But she pressed a hand to his heart. Shadows swirled over her fingers, tingling with warmth. "You saw me at my worst. I think I owe you."

You owe me nothing." He reached out, brushing the tips of his claws through her messy hair. "I wondered what your true form looked like for some time."

Aster gave him a little smile. "Impressive, huh?"

"A lot less...viscous."

Aster's laugh made the shadows around his face curl into a faint grin. "Yeah. I don't ooze like I used to."

He brushed his fingers across her cheek, the swirls of darkness kissing her flesh. "I prefer you like this. Far more...touchable."

The deep roll of his voice shook Aster right to the core. She swallowed, face heating. "I'd shoot you a compliment too if I could see you. You're like a walking Rorschach picture."

The fog curling his head stilled. Then it parted, revealing his face. By Artemis, he was terrifying. Terrifying and stunning. His skin was slate gray, his heavy brow sprouting large horns that curved gracefully over a mane of thick purple hair.

"Impressed?" Mischief twinkled in his golden eyes, their pupils slitted like a cat's. His smile flashed a pair of long gleaming sharp white fangs.

"Y-yeah." Aster swallowed the break in her voice. The primal beauty in his harsh planes, the carnality his gaze as he looked her over from head to toe. Suddenly she understood her siblings' attraction to somebody so inhuman.

Before she realized it, she had pressed her hands along his rugged face, the tiny scales smooth on her palms. A low purr rumbled from his throat, and he leaned into her touch like a needy cat. Aster shivered at the sound. Quickly, she tucked her miscreant hand behind her back. The shadows swallowed him once again.

"Cold?" he asked.

Aster shook her head. "Um no?"

"You're trembling. Your dress is so flimsy in this weather. It's a wonder you haven't turned blue." He stepped closer, tucking an unruly lock of her hair behind her ear. The edges of his shadows tickled her cheek, tasting her skin. "Do you need warmth, Kitten?"

Gods, the way he crooned her nickname in that deep, gravelly voice went right between her thighs. Aster was ready to leap back into his arms and let him cart her wherever he wished.

"Aster!" Her name was carried across the air by several voices. Finn and Ivy, Aunt Dahlia, and Aunt Rosemary. She stepped back with a sigh. "My family..."

The gargoyle cleared his throat, flicking his hand at her. "Get home, Kitten. They're worried, I'm sure."

"You should get going too. After the way you busted in, they won't be happy to see you." He bowed, sweeping his wings like a cloak then started away, the air rippling around him as he walked through the ward barrier. Realization hit Aster like a sledgehammer. "Wait. How did you get past my sister's wards?"

The gargoyle peered over his shoulder the corners of his shadows turning into a trickster smile. He waged a finger at her. "I revealed enough secrets to you today. I'll save that for, well, next time."

Her belly fluttered, a little laugh tickling her lips. "I'll hold you to that."

The force of his wings unfurling blew her hair back. "Just call for me, Kitten, and I will come for you."

She smirked. "I would if you gave me your name."

He winked "Thaddeus. You may call me Thaddeus." Thaddeus leapt, wings catching the wind as he flew off into the horizon.

Chapter 27

Rowan rubbed his leg, the pain there hardly noticeable in the spring sunshine. *Thank the Gods for the changing seasons.* Winter had passed in a blink, the sky clearing, the air warming, and things were...normal. He hmmed, a little smile touching him. No sisters in danger. No wraith hovering over his shoulder. No pressure to bury his past in work. Yeah. It was normal. And it was overwhelming. But slowly, Rowan had adjusted. Now he craved that mundane peace every day.

He absorbed the rays like he was solar powered, hammering away at the brand-new Broderick nook that sprouted off Ivy's greenhouse. His poor familiar still hadn't grown used to the indoors. They had even tried bringing him in again after the stag begged and begged. After having to buy Ivy a new couch after that chaotic romp, Rowan decided to build him his own place to keep him warm at night, one with windows for a ceiling and walls.

Rowan wacked another nail in place as a shadow passed over him. Hands slid over his shoulders, the familiar scent of pine pricking his nose. He lowered his hammer. "You're blocking my light."

"No. I'm saving your life." Callum's tail wrapped around his waist. "Didn't you tell me the sun is not good for your kind? Your lovely pale flesh is in danger. Thank the Goddess I found you in time before you cooked yourself."

Rowan smirked. "I'm wearing sunscreen."

"I *am* your sunscreen!" Callum stretched his arms wide, his broad shoulders blotting out the daylight. "Wear me!"

Rowan playfully gave him a shove. "Come on now. I've been waiting months for the warm weather. Let me enjoy it."

"But I can't let my Witch-boy boil!" Callum's bazillion pounds of muscle collapsed against him, pressing his back against the Broderick nook.

"Cal, you're crushing me!" Rowan half cackled, half wheezed. He gave the satyr's back a hardy slap only to have his arms pinned over his head.

"Once again I saved you!" Callum crowed, their chests pressed together. "A hero of the ages! Write a song for me, Rowan! Teach it to our children!" He laughed that wonderful vibrant laugh that made Rowan melt. And melt he did as soon as that wonderful, scarred mouth made its way across his collar bone.

Callum's smiles came easy now, his nightmares and panic attacks less frequently. And Rowan couldn't be prouder of him. After the mountain began to thaw, Ivy and Rowan had piled into her SUV and made the drive to his abandoned apartment in San Francisco, an invisible Callum in the backseat. Despite his nervousness the entire trip, the satyr was determined to help Rowan move what little he had in there.

"You'll need strong shoulders for such things," he insisted despite the cracks in his tone. Callum had remained dim the entire move, which made it complicated to explain to passers-by how boxes were floating down the stairs. Still, the fact that he came unasked made Rowan love him even more.

The last of Rowan's things were moved to Big Bear. His lease was officially broken. And his new job as healer for the witches of the city had begun. Now he was home, truly home, in a grand old house with his wackadoodle family, and a big, gorgeous satyr that loved him with all his heart.

Callum flicked his tongue up Rowan's neck. "I like how this heat feels on you. Taking you with nothing but the sunlight on your flesh sounds delectable."

"Um, you're aware we have an audience, right?" Rowan jerked his chin towards Broderick. The stag was sitting across from them. He tilted his head as if to say, "Don't mind me," his ears wiggling.

"He approves of our love," Callum simply replied before slanting his mouth over Rowan's in a toe-curling kiss. Broderick, the springtime, and his own name went forgotten as Callum's hands slipped down the front of his jeans to give his cock a hard stroke. Rowan's hips jerked, fists tightening under the satyr's hold on his wrists.

"Guess you want to play carpenter?" Rowan moaned.

"Depends on how you play such a game."

"Well, first we'll get hammered. Then I'll nail you." Rowan snickered at Callum's glare. "Get it? Cause I'm holding a hammer? Eh?"

"You are lucky I love you." Callum said before taking his mouth again.

"Is this what you meant by erecting a nook?" Ivy peered at them from over from the elevated deck with a wicked grin.

"What the hell, Ives!" Quickly Rowan untangled himself, stepping away only to realize his pants were undone and his hard on was way too obvious. He pulled Callum against him but when the satyr nipped Rowan's ear, his erection only grew more present. "How long have you been there?"

"Too long for my tastes," Ivy replied. "I was just going to tell you something. I didn't know my brother and his mate were doing squat thrusts in the cabbage patch, but here we are."

"Witchling! Are we tormenting our brothers? I must join!" Finn's head popped up beside hers. "Greetings Callum! Look what I have!" He lifted his hand, a pinecone clenched between his claws then bounced it off Callum's rump.

"Dammit, brother!" Callum snarled.

"I heard there was torment!" And there was Aster appearing on Ivy's other side.

Her cheeks were plump, her eyes bright and shiny. A crown of wildflowers was woven in her shiny hair as she gave the two an impish smile. Ever since her unintentional kidnapping, she was more herself, even venturing outside, but never past the barrier of the wards. And while she still hadn't used her magic, she seemed less frightened of the idea. *Baby steps are better than no steps,* Rowan thought. *She's going to be okay.*

"Tell me, Brother, are cocks out?" Finn asked.

"They could have been without your interruption!" Callum replied.

Ivy grabbed Finn's arm before he tossed another pinecone. "I wanted to give the heads up that Auntie Lia and Auntie Rosie are-"

"Don't mind us, darlings!" Dahlia announced with a tip of her huge sunhat. Rowan quickly zipped his fly as the dynamic duo tramped past, Rosemary setting potted herbs in the half-finished greenhouse while Dahlia unfolded deck chairs. "It will be like we're not even here."

Unfortunately, his new life had a very distinct lack of privacy unless they were hiding in the "West Wing" as Aster had dubbed it. She said it was in homage to Rowan's favorite Disney movie. He didn't have the heart to tell her their wing faced east.

"Well look at this adorable canoodling!" Rosemary beamed. "I'm just pleased as punch to see you two getting on so well!"

"Of course, they're getting on, Love. They're mated." Dahlia replied, giving Rosemary a little peck.

"What are you two doing here?" Rowan asked.

"We heard about this new addition and felt decorating was in order." Dahlia placed red plastic flamingos around the greenhouse, little vampire fangs sprouting from their beaks. "Familiars should relax in style as well. You should see the adorable bungalow we decorated for Maximus."

"We have an old futon mattress and plenty of blankets in the truck for your stag," Rosemary added. "Oh! And rain chains! So many rain chains to hang! It will be beautiful!" Broderick pranced in a little circle, bobbing his head in excitement. Well, at least one of them enjoyed the interruption. "Shouldn't you just ask the house for the addition, Rowan dear? It would be so much quicker."

"I wanted a project," Rowan replied.

"His project is already getting him burned by the sun." Callum poked his shoulder.

"You know, he is looking a little pink, Auntie Lia," Aster said. "I think he needs to reapply."

"Good point, Aster sweetling!" Dahlia dug into her massive scarlet purse and out came a giant bottle of SPF fifty. Before Rowan could protest, she squirted it onto his arm and rubbed it in.

Rowan shot a look to the deck above as Ivy and Aster batted their eyes. "I *love* my sisters!" he snapped. "I love them *sooooo* much! I'm *sooooo* happy to be living with them!"

"I believe it's time for our exit?" Callum whispered into his ear.

"Please." Rowan groaned.

"Indeed," Callum scooped Rowan up, flopping him over his shoulder. "I'm taking my Witch-boy inside to rest his skin and ride his cock. Farewell!"

"Cal!" Rowan covered his face. "You know what? Fine. Sounds good. Let's go rest my skin and...uh...ride my cock." Callum carried him around the house, towards the back entrance of the West Wing. "I really need to teach you the art of subtlety."

Callum gave his backside a swat. "And never see your beautiful blush again?"

The door opened without a command, the house having gotten sick of Callum kicking it in constantly, and Callum carted Rowan into their wing. Gone were the hunting trophies and heavy, unwelcoming furniture, and in came Rowan's colorful curtains, and Callum's branches and baubles. The oil portrait of Thaddeus was moved to the attic, replaced with the satyr and elf painting Aster had done. Rowan allowed it, finding it less embarrassing when it was in their private quarters.

Callum flopped Rowan in front of the fireplace, their sex tree sitting where the leather settee once was. That was where they spent their nights, despite the many bedrooms upstairs. Rowan had made it more hospitable with his mattress, mountains of blankets and throw pillows while Callum hung his mobiles of glass bits, shiny metal things, and the necklaces he'd pilfered from the shop from above. The perfect cozy nest or 'Forest-core chic', as Rowan called it.

Callum draped himself over Rowan, careful not to crush him this time. "There, you're safe from the sun and your skin is at rest."

"A hero for the ages." Rowan smiled.

"Indeed." Callum tapped his lower lip. "Now, what was the other thing I was supposed to do?"

Rowan tugged at his loincloth. "Ride my cock?"

"Oh yes! How could I forget?"

He wrapped himself around him, leaning in for a kiss when a heavy rumbling shook the floor. Windows rattled, the chandelier overhead flickering and swinging.

"What in the seven hells?!" Callum caged Rowan with his arms protectively.

Rowan blinked, about to scream earthquake but this was lasting way too long. Soon the shaking rolled to a heavy thunder over the roof, moving higher and higher. He nudged Callum off him, tugging him to his hooves. "Come on!"

They rushed into the main house, the ceiling over the grand stairs stretching in a vortex, walls forming. Floors sealing the chamber away from view. But the construction sounds continued.

"Holy shit," Rowan laughed. "I think I know what's happening."

He tugged Callum to the deck where his family clustered, staring slack jawed. An immense tower built itself board by board between Ivy's house and Rowan's wing. It stretched into the sky, beautiful and proud, a round balcony resembling a ship's crow's nest circling its peak. Its three stories each touting a sparkling stained-glass window, each a unique design. The house crowned it's masterpiece with a peaked, shingled roof then stilled, as if taking a deep breath.

Ivy smiled. "Well, looks like the house has plans again."

"For who? Who is supposed to live there?" Aster asked. All eyes fell on her, and she smirked. "That's not for me." She shook her head. "How could that be for me?! I'm not dating anyone! Hell, I can't even get up there!"

"Well, the house works in mysterious ways, Azzie." Ivy slung her arm around her baby sister's shoulders. "Come on. Let's see if we can get inside." Everyone hurried inside, leaving Callum and Rowan out of the deck to study the majestic structure.

Callum hugged Rowan's shoulders, chin resting on his head. "It must know something we don't know."

"We can figure it out if we looked at Aster's sketchbook," Rowan chuckled. He gave Callum's hands a squeeze "Want to help them look for a door?"

Callum grinned. He lifted Rowan off his feet twirling him around before dipping him back. "I think I'd prefer my earlier plans of taking you with nothing but the sun on your skin. What say you, my good little Witch-boy?"

"I say thank Hecate I reapplied my sunscreen."

Callum kissed him as he carried him off, determined to find them a private place in the sun.

I'm not alone. I'm never going to be alone again, and neither is Cal. This was all Rowan had ever wanted, what he had wanted all along. Happiness. Love. A past left in the past where it belonged. Nothing but brightness waited ahead of them now that they had each other. *Mates. I love the sound of that word.* And with that thought, Rowan Bennett finally accepted his fate.

Author's Note

Thank you all so much for reading An Irrational Lesson on Witch-boy Wooing! It means so much that you picked this book up in particular to read. For years, I've been wanting to write a M/M story and have set up several in my other series, *Wyrd Love*. But this is my first official gay romance and I'm pretty proud of it.

This book was a struggle, partly because my life was in a lot of flux (New day job, then another new day job, anxiety, family, etc.) but mostly because I kept getting in my own way. I'm straight and CIS and had a lot to learn. Also, my anxiety kept stalling me and stalling me... and STAAAAAALING me until I wanted to tear my hair out. Yup, this is my process, constant fretting until I get pissed at myself and write the book. Thank you, anxiety disorder.

But my sensitivity and beta readers were amazing through this entire process. They truly made Rowan and Callum's story so much better. A huge, huge, HUGE thank you goes out to Oz, Keith, Andy, Hailey, Stacy, Karine, and Bonnie. Thank you for your advice on keeping pronouns correct, how to get the spicy scenes even spicier, how to pour on the feels, and for your encouragement and cheerleading. You're the reason I got over myself and finished this book and I couldn't be more grateful.

Holy cow! Only one book left in the *Magical Husbandry* trilogy! *An Impossible Practice of Gargoyle Chasing* will be coming down the pike soon but for now, Aster and ol' Thaddy are going to simmer while I get some story ideas out of my head and return to the Wyrd.

Until then you can hang out with me and other readers' Facebook group, **Cynthia's Wyrdlings.** And since we all know how social media is, sign up for my email list, **Wyrd on the Streets** to stay updated on all my antics and new releases. If you liked this book, please leave a review, tell a friend and hey, why not check out my other books as well? Thank you all for reading and your support!

If you like crackling chemistry, sharp wit, and plenty of action, then you'll adore Cynthia Diamond's other luscious stories.

<u>Wyrd Love</u>

Siren's Song
Valkyrie's Spear
Dryad's Vine
Alchemy's Hunger
Starting Fires
Trickster Business

<u>Magical Husbandry</u>

An Impractical Guide to Satyr Charming
An Irrational Lesson on Witch-Boy Wooing
(Coming Soon)
An Impossible Practice of Gargoyle Chasing